I0749370

Always Rebecca

A Novel of Regency Romance

Teresa Sweeney

Courting Romance Publishing
California

Published in the United States by Courting Romance Publishing

ISBN 978-1-940319-01-8

First Edition

Cover Photography by Christina & Jason Brusaca

By Teresa Sweeney

Always Rebecca

A Love Match, Indeed!

To my most amazing son, Jonathan.
Kind, strong, smart. I am so very proud of you.

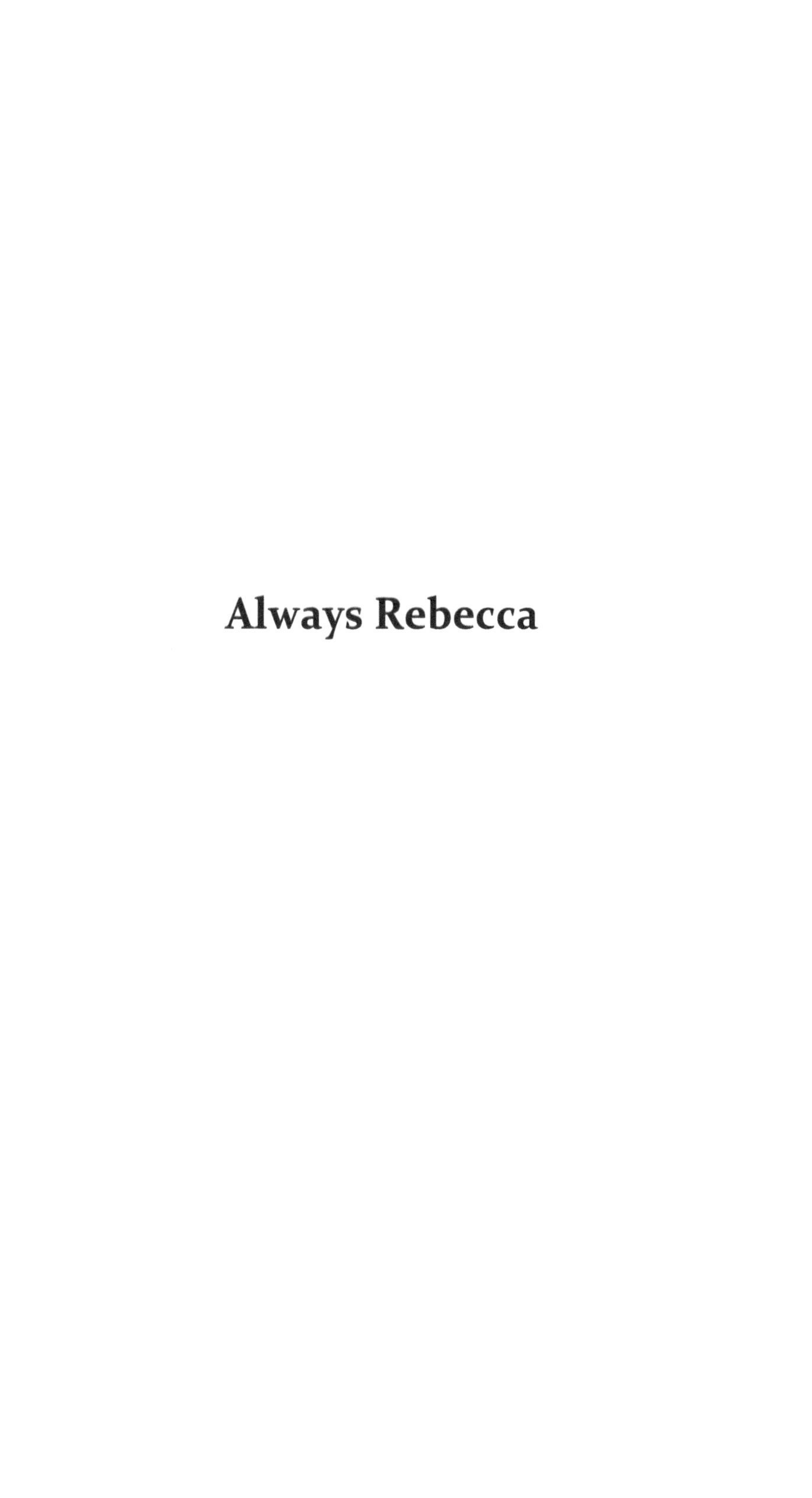

Always Rebecca

Prologue

1800
Ingall Estate, England

Lucy was still groggy when the housekeeper pulled her along the wide and ostentatious corridor to the mistress's suite. She had been sound asleep on a palette on the kitchen floor. Her sister, who was the cook's assistant, had taken ill. Lucy had been fetched to replace her in her duties until her sister was well enough to return. Like her sister, she went home at the end of each work day, but today the turbulent weather forced her to stay overnight.

In her deep slumber, Lucy's mind slowly jarred to attention and she became irritated that "Mary," for whom the housekeeper beckoned, did not answer. Over and over again, she heard, "Mary, come on girl, wake up!" It wasn't until Lucy's arm was practically pulled from her socket that she realized she was the one being fetched. She remembered too late that large households typically named their female servants "Mary," as there were too many of them to recall by their Christian name, especially temporary ones as herself.

Lucy could sense the housekeeper's anxiety and quickly realized it was because the Countess of Ingall was about to give birth to the anticipated heir. For some unknown reason, she was being called to attend the mistress. She wondered how the housekeeper knew she had assisted her mother when she gave birth to her youngest sibling. She thought it odd that she was being asked to help. At ten years of age she was far from experienced and she became petrified at what was being asked of her. She wanted to stop the housekeeper from dragging her forward, but she knew to argue with the woman would only get her a rebuke if not a box to her ears for her insolence. Her family greatly depended on the income her sibling's employment in the earl's household provided and they would not be happy with her if she lost her sister's position in the great house. She allowed herself to be hastily pulled, her mind searching for excuses to extricate herself. She was so lost in thought, she almost ran into the housekeeper when, having entered the countess's suite, the woman abruptly stopped. Lucy's eyes were wide with trepidation until she took in her surroundings. She saw that Lady Ingall had more than enough people around her to see to her needs. She expelled the breath that she unknowingly held and sighed in relief.

The housekeeper dragged Lucy over to the hearth and sat her on a small stool behind an embroidered fire screen. She pointed to a stack of wood and then to the flames. Lucy's eyes were focused on the finger that kept wagging in front of her face until the housekeeper grabbed and shook her shoulders to get Lucy's full attention. She berated, "Do not let that fire diminish, girl. If anyone in this room gets a chill, there will be little use for you or your sister in this household!"

Lucy nodded in understanding and then watched the housekeeper depart, leaving her to her task. She was positioned close to the fire and within moments her skin began to burn. She carefully inched her seat away to where she felt she would not overheat and immediately became alarmed when cool air assuaged her heated face. She looked to see where the icy breeze came from and noted that there was a gap between the large window sill and the heavy brocaded curtain that covered it. She quickly rose from her stool, grabbed a log from the stack, and thrust it into the blazing hearth. The weight of the new log caused the fire to crackle and pop. Lucy watched the flames climb as the dried wood quickly caught fire. She took the hem of her dingy grey skirt and wiped the beads of sweat that were forming on her face before she returned to her stool.

She felt like an intruder and kept her gaze on her shoes until she heard Lady Ingall beckon for her husband. She looked up and was surprised to see his lordship attending his wife. Lucy knew that men and unmarried women were not present at birthings, at least not in the peerage. Most noblemen hired the services of physicians and nurses to see to the needs of their wives, while they awaited the news of whether an heir was born in either their parlour or club. Commoners who owned little wealth, looked to daughters, neighbors, even husbands to assist. Lucy marveled at the affection she saw on his lordship's face as he held his wife's hand and cooed her with loving words. She remembered her sister telling her that the Earl and Countess of Ingall married for love and had not contracted a marriage out of convenience to merge their wealth and lands. She now understood the admiration the servants held for their master. There was love in this household and its goodness was felt through the ranks. She was glad she was here to help. She rose and checked on the fire. She knew this was the countess's first child and even at her age, she understood that it would be a long night.

Dawn was breaking when Lucy's droopy eyelids opened wide with cheers resounding throughout the room. Her stoic face broke with amusement as she watched a very jubilant master. He was following closely behind the nurse who carried his newborn infant over to the ablutions table to be washed. Lucy's grin grew into a full smile thinking his lordship would not be adverse to accepting the messy child. She could hear the nurse laugh at his ecstatic remarks and then her smile broke when the whispers pierced her ears informing her an heir was not born this day.

The countess gave birth to a girl, yet Lucy saw no disappointment in his lordship's face. Sons were important to the aristocracy. They guaranteed the succession of the title, wealth, and lands for the family. Lucy liked this lord who cared more for his baby girl than his title and watched him as he hovered with joy over the nurse tidying his daughter. Nurse Mary clothed the infant in a cotton lace cap and gown that according to gossip, his wife had made only a fortnight ago.

Lord Ingall watched Nurse Mary complete her task, bundling his baby girl in his mother's ancestral baby blanket. The treasured coverlet was embroidered in the corner with his mother's family crest and had been passed from generation to generation to welcome the first child born. Although the blanket was weary looking, his wife was excited to bestow the beloved article to her child and made sure it was on hand when she went into confinement.

Lucy jumped when she heard the booming thunder penetrate the walls. She walked over to the window to carefully look outside without allowing any chill to seep into the room. Her eyes widened at the ominous grey-clouded sky. Sheets of rain pelted an already saturated ground creating deep puddles and swift moving streams. The storm scared Lucy, not for her own safety, for the stalwart ancestral home of the Earl of Ingall was sturdy and could weather any gale, but a raging tempest had lethal power. Lucy hoped her family and neighbors were safe. She quickly turned when she heard his lordship bellow for the attending physician.

Roger, Lord Ingall, had been distracted with his daughter's ablutions and therefore, ignorant to his wife's malady. He was anxious to hold his baby girl and present the infant to his wife. As soon as Nurse Mary handed him his bundle of joy, Roger hurried to his wife's bed and placed their daughter in the cradle of her arm. Her lack of movement drew his concern and his happy countenance quickly faltered.

Jane, the Countess of Ingall, lay still. Her face was remarkably pale, cast against her raven black hair. Her forehead was swathed with pearls of sweat and her breathing was negligible. Lord Ingall fearfully called her name, relaxing a little when he saw her open her remarkable sapphire blue eyes. She said, "We will call her Elinor, after your dear mama." Within seconds of naming her daughter, Jane's eyelids fluttered closed and the arm that cradled her baby slackened.

In a panic-filled voice, Roger yelled for his physician, "Charles, come quickly!"

"She is weak, my lord," cautioned the physician. "It was a difficult birth, but with rest and care she will come around." Charles continued, "You must think of the child. The rain has not relented and soon the river will overflow making travel impossible. You must send the child to a wet nurse, immediately."

"No!" argued Lord Ingall. "You must bring the woman here."

"There is no time, my lord," said Charles hesitantly. "The river is too high now. It will be days before it recedes enough to cross—too long for the child to manage without nourishment."

Lord Ingall, exhausted and emotional, looked to his wife for counsel, but was flustered by her unconscious state. His mood changed from concern to anger and he lashed out at Charles. "Why did you not bring her with you when I sent for you."

Shocked, Charles beseeched him to remember that Lady Ingall refused to procure a wet nurse, reminding him that she intended to feed the infant herself.

Resigned, Lord Ingall acquiesced and ordered his carriage to be made ready. Nurse Mary was charged with Elinor's welfare and his coachman promised to conduct them safely to Farmer Bixby, whose wife would care for the infant.

Lord Ingall sighed deeply when he looked upon his wife and daughter nestled together. The fear that coursed through his body constricted his chest and made it hard for him to breathe. He bent down, kissed his wife and then picked up Elinor scrutinizing her face. He gently placed a kiss on her forehead asking God to bless her and keep her safe. Reluctantly, he handed her to Nurse Mary who placed her and secured her in a wicker basket, the ancestral blanket keeping her snuggled underneath a heavier quilt. Quickly, he picked up the basket that held his daughter and with great speed escorted Nurse Mary to his carriage. As the rain thrashed them, his coachman helped Nurse Mary to her seat while Lord Ingall gently placed the wicker basket on the seat next to her. His worried eyes looked into Mary's. Before she could say anything, he slammed the door shut splashing the beads of rain that ran along the casement. He yelled to his coachman, who had already taken his position, "Make haste! Do not fail me!" Drenched, Lord Ingall watched his coachman flick his wrists to slap the reins against the horse's flanks to start them into service. A heartfelt prayer silently left his lips while he watched them leave.

Roger returned to Jane's bed. He took a nearby seat, closed his eyes, and prayed. He was jolted into a panic, when he heard the servants screaming, "The bridge is gone!"

Chapter One

1815
Ingall Estate, England

Lady Ingall sat at her escritoire writing a "thank you" note to the Countess of Westfield for the crate of oranges she generously gifted her family. She presented an ethereal presence with her ebony coif aglow, her head a crown of sunrays from the daylight that passed through a nearby window. Even at the age of four and thirty, she drew the eyes of courtiers and commoners alike with her remarked upon figure, flawless skin, and silky black hair, though it was her sparkling sapphire eyes, beneath her long curled eyelashes, that were most admired.

Jane had been the *Toast of London* during her *come-out* Season at the age of eight and ten. Her husband Roger had been quick to seek her favor. A strikingly tall and handsome man at six foot one with chestnut brown hair and hazel eyes, he found no quarrel from the young debutante when he offered for her hand.

Some say the couple fell in love at first sight, but Lady Jane with her keen eyes and instinct, knew that this man who favored her among all others, was a man of stellar and sensitive character. Her heart told her she would be well loved, protected, and cherished. Unlike the other debutantes, Lady Jane did not take offense when Lord Ingall deliberately shoved her other suitors aside to reach her. She found his manner fearless rather than brutish. His touch was delicate, his strength remarkable, and his character surpassed every gentlemen of her acquaintance. He courted her with charm and wit, eliminating his competition with every ploy available to him. Whenever possible he showed them to a disadvantage, whether it be in athletic exhibitions or conversation. They married at the end of her Season with all the pomp and circumstance due their station. Aside from their tragic loss of their first born child, their marriage was happy and loving. They were eventually blessed with two sons, whom to Lord Ingall's delight, mirrored his wife's rich black hair and crisp blue eyes.

Jane put down her pen, separated another segment of orange, and bit into the juicy morsel. She grinned, her mouth indulgently savoring the refreshing sweetness. She licked her fingertips and smacked her lips in pleasure while silently thanking her neighbor Lady Amelia

Westfield for sharing the bounty of her orange harvest. Three years ago, Lady Westfield constructed an orangery on her estate after reading an article that professed the healing effects of oranges and limes. She visualized harvesting enough fruit to give to her tenants to eat, so as to ward against influenza. If limes could cure the scurvy of sailors, then surely she thought, the healing effects of fruits were powerful and should be widely used.

Unlike most marriages, Lady Westfield managed the family's business affairs. Amelia had the temperament to manage the estate that her husband lacked, so while she spent her days resolving land and tenant issues, he took pleasure in the abundant social and sporting pursuits the peerage offered. His idle life also gave Lord Harold Shelby, the Earl of Westfield, the freedom to spend an inordinate amount of time with his only child and heir, Jonathan. Although unorthodox, their arrangement worked well for them.

Amelia was a forward thinker. She was attentive in keeping apprised of the latest farm techniques and medicinal revelations. Jane admired Amelia who like her own husband was a conscientious and progressive landowner. They both considered each tenant an extension of their own family for most of the tenants had worked the land for generations. Their tenants would call them good land owners who habitually made the rounds to visit them to check on their welfare and livelihood, evidenced by their fit cottages and healthy crops.

Amelia's energy never surprised Jane who liked to compare her to a gale, a powerful force that overwhelmed anything in its path. If Lady Westfield was power, then Lady Ingall was peace, always presenting a calm and hospitable manner that made everyone feel welcomed and rejuvenated. They complemented each other like the sun and the moon. Over the years, their friendship blossomed.

Lady Ingall had just finished sealing her note when Palmer, their trusty and diligent butler, presented Lady Westfield's card on a silver salver. "Are you at home, my lady?" inquired Palmer. "Lady Westfield seems to have a man of the cloth and a young girl in tow."

"Yes, thank you, Palmer," replied Lady Ingall. "Please allow them entrance."

Palmer led Lady Westfield and her guest in, but before he could announce them, Amelia barked her greetings. "Jane, so good of you to see us. I was taking our new vicar around and thought you would welcome the intrusion. Allow me to introduce Mr. Stevens."

Jane saw an affable man of fifty years of age. He had brown hair mingled with strands of gray. His eyes were a soft brown that creased at the corners when he smiled in the pleasure of their introduction. He stood around five feet eleven inches and his stout build and remarkable posture presented a stark contrast to the young girl that stood next to him.

The girl was slender and slightly disheveled. Her age was masked by a simple straight cut muslin dress accented with a pale ribbon sash. A gold filigree locket on a long chain hung around her neck. Her hunched shoulders suggested her discomfiture as did her focus on the Aubusson rug that lay beneath her feet.

Mr. Stevens saw Lady Ingall's perusal of his daughter and offered an apology with his introduction. "Pray, forgive me, my lady, may I introduce my daughter, Rebecca?"

Upon hearing her name, Rebecca looked up and Jane was captivated with the vulnerability she saw in her face. She asked, "How old are you, my dear?"

With a whisper, Rebecca replied that she was five and ten years of age. Before any more questions could be asked, Amelia burst forth, "Yes, yes. Sweet girl. Lost her mama five years ago. I understand from Mr. Stevens that she is a great comfort and help."

Mr. Stevens nodded his head in agreement and placed an arm around his daughter's shoulder drawing her towards him with a hug. Jane saw Rebecca beam and a natural glow illuminated her face. She admired the love she observed, though she was shocked when she realized the knot in her stomach came from grief.

Amelia interrupted Jane's revelation and announced that in two weeks, she was hosting a country-dance for her son Jonathan. He was expected home, after graduating from Cambridge and was to embark the day after the gala on his *Grand Tour*. The festive event, she proclaimed, was to be a *bon voyage*, for her adored son and she expected everyone to attend.

For years, the peerage have sent their sons to tour Europe to gain life experience, sample new cultures, learn history, and more importantly, to hone their social skills. The *Grand Tour* was the rite of passage all young men of the peerage made to become distinguished gentlemen. Upon their return, England's Finest usually made their way to London where they procured a bachelor flat, indulged in Society, and rarely returned to visit their parents until a command dictated it or the time came to announce their betrothal. Debutante mothers waited in earnest for these young men to return and increase the *marriage mart.*

The moment Jane met Rebecca she felt overcome with emotion. She was not surprised that within the next two weeks, she found more than one excuse to invite the vicar and his daughter over for tea to visit with them. By the evening of the Westfield's fete, Jane was wound up with excitement. She had been waiting anxiously for her husband to meet the sweet girl and remembered her earlier conversation with him regarding them. *"I think Mr. Stevens will do quite nicely, Roger. He is an amiable sort of person, non-imposing and genuinely seems to care about our tenants. He shows an admirable devotion to his daughter, Rebecca, though I feel he has failed her miserably for engaging in society. The girl does not dress her age and demonstrates no social skills. I must say I feel much sympathy for her not having any maternal guidance. I am told she keeps house for Mr. Stevens. She has done so since her mama passed away. I also understand she copies her papa's sermons as she has the better hand. Clearly, she can read and write, but I don't believe she is schooled in any of the areas attributed to young ladies. Her posture is lacking and her conversation skills poor. I have yet to see her pour a pot of tea without some sort of calamity. I doubt if her papa ever hired any tutors to teach her to speak Italian, to paint watercolors, or to dance. I do not know if she embroiders or plays the pianoforte. I fear her lack of social graces will cast her beneath her rightful sphere in society. Roger, I hope I am wrong and I look forward to what you make of them when you meet them."*

Roger's schedule had not permitted him the opportunity to be introduced to Rebecca for estate business had kept him occupied. Each time Mr. Stevens and Rebecca came to call for tea, he had been either away from home or ensconced in meetings. Jane's nervous energy reminded him, how much it meant to her for him to meet the girl. He always worried when he had to leave her alone for long periods of time. Solitude tended to encourage reflection and he knew when the boys were away at school that Jane's bouts of melancholia often increased. Recently, he noted a marked sadness in her countenance whenever Rebecca took her leave. He knew that their daughter's tragic death still grieved Jane. The slightest cause could pull her into a somber mood. Roger understood her lapses for he often caught himself saddened when he remembered that joyous and tragic day when Elinor was born. He remembered how difficult it was when Jane opened her eyes and asked to see their daughter. How through unbearable sobs he confessed Elinor was gone, lost to the river. Confused, in denial, tormented, his wife lost all reason. When a flicker of life finally appeared in her eyes and brought her to a conscious state, she punished herself with guilt. She believed that had she not indulged in wanting to nurse her baby herself and had procured someone for the task, Elinor would never had been sent away to such a tragic demise. It took months for Lord Ingall to sway her, appease her guilt, enable her to forgive herself and in the end, to find solace that their daughter was in heaven. Even now, Jane's heartache was acute because unlike her husband, she did not remember cradling her daughter or beholding her face. She had no memory to temper the grief that often pulled her into a bleak state of mind.

Over the years, she mourned the relationship she might have had with her daughter when saw how her husband bonded with their sons, William and Henry. Father and sons in a club all of their own where the father passed his skills on to his heirs. Like his own father had taught him, Roger instructed his boys on those endeavors that a gentleman of Society needed to be skilled. Certain abilities rounded out a gentleman's education and Roger liked tutoring his boys in riding, shooting, hunting, fisticuffs, and swordsmanship. Duels were outlawed, but it was still important to be able to protect yourself against highwaymen and reprobates.

William and Henry enjoyed spending time with their father and as they matured, they were presented with more responsibilities in preparing for their fishing and hunting expeditions, and eventually with duties that oversaw their tenants.

Roger guided their development in learning both social decorum and estate management. He expected his sons to behave as gentlemen and to show the highest level of respect for their mother.

Jane marveled at how her boys were growing into fine men. She beamed at the love she witnessed, but she also longed for the same kind of connection that existed between the boys and their father. She craved for that mother and daughter relationship where her own girlish experiences could be drawn upon to mentor a child.

Country-dances were much more relaxed than anything London had to offer and Lady Ingall was sorry William and Henry were away at school and unable to attend Jonathan's party. The festivities started earlier at a country-dance and young boys and girls were welcomed. It was common to see a group of boys causing mischief or a bevy of fifteen-year-old girls doing their best to capture the attention of whatever titled young men were available. On this particular night the guest of honor, Viscount Jonathan Shelby, was the object of every young girl's and debutante's admiration. Lord Shelby's title was a courtesy title, an inferior title of his father, the Earl of Westfield. It was common practice for the peerage to give their children inferior titles in order to distinguish them among Society.

The age difference between Jonathan and Lord Ingall's sons did not keep the Westfields from accepting invitations to join the Ingalls in sporting pursuits. Jonathan showed an admirable degree of patience as William, age two and ten, and Henry at nine years of age, rivaled for his attention. They looked to him as a big brother who seemed to excel at everything he did. William and Henry tried to emulate him and Jonathan did his best to mentor them. He and his father enjoyed the family atmosphere that always prevailed when they joined the Ingalls.

The ballroom was a flurry of activity, but nothing could distract Lord Ingall from looking at his wife. He never tired of admiring her. She exuded a radiant smile that was usually reserved for him or their sons. It was the same smile that captured him so many years ago, though at this moment, he knew Rebecca was the reason she smiled.

Jane warmly introduced the new vicar, Mr. Stevens, and his daughter, Rebecca, to her husband. Lord Ingall immediately observed what his wife saw in Rebecca. Clearly unguided by a maternal hand, Rebecca's hair lacked the shine of a good brushing and the styling that a pretty ribbon provides. Her mode of dress was jejune, making her look like she belonged in the nursery instead of with girls her age. Her eyes held no one's attention and while Lady Ingall interpreted her discomfiture to shyness, Lord Ingall noted it was clearly embarrassment. He thought Rebecca knew that she stood apart from girls her own age. She was lacking and without a clue on how to engage in society.

Rebecca asked to be excused and headed towards the ladies' respite room. She smiled and decided that she liked Lord and Lady Ingall. There was something soothing in their manner. They exuded a warmth that made her feel welcomed. The Ingalls, she thought, were not *very high in the instep*, not too proud to accept her company, and it seemed they did not judge her unworthy.

As Rebecca walked through the hallway with her thoughts of the Ingalls for company, she stopped and was mesmerized by the young man that approached her. He was tall, lean, and handsome in a boyish sort of way. He sported a short cut hair style and had the brightest blue eyes she had ever seen. His brown hair owned golden strands that revealed he spent a great deal of time outdoors. She noted as he headed to the ballroom that he walked deliberately with a slight bounce to his step. Rebecca couldn't stop staring at him. If he had looked at her she probably would have shied away, but it was obvious when he brushed her shoulder that he didn't even notice her. Rebecca embarrassingly stepped back into the shadows of an alcove when the young man turned to see what he hit. With a shrug of his shoulders, he turned and continued on his path.

Jonathan was excited to show his mother his new suit of clothes and though momentarily distracted when he ran into someone, his attention immediately focused at the end of the hall where he spied her. He could tell that she was quite pleased with his finery. Recently arrived from London, he sported the newest style of black evening coat and black silk breeches. His valet had applied his expertise in folding his cravat and had placed a sapphire stickpin within its folds to cleverly match his eyes. Jonathan felt quite the arbiter of fashion and the look on his mother's face verified that she agreed.

Lady Westfield smiled when Jonathan embraced her. She said with good humor, "Yes, yes. You do quite well, Son." Before he could respond, she pushed him off, telling him to go and enjoy himself. Jonathan laughed and took in the crowded ballroom. He always liked his mother's parties. They were intimate with only the local gentry in attendance. He knew everyone and liked to play host. He socialized with a natural flair, having learnt the art of conversation and making people feel at ease from his father who enjoyed entertaining immensely. However, lately, he found himself annoyed with the young ladies recently introduced into Society. It seemed to Jonathan that once a young woman made her *come-out* she seemed to lose her personality. She transformed into a shy damsel with nothing better to discuss than the weather or the latest scandal. He remembered it was not that long ago when he could chat away in comfort with them, teasing them until they retorted back with their own witticisms. Now it appeared that all they knew how to do when in the company of an eligible gentleman was to flutter their eyelids and smile demurely.

Jonathan was not beguiled by their feminine flirtations. He missed the camaraderie they shared before they reached their majorities when they played in picnic games or schoolroom antics. Rather than engage in their *marriage mart* games, he chose to give his attention to their younger siblings who were still two to three years shy of making their *come-out*. To these awkward girls and boys, he bore a confidence and gallantry that enamored them. He took great satisfaction in being able to place a giddy smile on a girl's face, without having to worry that she misconstrued his kindness. He enjoyed helping the young boys stand a little taller by remarking on their recent accomplishments. He often felt like a big brother, trying to boost their confidences by encouraging them to practice their social skills. He was extremely patient with them, getting them to mingle and try their hand at conversation. The effort monopolized his time to the dismay of their older sisters, who would have liked nothing better than to partner with him in dance and be the center of his attentions.

Jonathan had just finished returning one of the darlings to her governess, when he saw his mother, Lady Westfield, wave him over to where she kept company with the new vicar. Rebecca, who was trying to make herself invisible all evening, had sat herself down in a chair behind her father and watched as Jonathan joined his mother.

"Jonathan," Lady Westfield introduced, "this is Mr. Stevens, our new vicar. Mr. Stevens, I present my son, Viscount Shelby to you."

Mr. Stevens responded with pride, "I am honored to meet you, my lord, as is my daughter, Rebecca." The vicar moved aside to acknowledge his daughter, who was seated behind him.

Rebecca had her eyes cast down and Jonathan wanted to assuage the shy girl. He used his friendliest voice, hoping a witty remark would get her to raise her head and smile. He said, "I say you must be totally bored and excessively tired to be dragged to these dull adult affairs. I am sure it is way past your bedtime, child." Jonathan expected to see the face of a grinning girl, but instead he saw Rebecca stand, curtsy, and whisper, "Pray, please excuse me," before running out of the ballroom.

Surprised, Jonathan asked, "Did I say something wrong?"

His mother replied, "No, Son. I am sure she is tired."

Mr. Stevens excused himself to find Rebecca. Lady and Lord Ingall having observed the scene, shared a compassionate and heartfelt look.

Chapter Two

Ever since Jonathan's *bon voyage* party, Lord and Lady Ingall found themselves discussing Rebecca's plight on a regular basis. Each evening as they relaxed before a warm hearth, they recalled the humiliation that Rebecca wore on her face, when Viscount Shelby referred to her as a child. Although Rebecca did her best to appear invisible at the party, they could tell behind her lackluster persona, there existed a smart and pretty girl.

During the next week, Lord Ingall found himself more often being able to observe the young girl. He immediately understood the pull Rebecca had on his wife. She was simply good. He saw for himself her caring and compassionate nature, managing her father's household and helping anyone else that required assistance. He noted she did everything happily and her good cheer was contagious, alighting those around her with smiles and laughter.

Without an intervention, Lord and Lady Ingall knew the gentry would bleakly welcome Rebecca into their sphere. The girl needed a woman's guidance and the Ingalls were determined to assist her in some way. After all, she was the daughter of their vicar and they resolved if the welfare of their tenants were their responsibility, then so was the vicar and his daughter.

Lord Ingall had another incentive for aiding Rebecca. He knew his wife regretted not having another daughter, not that she wished for one less son, only another baby girl, perhaps in her image. However, overtime, it became obvious that Henry was to be their last-born. Upon a heartfelt deliberation, Roger decided that Rebecca, as a companion, would be the perfect solution to his wife's maternal yearnings. Rebecca could be someone his wife could dote on and mentor, someone that would keep her from falling into her solemn moods. It did not surprise Roger to learn that Jane wholeheartedly approved of hiring Rebecca as a companion for her.

Lady and Lord Ingall decided to talk to Mr. Stevens and Rebecca to see if they would be amenable to their proposal. They planned to conduct a private interview with each of them. Jane would keep Rebecca with her while Roger took the vicar to his study to make his proposition, explaining the equitable benefits for each of them. He planned to emphasize Lady Ingall's need for company and how the position would give Rebecca the opportunity to learn decorum, dress, and those skills necessary to engage in the upper echelons of society. He would assure the vicar that Rebecca would be treated more like family than a servant, while in her own interview with Rebecca, Jane would learn more about the girl to ascertain whether she would be agreeable to their proposal.

They waited anxiously in their sitting parlour for Mr. Stevens and Rebecca to arrive. When Jane spied the vicar and his daughter, she went to pull the bell cord to summon a tray of tea while Roger welcomed them. Proffering his arm, Lord Ingall escorted Rebecca to a seat near his wife. He relinquished Rebecca to Jane's company and then he requested a private audience with Mr. Stevens, who immediately agreed. Mr. Stevens and Lord Ingall retreated to his lordship's study, leaving Rebecca and Lady Ingall to conclude their own interview.

As soon as the tea service arrived, Jane set to task pouring a cup for Rebecca and herself. She then assessed Rebecca, taking in her full countenance. She looked at her clothes, her posture, how she held her cup, and then she looked at her eyes. Hazel eyes. She was partial to them as they reminded her of Roger.

Rebecca knew she was being scrutinized and her knees began to shake, making her cup and saucer clatter. Lady Ingall smiled and tried to put her at ease by asking about her mother, "Tell me, Rebecca, do you look like your mama?"

Rebecca smiled and said, "I think I do. I am rather plain faced like her, though unlike me she had beautiful blond hair." After a hesitation Rebecca blurted, "However, papa insists I am not plain, but a flawless beauty." At her remark, Rebecca blushed and began to laugh, apologizing to Lady Ingall for her candor. "Clearly," she said "he sees me with loving eyes."

Lady Ingall was amused, thinking hidden behind Rebecca's facade of caution, existed a girl with sense and wit. She said, "Do not apologize, Rebecca. We should all be so lucky to have such adoring papas. Tell me, do you know how your parents met?"

Rebecca's eyes beamed. She thought her parents' betrothal was a great love story. She clasped her golden locket that hung from her neck in her right hand and then began her tale, "My papa met my mama as he is now, a vicar. He was visiting Baron..." Rebecca paused thoughtfully and then continued, "I can't remember his name, but that is not really important, what is important is that my mama worked in his household as a downstairs maid. My papa said her hair was much talked about and that when he saw her and her beautiful blond hair, he knew he was in love. You see, her hair was thick and had a natural wave. Papa said that when she let her hair fall down her back that it bounced when she walked. I know this to be true because I remember in the evenings, after my mama readied for bed, she would come to bid me good night and I would watch her long blond hair dance when she walked away. I tried once, unsuccessfully I might add, to make my own hair bounce like hers by hopping from one foot to the other."

Lady Ingall's smile encouraged Rebecca to continue. She said, "They married soon after they met. I remember my mama telling me that my papa rescued her from an uncomfortable situation and that she loved him for giving her a home and a family." Jane reflected that Rebecca's mother was a young woman of nine and ten when she married Mr. Stevens, already five and thirty at the time.

Jane noticed that when Rebecca recalled her story that she spoke in the manner of the old bards. Her eyes looked towards the far corners of the room as though the memory was a vision to be seen. With memories sparkling in her eyes, Rebecca eloquently narrated her parents' betrothal in a tale that equaled an Arthurian legend, where a Knight of the Round Table rescued a damsel in distress. Lady Ingall interrupted her, "It is clear that you love your parents very much. Tell me, what do you remember most of your mama?"

She was sorry she asked. The gleam Rebecca had in her eyes turned sad. Rebecca hesitated before whispering, "I miss her very much."

Lady Ingall reached over and squeezed Rebecca's hand. Before she could say anything, Rebecca continued in an affected voice, "My mama was full of life and laughter. We spent our days together while I helped her around the house and garden. She used to tell me about the wonderful parties she worked at the baron's house. Sometimes when we ate our simple meals, we renamed our dishes to reflect the supper set at the baron's table. It was great fun eating a turnip, but calling it a strawberry. At night before bedtime, mama would sing me a lullaby. She had a melodic tone that never failed to put me to sleep." Rebecca's eyes filled with tears. Cautiously, Lady Ingall asked how her mother died. Without hesitation Rebecca revealed, "Influenza. She never recovered."

Right at that moment, the doors opened. Mr. Stevens and Lord Ingall entered. Both of them stared with concern at the affecting picture of Rebecca and the countess. Lady Ingall quickly apologized to Mr. Stevens and said, "I inquired about Rebecca's mama," answering their unspoken question. "I am afraid we have become quite sentimental."

Rebecca looked at her father and offered a weary smile. Mr. Stevens walked to Rebecca and gave her a gentle hug and said, "You are a good daughter and deserve some amusement. How would you like to become a companion for the countess?"

Startled, Rebecca looked first at her father, then turned to look at Lady Ingall. She then shifted back to see her father. She whispered, "I do not know. May I think on it, Papa?"

Lady Ingall chimed in "Of course, my dear. There is no hurry. Take your time and let me know when you make your decision." On that note, Mr. Stevens and his daughter departed.

1818
Small parlour, Ingall Estate

Lady Ingall and Rebecca worked on their embroidery samples, warmed by the sun that filtered through the bay windows. For three years, since Rebecca agreed to become Lady Ingall's companion, she and her mistress spent the early evenings in quiet activity enjoying each other's company. Rebecca's journey from an awkward youth to a distinguished young lady who owned incomparable beauty and talents was a delightful surprise to all who knew her. It was hard to believe the young vicar's daughter with disheveled hair, poor dress, slouched posture, and a timid character was now a woman that could rival any lady of the peerage. Her hair shone and was styled in the latest fashion. Her clothes were made of the finest material, remarkably detailed with all the extravagances of fine lace, embroideries, and seeded pearls. Her posture was impeccable and she composed herself as one who knew she belonged. The only accoutrement that remained constant on Rebecca, from when she was first introduced to the Ingall household, was the locket her mother bequeathed on her before her demise. The once downcast discomfited and gangly girl, grew into a beautiful figured woman, who held her head high and presented a quiet air that radiated a warm and friendly demeanor.

Lord Ingall blessed the day that Rebecca agreed to become companion to his wife because she did something that he was not able to do. She bridged the Ingall family by unintentionally abolishing the boys' club of father and sons and creating a new institution that indulged men, women, and children in all activities.

The first family outing was the invention born out of need. Rebecca was distraught at not being able to see her father daily. As Lady Ingall's companion she was required to lodge at the Ingall Estate during the week because the vicar's cottage was located too far away for Rebecca to return home each day. She worried that her father would feel lonely. Mr. Stevens refused the offer of the Ingall's carriage to transport his daughter home each evening, feeling it was too much of a burden for all. He wanted Rebecca to be embraced by Lord and Lady Ingall and he thought that would only be possible if she lived with them. Rebecca was concerned her father would become melancholy in her absence, so she asked Lord Ingall if she could learn to ride and on occasion, visit her father during the weekday. Lord Ingall was a true benefactor and agreed. His lordship encouraged Rebecca's interest, especially since she insisted that Lady Ingall ride with her while she learned. Lady Ingall wanted to offer her a lady's maid for a chaperone, but Rebecca insisted that she was her companion. Rebecca argued that if Lady Ingall refused to accompany her on her lessons, then she could not agree to them, reasoning herself to be lacking in her duties as her paid companion. Lady Ingall was a mother that found it difficult to refuse a child's wishes, so she donned her riding habit and engaged in the activity she had forgotten she loved. It had been years since she rode with her husband, Roger. She stopped when he started instructing William to ride, staying behind to pacify Henry who would fall into a crying tantrum whenever his brother left him behind in the nursery. Jane could not leave her youngest son crying to be dealt with by his nanny. She knew her own absence would only make him feel more abandoned, so she fell into the habit of preoccupying Henry, whenever William and Roger went riding. Habit turned into expectation, so when it was Henry's turn to learn to ride, she stayed home, so as not to interfere with her husband's and sons' bond. She soon grew to envy that bond until a precious girl showed her how to become a part of it.

The early morning rides with his wife and Rebecca were Roger's favorite time of the day. He loved to see his wife relaxed and laughing. It reminded him of their early courtship before sadness hit them. He enjoyed the rides so much that he began to plan excursions for the whole family, for that was how Lady and Lord Ingall thought of Rebecca. When the boys came home from school breaks, they rejoiced in the plans their father made. They were surprised to learn their mother owned some athletic skills. Her horsemanship and shooting surpassed their own. They marveled of the misconception they had of her over the years. Their mother always seemed so distinguished and fragile. It gave them great pleasure to see that she had a competitive and hoyden streak that made spending time with her fun. Her humor and laughter were infectious and the boys were grateful for the changes that allowed their mother to join them in their outdoor pursuits. They especially enjoyed Rebecca's company, who unlike other girls of their peer, did not squeal at the sight of a frog or want to swoon when they baited their worms for fishing.

Rebecca relished her new life. She finally felt comfortable in her own skin, though that road to womanhood had been challenging. She probably would have given up, if not for the Ingall family, who all tutored and supported her.

Lady Ingall, with remarkable patience, showed Rebecca proper etiquette and form. Her ladyship had to overcome Rebecca's concerns that she was rising above her station and finally convinced her that good manners had nothing to do with class but with character. They spent many afternoons having tea where she could teach Rebecca the proper way to sit, to pour tea, to sip tea, and to engage in polite conversation. She reminded her that young ladies did not enter into masculine topics like politics, but were encouraged to discuss the weather and fashion among gentlemen of their society. A married woman could be tolerated to offer an opinion, but gentlemen expected young ladies to be naive and request guidance in forming their views. A woman showing intelligence was often labeled a *bluestocking,* an anathema for those ladies of quality who met to discuss politics and cultural interests. The label could be social ruin, so Lady Ingall tried to teach Rebecca to be circumspect of her opinions. It was a futile lesson because Rebecca loved to read. She had spent her youth helping her father with his Latin translations and sermons. Her natural inquisitive mind prompted her to investigate and to ask questions anytime something mystified her. Her honest outbursts often startled Lady and Lord Ingall into laughter. Try as they might, they were unable to check her forthright behavior and eventually, abandoned the effort for they came to love the genuineness of her character. Besides, Lady Ingall could hardly chastise her when she believed herself that knowledge was powerful. She was of the opinion that while one did not need to discuss everything one knew, one certainly should know as much as possible of whatever anyone else knew.

Lady Ingall encouraged Rebecca to read the newspaper, popular subscriptions, and the latest novels (those she deemed appropriate). Together with Lord Ingall, they would discuss the writings in the evenings. The casual after dinner discussions helped her hone her conversational skills. She learned how to introduce a topic, how to include others in a discussion, and how to deflect inquiries that proved uncomfortable. Each evening, Rebecca became more confident and accomplished to the delight of Lord and Lady Ingall.

Once her natural affinity for the pianoforte was discovered, Lady Ingall hired a master to coach her in music and voice. Rebecca was diligent in her practice and after three years of study, she regularly played before an audience. Lady and Lord Ingall enjoyed their private evening concerts with only William, Henry, and Mr. Stevens in occasional attendance.

William and Henry, like their parents, grew to love Rebecca. They helped her when possible with her transformation from a shy, awkward girl to a confident poised woman. Plenty of evenings were spent helping Rebecca balance books on top of her head to improve her posture. William and Henry worked as a team. For every book that fell off Rebecca's head, Henry was near to pick it up. William, as Rebecca's escort, had a book ready to replace each fallen one. It was a strenuous affair. William would quickly replace a book on Rebecca's head while Henry picked up the felled book and handed it to William for a reserve. William and Henry followed Rebecca around the room hoping she could balance the book with stellar posture. When she failed and the book fell, the process started all over again, until young Henry in exhaustion, cried, "Stop! I think I have broke my back!"

Aside from her beauty and talents, Rebecca was kind and generous with her time. She helped William and Henry with their homework, played games with them, listened to their concerns, and teased them as though they were her siblings. Over time, they began to think of her as the sister they never had and Rebecca cherished them in return.

Lady Ingall and Rebecca looked up from their embroidery samples when Lord Ingall entered the parlour.

Jane was ready to disabuse her husband for his tardiness when she saw the pallor of his face. “Roger!” she exclaimed. “Heavens what is it?"

When he did not answer, she quickly rose, placing her embroidery frame on her seat, before walking to him. She took his hand into hers and checked her inquiry when she saw him shake his head from side to side. She feared the worst, for it was unlike her husband to lose control of his emotions. She waited for him to gain his composure. Then watched when he opened his fist to reveal a crumbled parchment. She removed the paper from his palm and carefully unraveled the note. Her knees buckled when she finished reading the news. She was glad her husband had the sense to catch her. Her shock was such, that she would have collapsed to the floor had he not captured her and held her close. She looked up to her husband and was sure the sadness she saw in his face mirrored her own.

Rebecca alarmed at the scene before her, queried, "What has happened?"

Lord Ingall, solemnly answered, "Lord Westfield is dead."

A fortnight passed before a heart-wrenched Lord Shelby returned home. His father was laid to rest by then and his mother was closeted away in her darkened room. Her heavy red velvet drapes were pulled closed and only the glow from the fireplace illuminated the room. Lord

Shelby was told that she retired to her room shortly after Lord Westfield's burial and had not received any visitors, even Lady Ingall had been sent away. Since her retreat, Lady Westfield had consumed little nourishment and appeared to sleep most of the day. Lord Shelby was told that her most loyal of servants were beginning to worry.

The shock of her husband's untimely death had overcome Amelia and she found herself unable to rise from her bed. She spent the day asleep in her room, dreaming her husband still lived. Her mind was unable to bear the conscious truth of his death and she preferred her dreams to reality. When she was awake, she lay in reflection and remembered their courtship and marriage. They were a young couple when they met and married in London. Lady Amelia brought a small fortune with her when they married and his peers heralded Lord Westfield, Viscount Shelby at the time, with making a fine match. He knew they applauded the connections and wealth that Lady Amelia brought to the marriage, but Lord Westfield knew he found the woman that completed his heart. Where he was weak, Amelia was strong and yet their tastes were similar. They both enjoyed life with a passion. They liked to eat heartily, play games, entertain, laugh, and talk. They could energetically converse for hours about anything, or spend their day doing something serene, like looking at the clouds to discern the character of each one. They both loved athletic pursuits and rode daily together. It didn't matter what they did, it only mattered that they were together. Their life was free of worries and they spent their days in idle relaxation, enjoying each other's company, until the day that through his father's death he became the Seventh Earl of Westfield. The inheritance forced the new Lord Westfield to return to his ancestral home and assume the duties of his earldom.

His father had been widowed and ill for years. When the new earl returned home he learned that while he had always received a healthy allowance from his father, he did so without knowing the state of his inheritance. The Seventh Earl of Westfield found his properties in great need for improvement and his tenants severely neglected. The steward that worked for his father was nowhere to be found and left the new Earl and Countess of Westfield meagerly welcomed home by crisis. Lord Westfield was a man that liked to make everyone happy. The situation of his inheritance overwhelmed him and he slowly retreated from his duty. Amelia found herself in constant argument with her husband insisting that he take charge. It did not take long for their marriage to become strained.

In the end, it was Amelia's fortitude and savvy that enabled her to take stock and initiate the management of their estate. Amelia craved the comfortable and loving relationship that existed between her and her husband before he came into his inheritance. She decided that in order to reconcile her marriage, she needed to take over the management of their properties. Amelia removed the responsibility from her husband and learned that not only did she have an aptitude for business, but that she liked it as well. Her marriage resolved itself. Lord Westfield relieved of his burden showed magnanimity toward his wife and placed exceptional admiration on her and her decisions. He never questioned her choices and made sure no one else did. She had his full support and hearty praise. Their marriage was blissful and nine months later Jonathan was born.

Grief stricken, Jonathan cautiously entered his mother's suite. He was unsure whether to wake her if she was sleeping. The room was eerily quiet. He expected to hear her breathing and when he didn't, he panicked and called out her name. Lady Westfield thought she heard her husband's voice. She opened her eyes and dropped her mouth in astonishment. It took her a minute to discern it was her son calling her and it took another minute for her to realize the sobs she heard were coming from her.

Jonathan wrapped his grieving mother in his arms and apologized for not arriving home sooner. While his mother wept, Jonathan spoke softly, telling her that she wasn't alone and that together they would find a way.... Jonathan did not finish his sentence. He did not know how.

Chapter Three

Lady Ingall sat with Rebecca in her posh carriage near the steps that led to the Westfield Manor's portico. She anxiously awaited to learn if Amelia would see her. She had sent her calling card with her footman to inquire if Lady Westfield was receiving visitors. It had been over two months since she saw her friend and her concern for Amelia grew exponentially with each passing day. She had seen for herself, the week after Lord Westfield's passing, the impact the flood of visitors had on Amelia's health. Lord Westfield had been well-liked and admired among his peers, and news of his untimely death brought them all to pay their respects to his widow. Their profound sorrow fueled Amelia's own despair, eventually sending her into solitude. Jane understood Amelia's need to retreat and gain some equilibrium, but she did not understand why she was not the exception to her standing order of not receiving callers.

She hoped today would prove different, since she knew that Jonathan, the new Earl of Westfield, had returned home. Before his arrival, rumors had begun to spread through the servant grapevine that the mistress of Westfield was wasting away. Nothing had relieved her more than to learn that Jonathan had finally returned home. She hoped he was able to pull his mother back from the abyss where she had fallen. A squeeze to her hand brought Lady Ingall back from her reflections. Rebecca had reached to hold her hand in support when the footman returned with news. Jane sighed with relief to learn that the Countess of Westfield would receive her in her private suite. She quickly debarked from her carriage.

Lady Westfield had started to rally the moment Jonathan returned home. They spent hours reminiscing and the memories assuaged their grief. The pain was still there, but each day they remembered a word, a phrase, or a moment, and like a salve soothes a burn, they found relief in their recollections. Sometimes, they even caught themselves laughing when they imagined what Harold would have said, had he still been with them.

Time had no measurement as days passed into one another without notice, but eventually Amelia began to function. She called it "function" because she wasn't prepared to live yet, but she was able to rise and leave her room.

It was on one of these days that she learned her tenants were dropping off presents with their heartfelt sympathies. The gifts were simple: bands of posies, homemade breads, and jellies. She knew each tenant had a long and arduous walk to reach the manor. Not many farmers owned horses which meant they had to leave early in the morning to reach Westfield Manor with enough time left to return to finish their chores. She was overcome with emotion realizing the esteem her tenants held for her. She could picture each of them approaching her home with the tender gifts in their Sunday best clothes as a sign of respect. She felt a speck of guilt having indulged in her grief when they were most likely concerned for their future. They probably wondered whether Jonathan, the new Earl of Westfield, would be a conscientious landowner. They probably had plenty of questions, though she knew that their station would keep them from asking. These thoughts distracted her enough from her melancholy to seek out Jonathan to review the Westfield properties with him.

Jonathan almost laughed when he listened to his mother's concerns regarding his readiness to assume his duties as earl. He had to remind her that she had instructed him well regarding property management and while he spent many an hour in recreational pursuits with his father, he spent just as many hours visiting their tenants, reviewing ledgers, and reading the latest journals on farming and science.

He was in his study reviewing his account books when he noticed a maid passing by his door with a tea tray. He wondered who came to call and followed the maid who carried the refreshments into the parlour. He did not recognize the lady sitting on the settee, but found he held his breath at her beauty. Before him sat a genteel woman wearing a rose-colored muslin gown. The Empire cut day dress was accented with dainty cream-colored rosettes on the border of her puffed sleeves and flounced hemline. An antique locket hung from the end of a gold chain resting against her décolletage. Jonathan saw that her face was retrospective before she turned to look at him. A heartfelt offer of sympathy for the loss of his father left her lips. He stood mesmerized looking at her. She had brown hair mixed with streaks of raspberry blond. Her hazel eyes seemed to twinkle just for him.

"Pray, forgive me," he apologized. "Have we met?"

Rebecca bowed her head in embarrassment. She blushed having remembered their first meeting. Composing herself, she raised her head to make her answer and found Jonathan watching her. With aplomb, she said, "Yes, my lord, we were introduced at your *bon voyage* party that your mama hosted the evening before you left on your *Grand Tour*. I am the vicar's daughter, Miss Stevens."

Jonathan was surprised. Her regal dress and demeanor spoke more of the peerage than the child of a clergyman. Yes, he remembered the young girl at his mother's country-dance. Rebecca saw the glimmer of recognition and smiled when she said, "I see you remember our introduction, my lord, though you were then Lord Shelby. I fear I have grown up since you went away."

Jonathan raised his brows and answered with amusement, "Indeed." After a pause, he asked, "Is your father, Mr. Stevens, attending my mother?"

"No," answered Rebecca softly. "I am here with Lady Ingall. I have been her companion these past three years."

Their visit was cut short when Lady Ingall entered. Rebecca rose upon seeing her, but was waved down by her mistress, who said, "Pray, sit down, Rebecca, I want a word with his lordship before we take our leave." Jane extended her hand to Lord Westfield and asked, "Jonathan, how are you managing?"

Jonathan took Lady Ingall's hand and placed a gentle kiss to the back of it, before replying, "Much better. Tell me, how does my mother seem to you?"

"She is amazing, my lord. Though I had my concerns at first. She grieves and does not seem interested in the business affairs that so used to occupy her time. She is more concerned about you and the tenants. It is family and our little community that will rally her. Don't you worry, she will come around if for no other reason than because she knows your papa would not be happy to see her grieving. He was such a cheerful man and wished for everyone to be so."

Jonathan smiled at her comment, knowing it to be true. He asked Lady Ingall to sit and have tea, but she insisted that she had to go and that his mother had requested that he pay her a visit. Jonathan escorted them to their carriage. While he watched them drive away, he felt an ease in his breathing as though a weight had been removed from his chest. He recalled Lady Ingall's comments regarding his father and reiterated the remark, owning it as a truth, "Yes, father would not want us to grieve."

On Jonathan's orders, the heavy velvet drapes were pulled back each morning in his bedroom to let in the early light that woke him. He rose to find that his valet had his toilette and clothes ready for his ablutions and dress. It had taken Jonathan almost a fortnight, but today he would finish his visits to his tenants, inspecting his properties and listening to their complaints. He wanted to ease their minds by showing them he was an active and caring landlord. To his pleasure, his tenants responded with great appreciation and further endeared themselves by asking about the welfare of his mother, Lady Westfield. Jonathan informed them that as time passed she would be about inquiring after them as was her practice.

While Lady Westfield rose from her bed each day, she still received only a few visitors, Lady Ingall being one. She preferred the solitude of her private suite to the more public rooms, not wishing her grief to be on display for the servants. Rebecca had no wish to intrude on Lady Ingall's visit with Lady Westfield, so when she accompanied her mistress to Westfield Manor, she chose to wait in the Westfield library until Lady Ingall was ready to depart.

When Jonathan returned home from visiting his tenants, he was pleased to recognize the Ingall carriage parked in front of his manor house. He hoped that Miss Stevens had accompanied Lady Ingall on her visit to see his mother. He had enjoyed the few minutes he and Rebecca had shared together. She seemed comfortable in her own skin, able to laugh at their first and current introduction. Lately, it seemed that those members of the peerage that came to call were only interested in learning his political allegiance. He found it difficult to tolerate their disingenuous sympathy when it was clear to him that their purpose was to determine which party, Tory or Whig, he would give his vote when he took his father's seat in the House of Lords. He craved for the simple friendship that someone like the vicar's daughter could offer. If anyone could ameliorate him, it was Rebecca with her thoughtful and heartfelt consideration. Jonathan found her direct, honest, and liked the way she conversed easily. A warm feeling overcame him when he remembered her twinkling hazel eyes and he thought he would like to gaze on them once more.

Jonathan vaulted from his horse, handing the reins to his approaching ostler, and then brushed past his butler's greeting when his servant opened the door. During Jonathan's *Grand Tour,* he had learned to appreciate the flirtations and beauty of women. While abroad, his rank and noble blood garnered him more invitations to soirees and balls than he could attend. The ample society of women who were attracted to him eventually led him to his first liaison. Before long, Jonathan became quite experienced and confident in the company of women, so he was surprised at his jejune excitement at seeing Rebecca. He had to admit to himself that he was greatly attracted to her, but he also acknowledged any union other than a dalliance was insupportable. His title demanded an equal alliance of lineage and wealth, and he knew that duty forbid him to marry anyone beneath his station. Sadly, he believed she was too respectable for an affair of the heart. He shuddered realizing that any flirtation with the vicar's daughter could cause scandal.

With quiet, unnoticed moves, Jonathan stealthily searched each public room until he came across Rebecca in the library. He observed her from the doorway and smiled at her concentration over the book she read.

Jonathan thought Rebecca was an intuitive girl to seek out the most comfortable chair in the room. She wore a jonquil cambric dress accented with petite embroidered daisies. The square cut collar was trimmed in lace and her hair was styled in the Grecian fashion with a few curls loose around her face. Her gold locket hung from her neck and Jonathan thought her charming.

Rebecca felt someone's presence as though she was being watched and surreptitiously checked out her surroundings to see if anyone had entered the room. She was surprised to see Jonathan smiling at her and immediately blushed at her ill attempt at stealth. She franticly stood, blushed, curtsied, and offered a shy felicitation. She doubted his lordship heard her faint greeting and was taken aback when he made his way to her. He looked like a man on a mission, taking three deliberate strides to welcome her. He took her hand, placed a kiss on it and greeted her most warmly, "Miss Stevens, it is indeed a pleasure to see you once again."

Rebecca felt his warmth radiate from her fingers through her body. Her face grew even more crimson when he failed to immediately release her hand. Jonathan noted her discomfiture and being a gentleman he tried to put her at ease, by asking, "What are you reading?"

Rebecca answered, "I am reading Saint Augustine's *De Doctrina Christiana."*

Jonathan replied, "You surprise me, Miss Stevens. I thought one of the more popular novels would be your choice."

Rebecca beamed and giggled before she informed Jonathan, "Oh, they are. I like them quite dearly. In fact, I fear I gave young Henry and myself a fright the other night after reading a subscription by Mrs. Radcliffe."

Jonathan asked what happened and with good humor Rebecca told him that after reading the delicious mystery, she thought she heard a noise in the hallway and went to investigate. It appeared from sheer nerves, she was a clumsy investigator and had made enough noise to wake Henry, who took himself into the hallway where providence had them back into one another. Screams abounded and the whole household woke to find them, giggling and admonishing one another for their fright.

After controlling his laughter, Jonathan asked Rebecca where she learned to read Latin. Rebecca answered, “Surely, it should not be a surprise to you that a clergyman’s daughter knows Latin. I believe I am my father’s most attentive pupil. I take much joy in being able to confer with him regarding his sermons. He is a most passionate vicar and receives much satisfaction from his work, though he tells me I am his greatest joy.” Rebecca laughed at her last remark.

Jonathan’s eyes gleamed with amusement. He was amazed at Rebecca's unpretentious nature. He admired her candor and found her ability to laugh at herself refreshing. He stared at Rebecca and wanted to reply something clever, but nothing came to mind.

After a momentary silence, Rebecca reclaimed her composure and in a most ladylike manner asked, “Did you enjoy your *Grand Tour*, my lord?”

Jonathan smiled and guided her to the settee where they sat down together to begin their discourse. He answered, “It was quite educational. You might be happy to know that I visited the shrine of your most revered St. Augustine in Italy.” Rebecca was pleased and asked question after question. Jonathan found it easy to share his adventures, especially to someone who listened so attentively that she was able to interject her own ideas and readings into the conversation. Jonathan thought, *"She is really interested in what I am saying. Her eyes show so much enthusiasm for what I have seen. I wish I could show her all the places I have visited and discover all the pieces of knowledge she has stored away."*

She demanded, "My lord, are you laughing at me?" Apparently Jonathan's amusement to Rebecca's lengthy discourse about her readings was revealed in a large grin and she thought that he was ridiculing her *bluestocking* tendencies.

He replied, "Not at all, I am only smiling at your wealth of knowledge and wished I had known an iota of it while I traveled."

Rebecca laughed and said, "That is very kind of you, my lord. You have indulged me most graciously. I am sorry I have trespassed on your good nature."

"Nonsense," replied Jonathan. "I cannot remember the last time I have enjoyed myself so much."

Lady Ingall's entrance and apology for overstaying her welcome, completely surprised Jonathan. Her visit had severely surpassed the socially accepted quarter hour and she begged forgiveness. Jonathan thought. *"Surely, it could not be, it seemed I had just arrived to greet Rebecca."* To his visitors, he remarked, "No forgiveness is necessary. I am sure mother is far better for it. I know I have thoroughly enjoyed Miss Steven's company."

Lady Ingall looked at Rebecca and then back to Lord Westfield, before replying, "Very good, my lord, but we trespass no longer. Come, Rebecca."

Chapter Four

Jonathan was looking forward to his next visit with Rebecca when he received a letter that required his attention. Part of Jonathan's inheritance included some estate property in Scotland. His steward on that estate wrote to request his presence, in regards to solicit permission for some renovations that he wished to make.

The call to duty both excited and dismayed him. He had to admit, if only to himself, he yearned to escape the overwhelming sadness that still permeated his home. With his mother unwilling to take on the duties of mistress, he found himself seeing to the housekeeping duties, as well as the estate management. Even more draining was his obligation to host every visitor that came to pay their respects. A family and its home mourned the loss of a loved one for a year, less if the member was not much admired. That meant shunning bright clothing and parties. He knew some widows who after six months, dropped their black wardrobe and entered the social scene. Yet, there were those who mourned for a better of two years if not their lifetime and Jonathan cringed at that depressing thought. His father loved to live life to its fullest and his spirit beckoned Jonathan to shed his sorrow and join in the amusements Society offered. His only hesitation was in leaving his mother alone with only her grief as companion.

Jonathan went looking for his mother and as he expected, found her in her private suite lying on her chaise lounge in slumber. He hated to see her resigned to sadness. He wished she would rally and not let her sorrow defeat her. He knew it would break his father's heart to see her so brokenhearted. He did not wish to disturb her solace and was ready to make his exit when he saw her eyelids flutter open. She welcomed him to take a seat next to her.

He asked, "How are you?"

"You must not worry about me, Son," she replied. "Each day is a challenge, but I am well. I confess, I had a dream where your father was chastising me. Telling me to get up and enjoy each day for the gift it is. I fear I may have disappointed him gravely."

Jonathan saw his mother's tears and said, "Don't be ridiculous. Father loved you dearly and was amazingly proud of your ability to manage this large estate with little help from him. He constantly told me how grateful he felt that you condescended to be his wife."

Jonathan's eyes widened when his mother let out an unexpected guffaw. He found his own laughter bubble up when she lightly shoved him in the arm.

"Oh, my," she said. "That felt amazingly good. Only your father could make me laugh like that, condescend, indeed. Leave it to him to find a way to reach me with his words."

"Well," she continued. "I won't shame his memory by being the type of person he despised, someone who took life for granted. The way he greeted each day with gusto makes me wonder if he knew his life would be cut short and he wanted to make the most of the time he had."

Jonathan watched his mother rise and begin to make her exit. He asked, "Where are you going?"

"It's time I met with the housekeeper and saw to the manor."

Later that evening, after talking to her about Scotland, he felt better about leaving. She seemed improved after engaging in some industry, talking to the housekeeper to review menus and household accounts. She even helped to inventory the linen closet. His staff were so happy to see their mistress up and about, he was sure they presented problems to engage her counsel just so that she would not retreat to her room. He hoped his absence only encouraged her more to involve herself with the estate once again.

When Jane heard of Jonathan's departure, she immediately became concerned for Amelia. Her worries that she might fall into despair again led her to ask Rebecca if she would consider staying with Lady Westfield until Jonathan returned. Rebecca wanted to please Lady Ingall and assuage her fears. Since she believed her visit with the countess would be of a short duration, she gladly agreed. Even though Jane was sorry to relinquish Rebecca's companionship, she believed it was the right thing to do. The next day, Rebecca and Lady Ingall traveled to Westfield Manor where Lady Westfield received them in her parlour. While Amelia served them tea, Jane revealed her proposal.

At first, Amelia balked at Jane's suggestion, but eventually she relented. Lady Westfield admitted that she had been lonely since Jonathan's departure. She confessed a melancholy that veiled her in the evening hours. Rebecca felt great sympathy for Lady Westfield and was glad Lady Ingall was able to convince the widowed countess to invite her to stay with her. She warmly accepted Lady Westfield's invitation. Through teary eyes, Amelia remarked, "You are too kind."

In Scotland, Jonathan's business took longer than he expected, but after a month he was headed home on the North Road. He had ridden his own stallion Apollo and once again, began to regret doing so, having to maneuver his steed through the hazards of a well trodden road. Many horses fractured their legs and many carriages turned over when their cattle were unable to maintain their footing on the deep ruts. The inclement weather and the heavy traffic, like the hands of a sculptor, molded the road into potholes and ridges, playing havoc on its travelers and their mounts. Jonathan decided he was weary of Scotland and would not rest until he crossed the border into North Yorkshire, making his way to Northallerton. He chose to stop at the Black Bull, one of the smaller posting inns to take his repast. He planned to spend the night and allow his steed a night of rest. He hoped his valet and carriage would catch up with him at the inn before he made his way home to Westfield Manor. The market town of Northallerton was a busy hub with four posting inns that catered to travelers. Jonathan was fatigued and not in the mood to ensconce himself into the pandering society of the larger inns, so he was content to quench his thirst at the quieter Black Bull.

He was drinking a pint of ale and had just eaten a pigeon pie when he heard someone exclaim, "Shelby! Forgive me, Lord Westfield, how good to see you!" Jonathan recognized Mr. Arthur Willoughby right away. They had attended Cambridge together and Jonathan remembered him to be a pleasant sort of a fellow, a man more happy to cause mischief than not. Arthur was not of the aristocracy, he was the son of a baronet, so they did not travel in the same circles, but to Jonathan's recollection they had gotten along well at school. As memory served him, Arthur always had some *chit* on his arm, so seeing him alone surprised him.

"Sorry about the name," replied Arthur.

"Not necessary," said Jonathan. "I still think they are calling my father when I hear Lord Westfield. What are you doing here?"

"My parent's country home is nearby in the Vale of Mowbray," answered Arthur. "We just left London, closed up the town house. You know, end of the Season and all. My parents brought some guests home to entertain, but they completely bore me, so I was seeking more satisfying entertainment." Inspiration hit Arthur and he gleefully suggested, "Pray, come stay for a visit. My sister Belinda is in attendance and the three of us will make a fine party."

Jonathan agreed to an introduction, but not until he met Arthur's sister Belinda did he decide to stay. Like Arthur, Belinda had blond hair and blue eyes, but it was her full hourglass figure that captured his attention. On their meeting, Belinda expertly fluttered her long dark eyelashes. After three years on the *Grand Tour*, Jonathan was immune to the machinations of a pretty woman, but like any man, he was happy to enjoy them. Arthur was not amused seeing his silly sister try her wares. Belinda had just made her *come-out* and though she refused her first offer, she was actively interested in any aristocrat that crossed her path.

Jonathan spent most of his time with Arthur and engaged in those athletic pursuits that he once enjoyed with his father. They rode daily, Arthur showing off his countryside to his friend. If they were not riding, they were shooting grouse or fishing in the nearby streams. After the first week, Jonathan sent a missive to his mother to see if she could manage without him a little longer. When she responded with encouragement for him to stay and enjoy himself, he found the grief that had been hovering over him like a black cloud since his father's death, had lifted.

Belinda thought providence knocked on her door when her brother introduced the Earl of Westfield to her. She found him amazingly attractive, charming, and completely eligible owning a title, lands, and wealth. She decided he was the perfect man to marry, reasoning, *"Why bother with the Little Season when I have a most eligible and attractive gentleman at home?"*

Each night, she dressed in her finest gowns and flirted using every debutante's trick to her brother's dismay. When the earl looked at her, she acted modestly and when Jonathan expressed some wit, Belinda released a practiced lyrical giggle. Belinda took every opportunity to promenade across Jonathan's path to display her figure to advantage, swinging her hourglass hips to and fro. Throughout all her exhibitions, Jonathan smiled and made small quips, complimenting her beauty and style. He enjoyed the flirtations and made sure to compliment her when she struck a pose, "I say, Miss Willoughby, you create a stunning picture in your blue crepe dress. You must have many beaus at your door."

"Thank you, my lord. You are too kind, but I fear I am too reserved to encourage the society of too many beaus." Arthur held back his laughter and Jonathan smiled, for Belinda never failed to amuse him with her attempts at seduction.

When Belinda was not flirting, she did her best to showcase her talents, like presenting her watercolor paintings for review. This evening, her family was surprised when she announced she would play the pianoforte for their entertainment. Jonathan was told that she rarely performed for an audience and he felt honored that she chose to play for him. He took a seat where he could watch her hands and fingers dance across the ivory keys. He enjoyed watching the artistry of a pianist's hands lifting, crossing, and their fingers hitting the keys to create arpeggios, chords, and melodies. To him, the hand movement was as entertaining as the music produced.

On his *Grand Tour*, he had visited the Italian Opera and attended many *musicales* that featured accomplished pianists. He always found the music affecting and realized he heartily awaited Belinda's performance. She looked stunning in a primrose cambric dress. The candelabra on the pianoforte illuminated her beauty and Jonathan felt himself totally captivated. He leaned forward from his seat with alacrity.

He watched Belinda gracefully place her fingers on the ivory keys to begin her prelude. He nodded his encouragement when she favored him with a smile. By Belinda's fourth measure, Jonathan's body began to shake. He feared drawing attention to himself, so he relaxed back into his chair and bit his lip trying to control the convulsion that was bubbling from within. He looked around to see if he was the only one fighting to keep from laughing. He was amazed to find Arthur and his parents captivated by Belinda's performance. They looked spellbound. He thought perhaps his ears deceived him, until another note shrieked and his minute control crumbled. To his horror, he released a chuckle. He tried to compose himself by focusing on the flickering flames of the candelabra and trying to solve the conundrum of his hosts' hearing. After a few moments of concentrated effort, his laughter subsided and he began to marvel at Belinda's tenacity in finishing her piece. Regardless of her skill or lack thereof, her acute concentration on her music sheets impressed him. He suspected she forgot she was on display.

With a grand flourish, Belinda finished her piece, turned to face her audience and proffered a cheeky grin that gained her a standing ovation. Jonathan watched his hosts compliment their daughter. Arthur made his way to him and smiled. His high spirits broke Jonathan's shaky control and the bubbling convulsion he tried so hard to stifle earlier, finally bellowed out. Arthur joined in his laughter and soon everyone else did as well.

"She is much improved, my lord," remarked Lady Willoughby.

Arthur added, "We have a running bet on how long our guests can control their laughter. You won me a ten pound note, Westfield. I counted, you broke on the fourth measure."

Belinda punched her brother's arm and everybody started to laugh wholeheartedly again. In that moment, Belinda knew she would never receive an offer from Jonathan. He looked at her like a sister and to her surprise, she was not aggrieved. It was enough to know that he liked her.

Jonathan's visit ended when the Willoughbys prepared to return to London for the “Little Season.” On their last evening together, Miss Willoughby inquired, “Pray, tell me, my lord, will I see you in Town?”

“Perhaps,” responded Jonathan. “I need to return home first, but if I make the trip, I hope you give me leave to call on you.”

Miss Willoughby fluttered her eyelashes and teased, “But of course. I shall wait in anticipation for you to pay your respects.” And with her comment she laughed and then extended her hand to Lord Westfield who smiled and laughed as well. To Jonathan’s amusement, Belinda expected him to kiss her hand before bidding her farewell.

Since propriety dictated that Jonathan repay the hospitality Arthur bestowed on him, he invited his friend to accompany him home and immediately sent a message informing the Westfield household of their impending arrival. No sooner did Jonathan and Arthur dismount from their horses, did the Westfield butler open the front door in greeting.

Jonathan handed over his greatcoat and hat to his butler while inquiring the location of his mother. He was astonished to learn that she was in the parlour having tea with Miss Stevens. When Jonathan asked if Lady Ingall was visiting, he was further amazed to learn that Miss Stevens was a houseguest. Jonathan hurried to the parlour with Arthur following in his wake. He was anxious to learn how Rebecca came to be living in his home.

Rebecca wanted to rise and shout, *"Oh, Lord Westfield, I am so glad you are home!"* It took every ounce of her strength to maintain her dignity. She felt her body tremble and warm as her nerves overcame her. She prayed the blushing she felt would not rise to her face, but when she caught Lord Westfield's eyes widen and his smile grow ever bigger, she knew it was too late. *"He knows,"* she thought. *"He knows I am happy to see him."*

Lord Westfield saw Rebecca blush the minute he walked in and felt amazingly gratified. He realized he liked Rebecca and was sure she admired him as well. They were friends, he discerned, and he decided that he looked forward to spending time with her. While Jonathan indulged in his thoughts, his mother exclaimed, "Jonathan, dear boy, I am glad you are home!"

Arthur nudged Jonathan and coughed softly. Jonathan apologized, and said, "I say, I am sorry. Where are my manners? Mother, may I present Mr. Arthur Willoughby. Mr. Willoughby, my mother, the Countess of Westfield and her guest Miss Stevens. Miss Stevens is our vicar's daughter and the Countess of Ingall's companion."

Lady Westfield interrupted and said, "At the moment, Son, she is my companion. She has kept me in high spirits these past months that you were away and I fear, I do not know how I will relinquish her company."

Arthur approached Lady Westfield and Rebecca, stating the pleasure of their introduction. Rebecca dropped her mouth and was astounded to see the twinkle in Mr. Willoughby's eyes. She thought, *"He is flirting with me,"* while he took her hand and placed a kiss on it. She then realized he held it longer than Society dictated and blushed.

Jonathan noticed the rakish display and scowled at Rebecca. Lady Westfield saw Jonathan's face and asked, "What, dear Son, perturbs you?"

Jonathan rebounded quickly, "I am admonishing myself for staying away so long that you necessitated the need for companionship. Pray, forgive me."

"Don't be silly, Jonathan," replied his mother. "You are entitled to a life, you know, and I have found Miss Steven's company most refreshing and therapeutic. She has reminded me that I am most needed by our tenants and friends. That I have a responsibility not to waste the gift God has most generously bestowed on me. You will not see me so self-indulgent in my sorrow though I still grieve for your dear father." Lady Westfield held her sadness in check and swallowed before continuing, "Enough of personal matters that shall be discussed later. Pray, tell me, what you have been doing?"

Jonathan, with Arthur's quips thrown in for amusement, described his visit at the Willoughby country home. Rebecca listened attentively and while Jonathan narrated his romps through the countryside, Rebecca conjured up the beautiful Belinda with whom Jonathan had spent the last few months attending. She pictured Belinda in her wedding dress walking down the church aisle towards Jonathan who awaited her at the altar. Her mind was beginning to expand upon the theme when Mr. Willoughby interrupted her meanderings. "I fear we are boring you, Miss Stevens. Please forgive our gentlemanly rabble. Tell me, have you enjoyed your visit at Westfield Manor?"

Rebecca was surprised that Arthur noticed her reverie and took his intrusion into her mien as a compliment. She was moved by his charm and instinctively responded with a demure smile when she lowered her eyelids to reply, "Yes, thank you." Arthur smiled in return, pleased that he brought a blush to her countenance. Rebecca's ladylike manner pleased Lady Westfield, as well. Jonathan was the only one that seemed to dislike the whole scene entirely.

A thought occurred to Lady Westfield after she witnessed the interplay between Rebecca and Arthur. In a matter of seconds, Lady Westfield's life took new purpose. She liked Rebecca and decided she would help her make a suitable match. She would need to learn more of the character of Mr. Willoughby, but a match between a vicar's daughter and a baronet's son was a suitable prospect. Lady Westfield decided she would devise a test to determine Mr. Willoughby's character and whether he was a worthy suitor for Rebecca.

Jonathan asked about his tenants, interrupting his mother's thoughts and she considered it fortuitous. She said, "Dear Mrs. Williams slipped and fell, injuring her ankle. She is hopping about with a sturdy piece of English Oak for support. I have asked Miss Stevens to visit her tomorrow and take her a poultice that I think will help. Perhaps, you and Mr. Willoughby may accompany her."

To Jonathan's frustration, Arthur beat him in responding, "I would be most delighted to accompany, Miss Stevens." Jonathan's irritation increased when he saw Rebecca blush.

Lady Westfield took great satisfaction in creating a situation that placed Mr. Willoughby in Rebecca's company and could hardly wait to hear how Mr. Willoughby conducted himself.

Chapter Five

When Rebecca's abigail informed her the earl and his guest were waiting outside by the carriage for her, she beckoned Hannah to quickly finish her dress. She liked to call the servants by their actual names if they knew it, many maids grew up in servitude where the name Mary was the only identity they remembered.

Rebecca fidgeted while Hannah tied the bow of her straw bonnet under her chin. She did not allow the maid to tidy the bow to perfection. The minute she felt her hat secured, she grabbed her kid gloves, raced out of her room and down the main staircase, holding her skirt with one hand so as not to trip, without thought to her unladylike manner. Hannah ran to follow, for she was tasked to chaperone the vicar's daughter on her visit with the earl to the Williams's farm.

A footman checked the smile that twitched to reveal itself when he spied the pretty vicar's daughter owning a flushed and happy expression. He opened the front door with precision when she approached and accepted her thanks for his consideration. An unfamiliar gesture since a servant was rarely thanked.

Rebecca paused when she crossed the threshold, stopping at the top of the steps that led to the graveled drive. She marveled at having two dashing gentlemen awaiting her. She had never received any man's attention before and the idea that not one, but two noblemen wished to keep her company amazed her.

She hurried to them and made her felicitations. Jonathan and Arthur reciprocated with both greetings and compliments. She was wearing a sprig muslin dress with puffed sleeves and a matching spencer that would do little to protect her from the cold. She looked very pretty and when she noted she was being looked upon admiringly, she found a warmth spread through her body and she blushed. She quickly accepted Jonathan's hand to enter his luxurious carriage and took her seat. Hannah followed and sat next to her mistress. Normally, her place would be the seat with the uncomfortable position of having her back to the road, but the earl insisted that she take the forward facing seat next to Rebecca. Without censure, Rebecca remarked, "The day is so beautiful, I wish we could have ridden instead of closeting ourselves inside."

Jonathan asked, "Do you not like my carriage, Miss Stevens?"

"Heavens," replied Rebecca. "I do beg your pardon, my lord. I meant no offense."

"I take none, Miss Stevens," grinned Jonathan. "I confess on a day like today, I would prefer to ride but baggage, or I should say the baskets we carry to the Williams's farm make it impossible."

Arthur asked, "Do you ride, Miss Stevens?"

"Yes, and quite well. Lord Ingall and his sons have tutored me exceptionally."

"The Earl of Ingall," questioned Mr. Willoughby, "a tutor?"

Rebecca laughed, replying, "Yes, Mr. Willoughby, a most proficient one." Arthur reflected that Lord Ingall was a prized connection being the heir apparent to a dukedom. He knew the Earl and Countess of Ingall were relentlessly sought after when they came to Town. Their attendance to any event made it an immediate success. He marveled at the intimacy a vicar's daughter shared with the Ingall family.

Jonathan asked Rebecca if she would like to ride the estate with him tomorrow. He could tell by the smile on her face that his request pleased her and he was surprised how the idea of a private jaunt with her made him feel giddy. He had no time to examine his feelings because they quickly changed to frustration when Arthur exclaimed, "That is a capital idea!"

In the carriage, Arthur sat opposite Rebecca with Jonathan next to him across from Hannah. Rebecca took a good look at Arthur and silently noted, *"He is very good looking. I like his blue eyes and his full blond curly hair. It is quite the fashion with it cut short."* She then realized that his sister Belinda was most likely as beautiful as he was handsome, and the thought unnerved her.

Jonathan caught Rebecca looking at Arthur and became irked. His feelings surprised him as did his unkind thoughts, *"Are you bartering your wares, Rebecca?"*

Rebecca saw Jonathan scowl at her and was concerned she had done something to displease him, although she knew not what for he had only arrived yesterday and they had barely spoken.

Arthur did his own observations and knew exactly why Jonathan scowled. Rebecca was a beauty; *a diamond of the first water,* and her observation of him did not go unnoticed. Arthur wondered if a *tendress* existed between Lord Westfield and Miss Stevens. He made up his mind to ask Jonathan when a private moment availed itself. No need, he deduced, to affront his host or sever a perfectly good connection by trifling with her.

They arrived at the Williams's farm. Jonathan quickly disembarked from the carriage and offered his assistance to Rebecca before Arthur had time to realize the carriage had stopped. Arthur smiled at Jonathan's gallantry and his competitive nature stirred. He would not let his lordship outmaneuver him, so he quickly offered Rebecca assistance by carrying her basket.

Rebecca was not sure why Jonathan and Mr. Willoughby were lavishing her with undue attention. She had never been in a situation where suitors were vying for her favor, so their behavior was alien to her. She never had an admirer. The idea that these noblemen were competing for her good opinion never crossed her mind. Her focus was on the Westfield tenant. Any curiosity she had regarding the gentlemen that accompanied her diminished when she entered the cottage and saw poor Mrs. Williams.

The invalid, Mrs. Williams, was seated in her front room that acted as both parlour and kitchen with her foot propped. The cottage was empty except for the toddler that was too young to be unattended. Mr. Williams and his children were likely doing chores and would soon appear once Lord Westfield's carriage was spied.

Rebecca hailed Mrs. Williams who answered, "How good of her ladyship to see to my sufferings. I am unworthy of her kindness."

"Do not say so," chided Rebecca. "You are most good and greatly admired by friends and family. How are you this day?"

Mrs. Williams, a stout woman, tried to rise and grimaced as she did. Rebecca placed her hand on Mrs. Williams's shoulder and said, "There is no need to rise as his lordship would not wish it. Please allow me to introduce his guest, Mr. Willoughby."

Mrs. Williams smiled showing all her teeth as only a matron can and said, "Tis a pleasure, Mr. Willoughby."

Rebecca instructed Mr. Willoughby to set the basket he carried down and then instructed the gentlemen to find Mr. Williams while she prepared tea. Rebecca removed her spencer and put on a weathered apron that hung on a peg nearby. Arthur and Jonathan marveled how someone so ladylike as Miss Stevens, showed no disgust when she picked up the dirty dishes on the table left from breakfast and carried them to the sink to be washed.

Rebecca was no novice to chores. She had kept home for her father for years after her mother's death, so she did not ascertain Lord Westfield or Mr. Willoughby's distaste when she donned the dirty apron. Mrs. Williams, on the other hand was used to Rebecca's help (she was the vicar's daughter after all and a hired companion) and her manner towards Rebecca was nothing less than appreciative.

Lord Westfield was disgusted that a lady, for that is how he viewed Rebecca, should lower herself with such menial tasks. He thought, *"No lady of rank would ever do such a thing."*

Mr. Willoughby, however, saw it as an opportunity to further his advances of gallantry and offered his assistance. With a quirky smile on his face, he executed a small bow and implored, "Miss Stevens, do put me to task. I am quite capable you know."

Jonathan's temper flared when Rebecca replied, "How very kind you are, Mr. Willoughby, to engage in such wifely duties."

Before Jonathan could check his behavior he slammed the door on his exit. Upon reflection, he realized that Rebecca's comment had surprised him. He deduced that her station in life dictated her values regarding the management of a household. To the common man, her actions would favor admiration; a nobleman, however, could only abjure them. As he made his way to find Mr. Williams, he contemplated, *"Isn't that what I did by exiting the cottage? What a proud man I am to shun her behavior. She is only being kind and helpful."*

He then wondered, *"What the devil is Arthur doing in there?"* Jonathan started to laugh when he recalled Rebecca's words and pictured Arthur engaging in wifely duties, but he checked his humor when he realized that Arthur was enjoying Rebecca's company and he was not.

Lord Westfield and Mr. Williams returned half an hour later to find the cottage swept and straightened. The dishes were washed and put away, a poultice was placed on Mrs. Williams's ankle and the toddler was sitting on Mr. Willoughby's bouncing knee. Lord Westfield and Mr. Williams found the cozy group laughing and in high spirits when they entered. Since Jonathan's exit, Rebecca had removed the aged apron and was looking remarkably invigorated. She rose and greeted, "You are just in time for tea." She then turned to ask Mrs. Williams, "May I pour?"

Mrs. Williams beamed at the gracious offer and replied, "Yes, please my dear, if you would be so kind."

The day concluded with Rebecca feeling remarkably content, a complete contrast to Jonathan's testy mood that somehow Arthur found exceedingly gratifying.

Upon their return to the Westfield Manor, Rebecca was summoned to the countess's bedchamber where Lady Westfield rang for tea and biscuits. While they waited, her ladyship asked about Mrs. Williams and how her visit had fared. Rebecca was full of compliments for Mr. Willoughby, though she frowned when Lady Westfield asked about Jonathan. Rebecca said she worried that somehow she had affronted him because he had a disagreeable temper throughout their visit. Lady Westfield responded to her concerns, "Fustian, he is just too sensitive. Do not worry yourself. He will come about."

Lady Westfield and Rebecca finished their tea. Amelia thought Mr. Willoughby had proven himself well at the Williams's farm and decided that tomorrow's ride was a splendid idea. She then told Rebecca that she would host a dinner at the end of the week and invite the Ingalls and her papa, Mr. Stevens. Rebecca thanked Lady Westfield for her hospitality and retired to her own room.

The next day, while Jonathan, Rebecca, and Arthur were away on their ride, Lady Ingall's unscheduled visit preempted the need for Lady Westfield to write an invitation to her and Lord Ingall for her planned dinner.

Lady Ingall had heard of Jonathan's return and was most anxious for Rebecca to return home for that is what she called the ancestral Ingall Estate, Rebecca's home. Lady Ingall loved Rebecca like a daughter and missed her company. Now that Jonathan was home surely Amelia would not have need of her. Besides, she thought, Roger,

William, and Henry complained enough for allowing her an extended stay at the Westfield Manor.

Jane thought Amelia looked radiant. There was a glow of enthusiasm that had been missing since her husband's death almost eight months ago. Her curiosity got the better of her and she forgot her mission. "My dear," queried Jane. "What has caused that wicked smile that crosses your face?"

Amelia laughed and said, "You have saved me from penning an invitation for your company. As for my smile, sit, I will ring for tea and a cold collation, for surely you are hungry. Then, together we will orchestrate a suitable marriage for Rebecca."

Shocked, Jane asked, "Amelia, What have you done?"

Not a cloud prevailed in the remarkably clear morning sky when Rebecca pulled on the reins to bring her galloping steed to a stop. Her resounding laughter floated through the air when she crossed the imaginary finish line. Jonathan had allowed her to ride his favorite black stallion. Rebecca knew Apollo was the fastest horse Lord Westfield owned and after a night of reflection, she was determined to use his horse to beat him in a race as punishment for being moody at the Williams's farm.

She began by presenting herself to Jonathan at the stables as a demure lady, surprising him with an awkward attempt at coquetry. He watched her offer him a shy smile while fluttering her eyelashes. In a timid voice, so out of character for her, she requested the use of his treasured mount. He was so thoroughly amused, he could not help but tease her by questioning her motive.

"But, Rebecca," Jonathan asked while he held Apollo by the reins. "Why would you want to ride him? Apollo is my steed. Surely, you would prefer your own mount?"

Jonathan knew quite well that Rebecca wanted Apollo to best him. Hadn't they spent half the evening after dinner last night, debating who was the better equestrian? Hadn't Rebecca shocked him and Arthur by declaring herself the most proficient rider? Unbeknown to Rebecca, Jonathan had never allowed anyone else to mount Apollo. So why was he considering her request now? Jonathan knew she could handle Apollo. He had trained the horse himself and knew that if he placed Rebecca on him that his steed would obey her, but Apollo was his horse. No matter how charming Rebecca was, he was not about to relinquish his horse to her. He was ready to refuse her request when she lifted her head and looked him straight in the eyes. Before Jonathan realized it, he handed Rebecca the reins of his most treasured mount and watched her walk away with his horse wearing the most glorious smile on her face.

Jonathan and Arthur hailed Rebecca with platitudes and congratulations, though Jonathan noticed that Rebecca seemed to offer herself the most praise. Arthur remarked, "My, you keep your seat well, Miss Stevens, very good, indeed."

Jonathan coughed, thinking, *"An appropriate comment for a fellow man, but a gentleman never acknowledges a woman's seat."*

Arthur realized his blunder and apologized, "Pray, forgive me, I meant no offense."

Rebecca and Jonathan laughed simultaneously at Arthur's discomfiture. Rebecca said, "Do not worry, Mr. Willoughby. I dare say, you would not repeat the remark in Society and I take your words as the warm compliment you meant them to be."

Arthur beamed and Jonathan frowned, wondering, *"Is Rebecca attracted to Arthur?"*

The three of them continued their ride. Jonathan returned the hospitality that Arthur had bestowed on him during his stay at the Willoughby country home and provided an eloquent tour of his properties. Both Rebecca and Arthur marveled at the prosperous farms and verdant landscape marked by several creeks, meadows, and magnificent neighboring woods. The fields were filled with color and sounds. Spreading wildflowers dotted the lush grass where cattle and sheep grazed. Jonathan realized that Rebecca had never toured his property and it brought him joy to see that she was pleased.

Arthur suggested a race back to the Westfield Manor, but Jonathan nixed the idea not wanting to tax his horses, so they returned home with Arthur and Rebecca riding side by side. They talked idly while Jonathan, who followed in rear, surveyed his friend's demeanor to see what his intentions towards Rebecca might be.

Lady Ingall sat in front of her gilt wood mirror while her abigail finished styling her hair and accenting her coiffure with a couple of jeweled stick pins. Her husband, Roger, thought she looked pensive when he entered her private suite. Jane caught her husband's look, he smiled, and said, "Do not worry, Jane, tonight will go well."

"But, Roger," admonished Jane, "You must ensure that this Mr. Willoughby is worthy of our dear Rebecca. Have you any word from your investigation yet of his character? Remember you promised to speak with him and do whatever papas do to make sure he is suitable."

Roger interceded, "Dear Jane, I am not Rebecca's father, surely Mr. Stevens is most capable of tending to his daughter's future."

Jane replied, "That is beside the point. Rebecca has been part of our household for over three years and the responsibility is ours, since it is in our Society that she met Mr. Willoughby. Besides, you love her as much as I do."

"You are quite right, my dear," relented Roger. "I will oversee Mr. Stevens in this courtship that Rebecca seems to favor and make sure Mr. Willoughby to be of stellar character before any marriage settlements are discussed."

"Oh, my!" cried Jane. "Roger, I forgot about the marriage settlements. Does Rebecca have a dowry? If not, either Mr. Willoughby has besotted himself with Rebecca or he is a rake of the worst kind, playing on the affections of an innocent." With this last comment Jane began to cry.

Mr. Stevens was already at the Westfield Manor when the Earl and Countess of Ingall arrived. They ran a bit tardy for it took time for Lord Ingall to calm his wife. When they were announced, they noted two separate intimate groups. Mr. Stevens and Lady Westfield were hovered close, smiling, whispering among themselves. Across the room, Rebecca stood between Arthur and Jonathan laughing. Both gentlemen it seemed were doing their best to win the girl's favor. Rebecca was animated, cheerful, and seemed to enjoy their company.

She was the first to see Lady and Lord Ingall enter the parlour, and walked cheerfully over to greet them. "Oh! My lady! My lord! How I have missed your company. I am so glad you have come. Now that you have arrived my family is complete. You see, dear Papa, is here as well."

Jane filled with emotion almost cried again. She looked at her husband and Roger smiled back at her, reading her thoughts. To himself, he said, *"Yes, my dear, Rebecca is family."*

The rest of the company greeted Lady and Lord Ingall who put on their most haughty faces when Mr. Willoughby was introduced. Rebecca had to hold back a giggle, wondering about the aristocratic display. She had never seen anything but warmth from the Earl and Countess of Ingall, never thinking them at all *high in the instep*.

The supper bell rang and Lord Ingall knowing himself to be the highest ranking peer, being heir to a dukedom, offered his escort to his hostess, Lady Westfield, while Jonathan offered his arm to Lady Ingall. To Arthur's pleasure he escorted Rebecca into the dining room while Mr. Stevens entered last.

Jonathan sat at the head of the table with his mother sitting opposite him. On Jonathan's right side sat Mr. Stevens, Rebecca, and Lady Ingall. On the other side, sat Arthur and Lord Ingall. Small talk was made among the guests, each careful to spend equal amounts of time, talking to their respective neighbors. As the courses progressed, Lord Ingall began to question Mr. Willoughby, to Jonathan's amusement, most relentlessly. Since Lord Ingall and Arthur were engaged in conversation, Jonathan did his best to entertain his other neighbor, Mr. Stevens. However, it seemed everyone at the table was more interested in Arthur's answers to Lord Ingall's questions. The room seemed eerily quiet when Lord Ingall raised his brows and looked down his nose to inquire, "So, tell me, Mr. Willoughby, am I acquainted with your parents?"

Arthur knew the question well and its intent. He had been active in Society for over three years and understood the question was one that was used in Town to determine suitability. Arthur knew his worth. His good looks and prospect of inheriting property made him an eligible bachelor, giving him *entrée* to the homes of the top ten thousand, affectionately known as the *ton*. His respectability and charm, if nothing else, made him a good fourth for a card game. Arthur was used to the question, though he thought it strange that Lord Ingall was interested in his background. After all, he was a guest of Jonathan's, not a suitor. Besides, no unmarried lady of quality was in attendance.

So, without further thought, Arthur answered his stock reply, not realizing its effect. "My father is Sir Miles Willoughby of Bedale in North Yorkshire. He is not a peer, sir, he holds no seat in the House of Lords, but maintains a residence in Town and is received by many, so your paths may have crossed. My sister Miss Belinda Willoughby made her *come-out* this past season and hopes to receive a most brilliant offer. Since I am among friends, I shall confess my father has similar hopes for me." Arthur smiled thinking his response quite clever and then saw the pity in Lord Ingall's eyes. He scanned the table and was stunned to see Lady Westfield perplexed, Lady Ingall emotional, Rebecca blushing, Mr. Stevens embarrassed, and his host, Lord Westfield, angry. Unsure of what happened, Arthur apologized and asked, "I am sorry. Did I say something to offend?"

Lord Ingall sighed, "No, Mr. Willoughby, not at all."

A subdued dinner continued until Jonathan signaled his mother to make her exit and lead the women into the parlour to take their tea, while the men made their way to the library for their customary indulgence of drinking port and smoking cigars. The minute the heavy doors closed, Arthur pulled Jonathan aside and asked, "What did I say that caused such a ruckus?"

Jonathan answered, "We thought you wished to pay your addresses to Rebecca and were surprised to hear otherwise."

Arthur rebounded, "Rebecca? Why of course I like her very well. She is a genuine article, but Jonathan, you must know that I could not marry without prospects. My father would never allow it. He expects a great match for me." Arthur saw anger flash again in Jonathan's eyes. He thought his answer had somehow offended his host, especially when he saw him fist his hand. He thought Westfield was about to throttle him and in an attempt to rationalize the situation, he asked, "Would you marry her?"

Jonathan released his fist in a defeatist manner and pondered, *"Would I?"* When he answered Arthur, it was with a resounding "No!" and at that moment his body trembled with anger.

The men did not languish long. They joined the women after the half hour. Both genders were remarkably uncomfortable, especially Mr. Willoughby, who now understood the reason behind the emotional charge that had filled the evening. He was mortified that his gallantry was mistaken for courtship and that in his folly he had injured Rebecca for whom he liked exceedingly well. He was not attracted to her in a romantic fashion, but heartily acknowledged that he enjoyed her company, more so when he caused Jonathan's discomfiture by flirting with her. He felt terrible that his self-indulgence had misled Lady Ingall's companion and he wondered how the Ingalls and the Westfields could think he harbored any intentions towards her. Was there not a tacit agreement, among the noble that marriages were contracted for mutual benefit? He understood how Rebecca would prosper from an alliance with him, but she owned nothing that would benefit him. It was not, after all, a love match and then he balked. Did Rebecca think he loved her? Had he wounded her heart and not just her pride? No wonder Jonathan wanted to throttle him.

Arthur agreed that he should retire early and leave the next morning so as not to suffer the Ingalls more than he had already done. Upon entering the parlour, he went directly to the group of women who sat in close proximity to one another and giving Rebecca his primary attention, he said, "I am to leave early tomorrow, so I must now retire, my ladies. You will forgive me...will you not, for leaving your esteemed company?"

Arthur had paused between the words "forgive me" and "will you not." He looked solemn and the women pitied him for they knew they had placed him in an odious position. Rebecca smiled and said, "You are forgiven, Mr. Willoughby. I wish you safe travel."

"You are too good, Miss Stevens. Thank you," he replied. He then left the parlour. Jonathan watched the discourse and felt wretched. He blamed himself for introducing Arthur to Rebecca's society. As soon as Arthur left, he heard Lord Ingall remark, "I fear we must bid you good evening, as well, Westfield. You will excuse us, of course."

Jonathan replied, "Of course." He watched his mother's party break up and retired with a heavy heart knowing that Rebecca had suffered greatly.

Chapter Six

Rebecca practically skipped into the Ingalls' ballroom. She could smell the fragrant ferns and flowers before she even crossed the threshold. Tonight, the room would be filled with laughter. Each year, the Countess of Ingall hosted a Christmas dinner and dance. The annual fete was a tradition that the countess herself initiated the first year of her marriage. The event was dear to her heart as it brought family and friends together to celebrate Christmas.

She asked Rebecca to give the ballroom a final inspection to make sure it was decorated per her instructions. The Ingall staff were familiar with their mistress's preferences, so Rebecca was confident that everything would be set perfectly to her ladyship's wishes. She hoped the task might calm her. Her excitement had her roaming from one room to another all day in anticipation of the coming evening and she feared she would exhaust herself before the festivities even began.

She had been in high spirits ever since William and Henry came home. Their energy enlivened the household, breaking the often tedious solitude, with their noisy presence. She was content knowing that everyone who was important to her would be in attendance for Lady Ingall's Christmas dinner and dance. She thought, *"Even Jonathan would be here."*

Rebecca had not seen Jonathan since the evening where Arthur announced that his father hoped he would make a great match in marriage. She remembered how embarrassed she felt when she became aware that everyone thought he meant to pay his addresses to her. For heaven's sake, *she*, believed Arthur was about to offer for her. She had never been sought-after, so naturally she mistook his attentions of gallantry and devotion as a mark of affection. In retrospect, she realized what she perceived as admiration was nothing more than fancy. Arthur never professed his love or made an offer of marriage. He flirted and charmed her. She enjoyed every moment, for a man had never singled her out before. The newness of being admired made her think that she returned his feelings.

She remembered how Lady Ingall earnestly arrived the following day to take her back to the Ingall Estate. It was then that she learned Jonathan and Arthur had left to finish the "Little Season" in London. She was embarrassed with all the sympathy and apologies placed upon her. Lady Westfield specifically begged forgiveness for encouraging a union between her and Arthur, while Lady Ingall showed remorse for not mentoring her in the ways of a gentleman's rakish manner. The scene was quite emotional and Lady Ingall brought the awkward discourse to a close by exclaiming, "Mister Willoughby is a fool!"

The surprising remark broke the tension that was beginning to overcome them. Rebecca and Lady Westfield erupted into chuckles with Lady Ingall joining them a moment later. The room resonated with snorts, guffaws, and sighs as they all tried to bring their unladylike manner under control before one of the servants entered to see what the ruckus was all about. It was obvious to each of them that the outburst was a soothing balm to their raw emotions and was just what they needed to dissolve their anxieties. Rebecca wiped the tears that had pooled in her eyes from laughing so hard and confessed, "I must admit I was embarrassed that I had so misconstrued Mr. Willoughby's intentions, but do not grieve on my account. I do not know if I could have fallen in love with Mr. Willoughby, though I will admit I tried. He made me feel special. I had so much fun in his company. He is a very amiable gentleman and the experience of having a man show me such singular attention was wonderful. I do not regret my behavior, it was genuine and beyond reproach."

"Do not worry, Rebecca," said Lady Westfield. "Jane and I will look for a suitable candidate. We still have a couple of years to find someone before you are considered on the shelf."

With warmth Rebecca responded, "Thank you. You are both too generous, but I must tell you that I decided a long time ago that I would not settle for less than love. How could I with such magnificent examples as both your marriages and my own dear parents? Do not worry for me. I am most content with only dear papa and you in my life. As for my security, I must tell you that since I have been Lady Ingall's companion, I have acquired quite a nest egg."

At this remark, Lady Ingall exclaimed, "Oh, my! I forgot all about your allowance."

Rebecca continued, "Lady Ingall allows me to want for nothing, so I have accumulated a tidy sum. Even my papa will not allow me to contribute anything to his living. He says the salary is for my retirement. Can you imagine such folly?"

Lady Ingall interceded, "Your papa is a wise man, but I hope Rebecca that you know that you always have a home with Lord Ingall and myself. I am glad you have a tidy sum, but pray, never fear for your welfare because it is in good hands with us. In our hearts, you are a daughter to us and we love you very much."

Rebecca let out an uncontrollable sob, and said, "I love you, too!"

Lady Westfield feeling like an outsider exclaimed, "I love you, too!" and then everyone laughed.

The evening found the Ingall ballroom aglow with burning candles illuminating the merry festivities of the Christmas fete. There were two large crystal chandeliers that hung from the ceiling, each holding a hundred tapers.

Between each of the tall French arched doors that flanked one side of the ballroom was a gold gilt wall mirror with a three-arm candelabra sconce. These mirrors reflected even more light unto the party. Lady Ingall had her servants festoon the room with evergreen marked with red berries, holly, and ribbon. Keeping with tradition, she ordered a fir tree to be placed in a tub next to the musician's stage. She had her maids garnish the tree with wax candles and the treats of sweetmeats, raisins, and almonds that cook had bunched up in paper to be enjoyed later by the guests. Rebecca marveled at the magnificence of the night and scolded herself for letting Jonathan upset her. She was disappointed that the earl had kept his distance all evening. She questioned whether the time he had spent with her at Westfield Manor was at his mother's bidding. She knew that under normal circumstances, he would not even acknowledge her. After all, she was the vicar's daughter and technically a paid servant in her role as companion, but she thought they had become friends, transcending those class of stations that placed her outside his society and notice. Lady Westfield had told Rebecca that Jonathan had been quite a success during the "Little Season" among the *bon ton* in London and received many notable invitations, one that included a countess with an eligible daughter. Apparently, the young debutante would be making her *come-out* next Season and it seemed that Jonathan had taken a fancy to her. Lady Westfield thought it would be a brilliant match. She expected to entertain them in the new year, before they headed to Town for the Season. Rebecca with her thoughts for company, walked outside to look out into the rose garden.

Jonathan saw Rebecca walk out into the terrace and followed her. He had ignored her all evening because he thought for sure she would inquire about Arthur and he did not want to lie to her. Arthur finished the “Little Season” exceptionally well, and had acquired a number of invitations from the nobility that would keep him traveling until the London Season resumed. Jonathan had received the same invitations, but he preferred coming home. He told himself he had to check on his mother, his properties, plus he wanted to see Rebecca.

“Good evening, Miss Stevens,” greeted Lord Westfield. “Are you enjoying the evening air?”

Rebecca turned and was surprised to see Jonathan offering an awkward smile. She thought, *“He is uncomfortable, perhaps he is embarrassed to be seen in my company.”*

With her usual candor, Rebecca announced, “Pray, do not be uncomfortable with me, my lord. While I am not of your Society, I did think, we once called each other friend. Your mama tells me that an announcement may soon be made regarding you and Lady Miranda. May I offer you my felicitations on your upcoming betrothal."

Rebecca's declaration surprised Jonathan. He once again marveled at her directness, but then he thought,

"Why should I be surprised when it is her honesty that attracts me to her?" He was disturbed that she thought herself beneath him, nothing could be farther from the truth. Then, why, he pondered, *"Is she not a suitable wife?"*

In that same instance, he became aware that she was under the false impression that he was going to offer for Lady Miranda and her mistake made him happy. He thought, *"I can enjoy her company without worrying that my conduct might be misconstrued."* He managed to circumvent her felicitations by returning the conversation to her previous remark. "I beg your pardon, Miss Stevens, but I do call you friend. I would understand if you prefer not to call me friend, for a poor one I was in introducing you to Mr. Willoughby. I am sorry for any grief you suffered."

"Oh, dear!" exclaimed Rebecca. "You do not own the blame. It was my inexperience that allowed me to misjudge Mr. Willoughby's attentions. I am not injured, my lord, and ask you not to concern yourself any further. In fact, it is I who should thank you for introducing me to a most charming man, one who provided me with much amusement. You see I have never been the object of any man's attentions."

Jonathan dropped his jaw before blurting, "But, you are so beautiful!"

Surprised, Rebecca blushed. She offered an unfashionably large smile and exclaimed much too loudly, "Thank you, my lord! No one has ever called me beautiful!"

A few guests that stood inside the ballroom by the French doors looked out to see who yelled and then they began whispering, trying to deduce what might have happened. The *gossipmongers* caused Jonathan to turn to them and silence them with a haughty stare, intimidating them into moving away from the terrace. When he looked back at Rebecca, he had to check his own behavior when he noted her body shaking from trying to keep her laughter from bubbling out. Seeing her amusement relieved him greatly.

He said, “I am very happy that you are not injured. Willoughby will be much relieved that you harbor no ill will towards him for he does indeed hold you in the highest esteem." He then extended his hand and asked, “Will you honor me with this dance, Miss Stevens?”

Rebecca never expected Jonathan to ask her to dance after he spent the evening keeping his distance from her. She was struck speechless at his offer, standing in shock with her mouth and eyes wide open. She found she had no voice to reply. She did not break her trance until she saw Jonathan's eyes gleam and quirk a smile in amusement. He could tell she was too enamored to answer his request and her discomfiture pleased him. He was glad he could affect her and extended to her his open palm. He enjoyed watching the once forthright vicar's daughter turn into a demure debutante. Unable to find her voice, she closed her mouth, and shook her head up and down to accept his offer.

Lady Westfield had loved her husband dearly and to honor him was committed to observe a proper mourning period. She wore the traditional black bombazet gown and refrained herself from Society's balls and fetes; however, she was not blind to her son's and Lady Ingall's increased concern for her over the holiday season. She knew they feared she would fall into despair over this first Christmas without her husband. Amelia did not want Jane or her son to worry about her, so she agreed to join them for the Ingall's Christmas dinner. Jane promised an intimate affair and Amelia thought she was above reproach from the *gossipmongers*, as long as she retired before the dancing commenced, which she did.

The following day, Lady Westfield's abigail shared the gossip she heard from the butler, who heard the *on dit* first hand from Palmer, the Ingall's butler, that Jonathan had made quite a spectacle of himself with Rebecca on the dance floor. Well, to be more precise, Lord Westfield asked Rebecca to dance a waltz and they seemed to enjoy themselves immensely, not adhering to the twelve-inch rule of separation. Lady Westfield was beside herself and summoned Jonathan to her bedchamber, post haste.

Jonathan entered his mother's private suite, humming the melody of the waltz that he had danced with Rebecca the night before. He saw that his mother was still abed in her nightclothes, breaking her fast with tea and toast. He saw her sip from her teacup and wondered why she scowled at him, looking like she was ready to spew the tea from her lips at seeing him. She admonished him, before he could greet her. "What were you thinking? I want you to know that I like Rebecca very much. In fact, in a moment of hysterics, I think I told her I loved her. She is a sweet girl and I do not want Society thinking she is a bit of muslin for your fancy."

Jonathan's surprise turned to anger as he exclaimed, "What?! I would never disrespect Miss Stevens!"

His mother continued, "Then, what were you doing last night with Rebecca when everyone knows that you are practically engaged to Lady Miranda."

Offended, Jonathan stated, "A misconception, Mother. Trust me, no offer has been made or any allusions to a promise. Lady Miranda is a charming woman, but I have no desire there."

Flabbergasted, his mother remarked, "But you have invited her party to visit us in the new year. I thought it was your intention to garner my approval."

Jonathan intervened, "I am sorry, if my invitation misled you. The invitation was at the behest of Mr. Willoughby who has an admiration for Lady Miranda. He hoped to extend his company with her by securing an invitation for himself and her party to Westfield Manor. I abhor interfering in other people's personal matters; however, for some reason I could not refuse. Aside from the debacle between him and Miss Stevens, Arthur has been a good friend to me this past year. I actually believe he fancies himself in love with Lady Miranda and they seem to suit quite well."

"But, what about Rebecca?" asked his mother.

"I do not know, Mother," replied Jonathan. "As Lady Ingall's companion and your guest she has been introduced into our Society and accepted as an equal, though she would argue the point. While the *ton* would reject her based on bloodline, I find myself drawn to her. I have feelings with which I do not know what to do."

Sympathetically, Lady Westfield said, "You are right that the *ton* would not accept her. I do not believe Rebecca has the polish or the sense to captivate them. She is much too direct and genuine for Town Society. She is however, an incomparable beauty, if she had any nobility in her, then her *faux pas* would mark her an *Original* rather than gauche. The aristocracy is a fickle group you know." With emphasis she continued, "You must consider her happiness before engaging in anything that could cause her ruin. Please be careful, Jonathan."

Sorrowfully, Jonathan replied, "I know, Mother, that is one reason I did not correct the gossip regarding a connection with Lady Miranda. I want Rebecca to feel at ease in my company while I determine my feelings. Besides, all will be made clear when we entertain in the new year."

Rebecca sat next to Lady Ingall in her carriage and listened to her voice her concerns for Lady Westfield. The weather had been bleak since Christmas, too harsh for travel and she felt bad that she had not been able to visit until well into the new year. Lady Ingall wondered how Lady Westfield fared. She remarked, "You know, Rebecca, her husband, the late Lord Westfield, has been gone eleven months today."

Rebecca nodded. She was not sure what Lady Ingall said, for she was preoccupied with her own thoughts. She tried to look unaffected sitting with remarkable posture, her back stiff, her chin lifted and her laced gloved hands clasped in her lap. She did not want to reveal her anxiety. She hoped the churning in her stomach and the warmth that was radiating throughout her body would not betray her countenance by revealing a blush. She did her best to calm her rapid heartbeat. There was little she could do to stop the perspiration that was beginning to soak through her gloves. She could not stop thinking of the dance she shared with Jonathan on Christmas, a waltz to be precise: a most exhilarating and beautiful waltz. She remembered his assured stride when he led her to the dance floor. She knew people were watching, but she only saw Jonathan. Overwhelmed, she relied on his strength to hold her up and lead her. She submitted to his every step, turn, and embrace, for that is what his dance hold felt like, an embrace. She could feel the pressure of his hand on her back and the warmth that emanated from him. His eyes held hers and never wavered. The room became a blur and she was exquisitely happy. Nothing in her life compared to that moment and then, just like that, it ended: the dance and the evening. Jonathan had bowed, kissed her hand, and thanked her. He escorted her to the Earl and Countess of Ingall where he thanked them for a wonderful evening and bid them good evening. Lady Ingall asked that he give her regards to his mama and to tell her that she would visit before the new year.

Jonathan thanked her again for all the care and compassion she had shown his mother, remarking, "I do not believe she would have rallied had it not been for your care and devotion. Sending Rebecca to her while I was away was inspirational."

Lady Ingall looked at Rebecca and then to Jonathan. She said, "She has been a blessing to us all."

The Ingall carriage stopped and her footman opened the door, dropped the carriage steps, and assisted her ladyship's descent. The Westfield butler had already opened the front door and was prepared to greet them. Being regular visitors, Lady Ingall and Rebecca did not wait on ceremony to be announced, but followed the butler to the parlour where Lady Westfield sat with Jonathan.

Jonathan had been plotting all morning trying to scheme a way to see Rebecca. He could not call on her without drawing speculation unless he had a good reason. He could not accompany his mother because she planned on staying sequestered to honor his father. Christmas dinner was an exception his mother made for his sake. She wanted to ameliorate the holiday for him. Christmas had always been celebrated with much fanfare and Jonathan knew his mother wanted to distract him from grieving for his father. He struggled with his thoughts and let out a sigh that caught his mother's attention. At that moment, Amelia saw Jonathan's face brighten with joy. She was not surprised to see Lady Ingall and Rebecca enter the parlour following her butler who announced them, "the Countess of Ingall and Miss Stevens."

Jonathan stood and greeted them. Lady Westfield rose and rang for tea, asking them to sit. Lady Ingall was too overwrought with concern. She took Lady Westfield's hands in both of hers, and asked, "My dear Amelia, you have been in my thoughts. Tell me, how do you fare?"

Amelia smiled at her friend's concern and responded, "I am coming around, Jane. My memories of my husband bring me more joy than grief. I count my blessings for the days we shared, rather than the days that might have been."

Jonathan looked at his mother and smiled. Jonathan and his mother had taken stock of their lives on New Year's Eve. When most families dismissed the past and looked forward to the new year, Jonathan and his mother spent the evening relishing their past. Every eventful memory they each had of the late Lord Westfield was exchanged and discussed. They laughed, cried, and in the end appreciated the time they had spent together as a family. They decided they would not let his death overshadow his life. Instead, they vowed that his life would be a beacon to guide them. They would live life to its fullest and enjoy it as they remembered he so faithfully did.

Jane immediately saw the change in Amelia's demeanor and was assuaged. She knew she didn't have to worry about her friend anymore and let go of her hands. She instructed Rebecca to sit while she sat next to Amelia on a nearby settee. She asked, "Have you read the latest Women's Home Journal?"

Amelia replied, "Yes, that reminds me. Jonathan dear, why don't you escort Rebecca to the orangery. Give her a tour and ask our gardener to pick a crate of oranges, so that I may send them back with Jane." When no one was looking she winked at Jonathan who smiled in enthusiasm.

As Jonathan proffered his arm to Rebecca and began to lead her from the parlour, he heard Lady Ingall exclaim to his mother, "You are such a forward thinker, Amelia. Imagine my surprise to see a whole article on the benefit of consuming oranges. Why you have been exclaiming that for years."

Jonathan and Rebecca grinned at each other as they exited the parlour. Rebecca realized that she had never visited the orangery the months she was a guest at Westfield Manor. Jonathan opened the door of the glass building and escorted her through. Her body sensed the change immediately, going from a brisk cold to a sultry warm that pinked her cheeks. Aside from the warmth, her other senses keenly picked up the sweet fragrance of the oranges. Her eyes beheld a private Eden that revealed thick bunches of leaves with splotches of orange orbs poking through them. Everything was tidy. The rows of trees were straight and the ground clear of any debris. As Rebecca touched an orange that hung on a low branch, Jonathan hailed the gardener and bid his mother's request.

The gardener picked up an empty crate and started picking oranges. Jonathan escorted Rebecca down the lane away from the gardener. She trembled and Jonathan felt her pulse quicken when he laid his hand across her wrist. He stopped, turned to look at her and whispered, "Rebecca?"

He said her name as a question and Rebecca answered in her most direct way, "What is wrong, my lord?"

Jonathan smiled and shook his head in the negative. He said, "You are so genuine that I am overcome each time I am with you."

Rebecca looked at him intently, saying, "I am sorry, my lord. You must be direct. Are you saying I am a good or bad influence? Pray, tell me, how I should be not to offend because I do enjoy your company. I would be sad if it was to be denied."

Jonathan felt wretched. Rebecca was an innocent. Her body gave every indication that she liked him, but he knew she was inexperienced. Had she not almost surrendered to Arthur charms?

He simply responded, "I like you too, too much I am afraid."

Rebecca answered, "I am confused, my lord, are you not in love with Lady Miranda."

Jonathan blurted, "No!"

And with that he turned Rebecca around and escorted her back to the manor. Nothing was spoken between them. Jonathan was frustrated. Rebecca was confused and she wondered, *"What just happened?"*

By the time Jonathan returned Rebecca to the parlour, Lady Ingall was ready to depart. Jonathan bid farewell and escorted them to the door while his mother remained seated. When Jonathan returned, she asked, "Well?"

In a distemper, Jonathan barked, "Well, what?!"

His mother laughed to see her son so out of sorts with the first pangs of love. She then rephrased, "Did your visit to the orangery with Miss Stevens enlighten your feelings towards her?"

A tightlipped Jonathan, bellowed, "No!" before he left the room.

Jonathan's emotional response, much to his mother's delight, was enough of an answer. She was never *high in the instep,* never one to look down on someone outside her sphere. While her and her husband's betrothal was a noble match, she knew her marriage was far from conventional. She had no qualms about Jonathan following his heart. Miss Stevens was beyond reproach and Jonathan had enough wealth that he did not need to marry for money. Besides, like his father, Jonathan preferred residing in the country to living in London, and the gentry were far more accepting of a nobleman marrying beneath his station.

Chapter Seven

Jonathan made his way along the dirt lane to the vicar's cottage, matching his own movements with Apollo's canter. The fresh air and cadence lulled him into reflection as the week marked the anniversary of his father's death. His idle life was immediately transformed when he became the Earl of Westfield. He took on the responsibilities for his mother, his tenants, even his country, now that he took his seat in Parliament and with his heart becoming engaged, he would soon have another loved one for which he was responsible.

He was glad to see his mother relinquish her black wardrobe for a somber yet attractive gray. The lighter color reduced the contrast with her fair skin, so she no longer looked pale and weary from wearing the heavy bombazet mourning dress. She seemed to walk more gracefully with a lightness of step.

The vicar planned to acknowledge the late Lord Westfield's memory during the Sunday Service and Lady

Westfield had sent Jonathan to ask the vicar to include one of his father's favorite psalms. While Jonathan traveled, he realized he was whistling and to his bemusement, happy. Thanks to his mother, he had the chance to explore at length his feelings for Rebecca. It all began when he was sent to the Ingall Estate with a cart loaded to capacity with oranges, only to discover Lady Ingall did not know what to do with them. The look of Lady Ingall's and Rebecca's faces were priceless. It was like putting a heaping plate of food in front of someone that wasn't hungry. Lord Westfield took them out of their misery by suggesting, “Perhaps you have some tenants that could benefit from the cures that only oranges provide. If Miss Stevens could accompany me, I could assist in the delivery per her instructions.” Lady Ingall thought Jonathan’s idea splendid. The open cart and driver satisfied all propriety and Rebecca was sent to retrieve her bonnet and pelisse.

Jonathan assisted Rebecca unto the cart seat next to his driver. He wished he had not decided to ride Apollo. He envied his servant and almost laughed aloud when he saw Rebecca's eyes revealing that she envied him riding. Unlike the trip over, where he rode in front of the cart, he found himself trying his best to keep beside it with Rebecca in his view. He noted her nose and cheeks were pinked from the winter wind and he wanted to warm her face with his hands.

Rebecca was highly cognizant of Jonathan watching her and tried to focus on giving the driver directions to which farms she wished to visit. At each stop, before she even had a chance to debark, she found Jonathan with his arms extended to assist her down. She relinquished herself into his hands and blushed from the intimacy of the action. Jonathan held her by the waist and did not release her right away, almost as if he was looking for something. She knew she should reprove his advances, but his warm eyes told her that he was sincere in his attentions.

Rebecca fluttered with a nervous energy, so affecting that she feared she would swoon if she could not find a way to harness it. Their last stop provided the opportunity. Mr. Jones, the last tenant on her list, greeted them soberly.

He informed them that his wife was ill and could not invite them in, but thanked them for their goodness. To Jonathan's amazement, Rebecca brushed Mr. Jones aside and entered his humble abode. She went directly to the side room where she surmised the Jones's bed occupied. Jonathan followed Rebecca to the threshold, not entering out of propriety. He could hear Rebecca say, "Pray, dear Mrs. Jones, I hear that you are not well. Tell me, what ails you?"

Mrs. Jones weakly said, "I have the ague, dear girl, you should leave. I am feverish and cannot eat. I fear I am for dead."

"Nonsense, " replied Rebecca. "I will urge you on. Rest for a moment while I speak with my escort." Rebecca exited the bedroom and found Jonathan close at hand.

His disconcerted look made her giggle, and she said, "Do not fear, my lord. It is the weather and an overworked body that makes Mrs. Jones prey to illness. A little caring and nourishment will see her through. I beg you to ride to inform Lady Ingall that I am charged to stay and care for her. Ask her ladyship if she will send me Hannah to chaperone and a list of teas that I feel would remedy Mrs. Jones."

Jonathan rebuked, "You cannot mean to stay the night?"

Rebecca countered, "You forget, my lord, I am a vicar's daughter. Many a night I have sat with an invalid or companioned someone who God calls. I am quite comfortable with my task. Will you do my bidding?"

"Of course," replied Jonathan unsure of his feelings. Was it reluctance that he left Rebecca or amazement at her generosity of spirit? He was not sure, but he sent his driver home with a note to his mother and duties to fulfill, while he rode to the Ingall Estate.

Lady Ingall did not seem alarmed, if anything she was used to Rebecca aiding her sick tenants. She packed a bag of clean linen and clothes for Rebecca's use, as well as the remedies she requested. Hannah was charged to aid Miss Stevens and was soon ready to depart. Jonathan mounted Apollo to escort her when Lady Ingall remarked, "Lord Westfield, I can have our own manservant accompany my abigail. You need not trouble yourself."

To Lady Ingall's surprise, Jonathan said, "It is no trouble at all. I plan to stay in the barn if Mr. Jones allows.

I desire to stay close in case Miss Stevens requires assistance. If all is well, I shall bring her to you tomorrow. My own man returns to me this evening. If Rebecca is required to stay longer, I will send word to you through him." With a tip of his hat, Lord Westfield bid goodbye. He urged Apollo into motion when the Ingall coachman, transporting Rebecca's chaperone, slapped the reins to start the carriage on its way. Astonished, a moment passed before Lady Ingall realized she was standing in view of her servants with her mouth open.

Rebecca wasted no time in assessing what needed to be done to care for Mrs. Jones. She immediately donned a well-used apron hanging on a wall peg in the kitchen. Then, she stripped Mrs. Jones bed and applied fresh linen. Mrs. Jones was not happy about that task. It was her only spare linen and she wanted to save it for when they laid her out for view. Rebecca assured her that she planned to set a pot of water to boil to wash the soiled sheets, so she did not have to concern herself about her best spare sheets.

Next, Rebecca bathed Mrs. Jones's body with tepid water to cool her temperature. She wished she had asked Lady Ingall to send some fragrant water, but she thought she could save that bath for another time. Rebecca put a clean gown on Mrs. Jones and peeled one of the oranges Jonathan had left with her. Rebecca said, "If you cannot eat the orange, Mrs. Jones, just bite and squeeze the juice into your mouth. The juice has healing properties. While you try, I will set a stock going on the fire to brew you a nice broth. Lord Westfield shall return shortly with a remedy that I think will cure your headache and fever. Try to eat the orange. I shall return soon."

Mrs. Jones simply nodded and bit into the orange. She had heard that Lady Westfield sent oranges to her tenants to keep them well and that they were supposed to be delicious. She thought the sweet orange a miracle worker since after the first bite she felt revived. Mrs. Jones did not realize that the worst of her illness was over and that the sweet juice was her first nourishment in days. She considered that perhaps she was not at death's door and after she consumed her orange, relapsed into a peaceful nap.

By the time Jonathan returned, Rebecca had just dropped a hot soapy sheet into a pot of clean boiling water to rinse. She alarmingly looked up, when Jonathan exclaimed, "What the devil do you think you are doing?!"

Rebecca chuckled. She was amused at Jonathan's scowl and answered, "Why, my lord, you know perfectly well, I am laundering the sheets."

Jonathan was not amused, in a frustrated but calm tone, said, "Yes, I know you are washing linen, but I do not wish it." He paused as if thinking and then continued, "I will allow you to nurse Mrs. Jones, but nothing else."

Rebecca was astonished at his impertinence, "I do not understand, my lord. Do I need to seek your permission for my actions?"

Jonathan retorted, "Yes! I mean, no! For heaven's sake, Miss Stevens, you know very well you do not answer to me, but I have taken the liberty to avail myself to you. Please allow me to assist by having these simple chores done. My servants are instructed to bring breakfast and clean linen at dawn and supper at noontime. There will be plenty to carry us into the evening. They can pick up any laundry at that time. Grant me this favor as it would please me greatly to be of assistance." Rebecca was warmed by his generosity and smiled. Jonathan smiled in return and was most pleased with himself. At that moment, two carriages bearing the Westfield Crest approached. Among the footmen was Lord Westfield's valet, Stuart, who ordered them into industry as Lord Westfield approached him. Rebecca heard him say, "Stuart, I did not send for you."

His valet replied, "No, milord, but I have attended you since you left the nursery. A day has not gone by that I have not prepared your dress. Please do not send me away for it would break my record and that would be insupportable." Jonathan was amused at Stuart's rant and struggled to keep a straight face. He held a strong affection for his valet and found he could not send him away, so he granted him permission to stay. Stuart resumed his orders and before long, Lord Westfield, Miss Stevens, Mr. Jones, and his family were seated for supper.

Mr. Jones did not know what to think of the lavish full courses of food. He did not eat this well on a holiday. He was not sure what it meant, but he was not about to affront his lordship or disappoint his children. He said nothing and ate the best meal he ever had. He was only sorry his wife was too ill to enjoy in the feast.

Before food began to be served, Rebecca said grace. Jonathan was touched by her spirituality and began to question his own. His thoughts were interrupted by the incessant chatter of the children asking if their mother had died. Shocked, Jonathan looked to Rebecca for counsel, but she laughed at the absurdity. "No, dears, our feast is a gift from Lord Westfield. He is all goodness and we must mind our manners, so that he might offer us dessert."

Jonathan smiled and said in support, "Yes, let us see those good manners and perhaps, there is pie for dessert."

The meal ended. Mr. Jones and his children returned to their chores. Rebecca went to release her abigail's watch over the sleeping Mrs. Jones, so that she could eat. Jonathan gravitated to the barn where Mr. Jones worked on the harness for his plow. The earl asked multiple questions regarding Mr. Jones's farm. He asked about his planting season, his irrigation methods, his soil treatment, and other techniques regarding scientific farming. "Do you use phosphates, Mr. Jones?" asked Lord Westfield.

Mr. Jones did not know what a phosphate was, but wondered how much work would not get done because of Lord Westfield's stay. Mr. Jones simply smiled, shook his head occasionally, hoping to appease Lord Westfield.

Inside, Rebecca found Mrs. Jones fever had diminished. She swabbed a cool rag across her forehead and Mrs. Jones eyes opened. She said she was thirsty and Rebecca helped her to sip some tea that had cooled while it sat on the nightstand by her bed. After Rebecca situated her more comfortably on the pillows, she asked, "How do you feel, Mrs. Jones?"

"I am at death's door no more," replied Mrs. Jones. "I do believe it was the miracle of the orange that brought me around."

Rebecca smiled, and said, "That is good news, Mrs. Jones. I am here for the night and perhaps a few more days, as I feel a bit of nourishment and rest will bring you about to your own stout self. What do you say to having myself and Lord Westfield as your guests?"

"Lord Westfield?" asked Mrs. Jones.

"Yes," replied Rebecca. "He has taken an interest in being of service to myself and your dear family."

Mrs. Jones simply stated, "Oh, my," and pondered what it could possibly mean that Lord Westfield had an interest and what about Lord Ingall, she was after all his tenant. She wondered what was Lord Westfield's interest and whether she was being disloyal to Lord Ingall in accepting it. Mrs. Jones tired as these thoughts rambled through her brain and she fell into slumber.

With her abigail once again watching over Mrs. Jones, Rebecca walked to the barn where she thought Jonathan would be. What she walked in on made her giggle. Lord Westfield was shoeing a horse. Apparently,

Mr. Jones was tired of Lord Westfield interrupting his workday, so he somehow managed to engage his help by arousing his curiosity regarding his scientific methods on "horse shoeing." It seemed that "relaxation techniques" could calm a horse, thereby allowing the ostler less resistance in applying a horseshoe. Mr. Jones stood idly by watching Lord Westfield when Rebecca entered the barn. Mr. Jones looked at Rebecca and shrugged his shoulders. Rebecca masterly turned her laughter into a small cough and then waved her arm to get Jonathan's attention. She begged his forgiveness for interrupting him and asked if she might have a word with him. Lord Westfield excused himself, most content that he had helped Mr. Jones. He dusted off his clothes and proffered his arm to Rebecca. He escorted her outside, away from the smell of the barn and said, "Pray, forgive me, Miss Stevens, I fear I am not suitable for company."

"It is not necessary, my lord," said Rebecca trying not to laugh. She continued, "I am accustomed to the look of a man at work."

Lord Westfield asked with a wide grin, "Really?"

Rebecca laughed, "Do not tease me. I have come to tell you that Mrs. Jones is much better. A few more days of rest and she should be back to her old ways. I shall stay to continue her care, but the worst is past. You need not feel it necessary to stay."

"Nonsense," said Lord Westfield. "I promised Lady Ingall that I would return you home when our visit ended. I stay as long as you. Besides, the visit provides me ample opportunity to test some scientific methods on farming that I am curious about."

Mr. Jones had just walked out of the barn in time to hear Lord Westfield's last comment. He sighed, realizing that if Lord Westfield kept helping him, his work day would extend into the evening hours. Rebecca saw Mr. Jones's frustration and stifled a chuckle.

Lord Ingall was in London on business when he received an urgent summons from his father. He was alarmed at the imperious command, feeling that odd turmoil in his stomach, much like when he was a boy in short pants about to be scolded. He knew his father rarely had time for anything personal when he was in the prince's company, so he did not hesitate to make his way to Carlton House. "What is wrong, Father? This is not like you to summon me without issue."

The duke replied, "That is my question, Roger. Tell me, what is wrong that requires Lord Westfield to manage your tenants. Are you unwell? Though you look perfectly apt to me. By chance, are your tenants uprising?"

Roger interjected, "Stop, Father! I know not what you are talking about. What makes you think I have trouble with my tenants and that I have asked a youngster like Westfield to help?"

The duke railed, "Where have you been, Roger? The whole Town is gossiping about how Lord Westfield is living on one of your tenant's farms and tending to your business! The speculation regarding your health is unbearable. Tell me, what is wrong because I cannot imagine why Lord Westfield would involve himself with your tenants unless by your request."

Concerned, Roger remarked, "Neither do I, sir. I beg your leave as I hasten home to determine for myself what has transpired in my absence." The Duke of Hartford waved him off and Lord Ingall returned home without delay.

It was an odd sight for Lord Ingall to see his tenants seated on stumps and other makeshift chairs in the barn, reminiscent of a classroom setting listening to the Earl of Westfield. Jonathan appeared to be instructing them on something, it wasn't until Lord Ingall got closer, that he heard the word "hybrid." Astounded, he looked around to assess the situation. One of the barn stalls was clearly turned into a living quarter, complete with a washstand and a bunk bed. On the floor lay an Oriental rug. A pair of damask curtains, altered in length, hung across the stall's opening and were tied back to act as a door. The alteration of the stall, the layout of the toilette, told Lord Ingall that Stuart, Lord Westfield's valet, was attending his lordship. The rest of the barn pretty much looked the same, except presently no animals were sheltered within and there was little evidence of them being there. Unknown to him, Stuart had the animals taken outdoors during the day and the barn cleaned. Each stall was chucked, swept, and replaced with fresh straw to reduce any offending animal smells.

Lord Westfield enthusiastically dismissed the tenants when he saw Lord Ingall. He made his salutation to him and offered his hand in greeting. Lord Ingall did not take Jonathan's hand. He stood with his arms crossed, looking quite put out. With a raised a eyebrow, he inquired, “May I ask what the deuce you are doing with my tenants?”

The heated question sobered Jonathan instantly. “Oh, I beg your pardon, Ingall. I am afraid my exuberance got the better of me and I took liberties without thinking.”

Lord Ingall’s manner softened and with an open mind, he listened to Jonathan tell his tale. How he and Miss Stevens found Mrs. Jones ill. How Rebecca insisted on her care. How he insisted on helping her. How to occupy his time, he thought he might help Mr. Jones by utilizing some of the scientific farm techniques he studied. How word passed of his existence and of his tutoring at the Jones's farm. He finished his soliloquy, “Before I knew it, I was holding classes.”

Not until later when the supper bell rang, did Lord Ingall understand why his tenants came to hear the Earl of Westfield speak. It was not his scientific theories. Lord Ingall believed the concepts were more than they could grasp, but food was another matter. What farmer could resist a banquet, larger than anything they have ever seen for a noon meal.

Lord Ingall told Jonathan that he had some good ideas and was prepared to listen to them, but not here or now. He invited Jonathan to visit him in a couple of days. Then, he commanded that it was time for all to leave.

Rebecca was surprised to see Lord Ingall. It took all her skill to remove the tension that resounded from him. She quickly assured him that all was well. Mrs. Jones was up and about and that she had been well chaperoned throughout her stay. She emphasized that Lord Westfield had been a perfect gentleman. Lord Ingall heard enough explanations and the moment she paused for breath, he told her that it was time to leave. He decided he would let his wife, Jane, talk to Rebecca and determine what folly, if any, existed between Lord Westfield and Rebecca.

Lady Ingall found a most contented Rebecca at her toilette table, preparing for bed, when she entered her suite. She asked her, "Rebecca dear, tell me, what puts you in such happy spirits. I would have thought you would be exhausted after a sev'night at the Jones's. Tell me, how is Mrs. Jones?"

Rebecca said, "Mrs. Jones is quite well and endorses Lady Westfield's oranges as the cure all." Rebecca laughed when she told Lady Ingall how word passed of Mrs. Jones's miraculous recovery and how Lady Westfield is now bombarded by all the local tenant farmers with requests for oranges. She went on to tell Lady Ingall that her week at the Jones's was no hardship. She said Lord Westfield was most benevolent. He took charge ordering this and that, his servants doing all the work, cleaning and cooking to everyone's delight. Mrs. Jones told Rebecca that she was sorry to see her go and hoped that Lord Westfield would take an interest in her family again because she said she lived like a queen, even if it was for a sev'night and half the time she was asleep.

After the laughter died, Lady Ingall asked Rebecca if Lord Westfield had acted with decorum. "Unfortunately, yes," said Rebecca with a sigh.

Stunned at her candor, Lady Ingall asked, "Rebecca, what do you mean? Are you telling me you have feelings for him?"

"Yes," said Rebecca. "I have feelings. That is the only way I can describe it. I am happy when I see him or maybe I am excited or perhaps both. My stomach flutters, my hands get clammy, my heart beats quicker, and he is constantly on my mind. I rethink everything he says, wondering if it could have a meaning with emphasis and I find myself planning what I might say to him. Do not look so worried, Lady Ingall. Our behavior is beyond reproach. I just long for something more because I cannot imagine him not part of my life, yet, I do not know exactly what our relationship could be. I know he likes me because when we are together, there is an ease between us that allows us to tease one another, anticipate each other's thoughts and confide in one another. We can talk about anything. I find we both listen to each other and I believe we each care what the other is saying. He once told me, he liked me 'too much,' to be more specific, he said, 'too much I am afraid.' Since then, I have tried to understand the duplicity of the meaning by evaluating his behavior towards me. This past week has been wonderful. He is kind and caring. He is strong, smart, and he makes me laugh. I feel so much better when I am around him. When we are apart, I am wanting to see him, so, yes, I have feelings for him."

Lady Ingall marveled at Rebecca's ardor and she worried that Lord Westfield might be trifling with her, in the same manner that Mr. Willoughby did. That deduction angered her and made her think what she could do. She couldn't have Roger call him out. No, that was insupportable, but Roger could definitely talk to him and find out what his intentions were towards Rebecca. Jane became even more angry and mentally exclaimed, *"For his sake, those intentions better be honorable."*

Chapter Eight

When Jonathan reached the vicar's cottage he was happy to see two familiar mares secured to a hitching post. He would recognize Rebecca's sweet chestnut mare and her maid's horse anywhere, as they had taken many rides together since their stay at the Jones's. It took a private beseeching from Rebecca to persuade Lady Ingall to allow her to ride with Jonathan over their two estates, to deliver the widely requested bags of oranges to their tenants. Her ladyship's only requirement was that Rebecca's abigail accompany them as chaperone.

Lately, all Jonathan did was think about ways to spend time with Rebecca. When he wasn't thinking about ways to be in her company, he was recalling the moments they shared. He was glad the tenants' request for oranges provided him with an excuse to be with her.

Their rides together were pure enjoyment though their chaperone, Hannah, felt differently. After three days, she gave up trying to keep her seat to catch up with the equestrians. She ended up releasing them to their own protection and used the time to visit her family whom she rarely saw. They agreed to meet up later in the day, so Hannah could return with Rebecca to the Ingall Estate. Rebecca appreciated Hannah's trust and discretion, faithfully meeting up with her at their prearranged time.

It was Rebecca's and Jonathan's habit to rest their mounts at the end of their races. They would drop their horses' reins and let them nip at the thick grass while they meandered about in conversation. Jonathan would always help Rebecca dismount, grabbing her waist to bring her to the ground. On one particular day, he found himself spellbound watching Rebecca laugh with glee. At Jonathan's raised eyebrow, Rebecca confessed that she knew that Jonathan was letting her win their races, having seen him on more than one occasion, pull on his mount's reins to slow his speed just before their designated finish line. She applauded his gallantry, but admitted she could no longer in good conscious accept the accolades of victory. When he attempted to disabuse her of her notion, Rebecca laughed with such liberty that her whole face lit with joy. Her cheerfulness ignited his own happy countenance and without thought he pulled her into an embrace and kissed her on her lips. His senses returned immediately and he released her, cautiously awaiting her reaction. He could not tell if her shocked look was due to disgust or joy. He saw her tremble and expected her to slap his face for his ungentlemanly behavior.

Rebecca desperately wanted to kiss Jonathan back, but she did not want him to think her wanton, so she had hesitated and regretted her indecisiveness immediately, when she felt his arms start to release her. She looked into his eyes and saw a tenderness of affection that made it easy for her to respond in kind. She placed her arms around his neck, pulled him back into an embrace and pressed her lips against his. She was not sure what to do; but any concerns she had vanished when Jonathan earnestly pressed his lips against her own.

Jonathan could hear Rebecca's chortle resound from the vicar's cottage. He loved her robust laughter and looked forward to a future filled with it. He could hardly wait until next week when his mourning period would be officially over and he could ask Mr. Stevens for Rebecca's hand in marriage. Both he and Rebecca had decided to wait to request the vicar's permission to wed, respecting a year of mourning for his father, the late earl. Jonathan expected his friend, Mr. Willoughby, and his party to arrive for a sojourn. He thought a house full of guests and the local gentry together for a ball would be the perfect venue to announce his betrothal to Rebecca. He suspected that everyone would think he hosted the gala to honor his guests and that was fine with him. Until he secured Mr. Stevens's permission to marry his daughter, he did not mind the misconception.

Jonathan knocked on the vicar's door and smiled when Rebecca opened it. She beckoned him forward to greet her father. Mr. Stevens noted the intimacy that resonated between them. He knew Lord Westfield and Rebecca were spending a considerable amount of time together and the admiration he saw the earl display for his daughter pleased him. The Countess of Ingall confided to him that Rebecca held tender feelings for his lordship and he was glad the earl appeared to reciprocate them.

Jonathan placed his mother's request for his father's favorite psalm before the vicar. He then discussed his father's memorial service in greater detail with him. Before taking his leave, he informed the vicar that he had guests coming to stay at Westfield Manor and he invited him to attend the upcoming ball he was hosting. Mr. Stevens inquired the name of his lordship's guests and Jonathan informed him that Mr. Arthur Willoughby, the Countess of Raleigh and her daughter Lady Miranda would be visiting.

Jonathan saw Mr. Stevens's expression falter at his announcement, but thought nothing more of it when Rebecca rose to bid her father goodbye. He extended his own warm parting and escorted Rebecca and her abigail to their mounts.

Mr. Stevens lost no time in seeking a private audience with the Earl and Countess of Ingall. He waited anxiously in Lord Ingall's study and blurted out his question to them as soon as they entered the room, "Have you heard?"

"Dear Mr. Stevens," answered Lady Ingall. "What troubles you? Have I heard what?"

Mr. Stevens continued, "Have you heard that Lady Miranda and her mother are to be guests of Lord Westfield and that he plans a ball in her honor?"

"Oh!" remarked Lady Ingall with distress.

"Is this not the lady that we heard everyone speak of at Christmas?" asked the vicar. "Is she the one for whom Lord Westfield made an offer? Is he betrothed to her? What does this mean? What about Rebecca? What are we to do?"

Lord Ingall saw the hysteria that was about to explode. He had not been taken into confidence regarding Rebecca's feelings, but was not about to let guesswork get the better of him. He went and pulled on the bell cord that summoned his butler. He sent his servant to inform Rebecca that he wished to speak with her. An astonished Lady Ingall and Mr. Stevens looked to Lord Ingall for an explanation. The earl remarked, "Enough speculation. We will ask Rebecca what is going on and if Lord Westfield has done anything to mislead her or to dishonor her, I will see to him, myself."

"Roger," whispered Jane with fear, "What will you do?"

"Never mind," he said, "but be assured I will handle it."

Rebecca entered a very tense and emotional room. Lady Ingall looked teary eyed. Both her father and Lord Ingall looked angry. She asked, "Have I done something wrong?"

After an intense interview that wrenched Rebecca to the core, it was decided that Lord Ingall on behalf of Mr. Stevens, would have a private audience with Lord Westfield. Mr. Stevens thought it would be awkward interviewing his lordship, considering it was partly under his beneficence that he earned his living. Plus, Lord Ingall insisted the responsibility was his since Rebecca lived in his household. Roger was appalled that Jonathan had proposed to Rebecca without approaching Mr. Stevens. As much as Rebecca insisted that Jonathan's intentions were honorable, Lord Ingall commanded she sequester herself until he had met with Lord Westfield. Out of respect, she reluctantly obliged him.

Roger barely controlled his fury, waiting to be announced by the Westfield butler. He was escorted into the parlour to be received by Lady Westfield. He noted she kept company with another matron whom he quickly learned was Lady Raleigh. The introduction fueled his rising anger. Before Amelia offered him any form of hospitality, he tersely requested an audience with Lord Westfield and his ire piqued when he was told that Jonathan was giving his guests a tour of his property.

Lord Ingall insisted a groom be sent for Jonathan. He told the stunned Amelia that he had an urgent matter to discuss with him and Amelia knew better than to prevaricate. She read Roger's manner to be of an urgent and serious nature. She did not summon her butler, but saw to the matter herself, leaving him in the company of the Countess of Raleigh.

Lady Raleigh wasted little time or tack to inquire, "May I ask what business you have with Lord Westfield that takes his company away from my daughter?"

Lord Ingall, in a very haughty tone, replied, "Yes, I do mind. I see it to be none of your business, any dealings that I may have with my neighbor."

Offended, Lady Raleigh retorted, "I beg to differ as I expect to call him family very soon."

With that remark, Roger left the parlour in three diligent strides and exited Westfield Manor without a farewell to its mistress. Lady Raleigh was quite perplexed to answer when Lady Westfield returned and inquired where Lord Ingall had gone.

With a heavy heart, Roger returned home and held a private conference with his wife and Rebecca. He informed them of Jonathan's upcoming betrothal to Lady Miranda.

"I don't believe it," said Rebecca in a marked tone. "He would never offer for me if he were already promised to another. Besides, I know he loves me."

"I do not doubt that he cares for you, Rebecca," Lord Ingall offered. "I have known Jonathan since he was a child and this behavior goes against his character and upbringing. I find it hard to believe it as well, but I heard directly from Lady Raleigh that she was, her words exactly, 'to call him family very soon.' She would not make such a public declaration making her and her daughter open to humiliation, if it was not true."

"She is mistaken or confused," interjected Rebecca.

Lord Ingall approached Rebecca and placed his hands on her shoulder. He said, "My dear Rebecca, even the servants are talking that an announcement is to be made at the ball."

"Yes," she cried. "Jonathan is to announce our betrothal."

"Without asking Mr. Stevens permission to marry you?" he barked.

"Well, no, of course not," she answered. "He was waiting for tomorrow's service, before seeking an audience with my papa."

"Very well, Rebecca," he said. "For your sake and out of respect for his father, the late Lord Westfield, I will give him the benefit of the doubt. However, I insist that you let me take you to London for a sojourn. The Season is about to begin. Jane has not made an appearance for quite a while and I believe the trip will do you both good."

"I cannot leave Jonathan without seeing him," she begged. "I know that only a misunderstanding exists."

"I will not see you hurt, Rebecca," he remarked soberly. "If Jonathan, is who you know him to be, then he will prove himself at the Westfield Ball by not announcing his betrothal to Lady Miranda. If you are wrong, then you will be safely away in London where country gossip cannot harm you under our protection."

Rebecca replied, "I will go if you promise to attend the ball and speak to Jonathan. I trust no one to deliver the news, aside from yourself and my papa, whom I know is not up to the task. Please, Lord Ingall, will you grant me this favor?"

"Of course," he relented.

The week had not gone as Jonathan planned and he was unsure what to expect at his ball this evening. He worried over what transpired to make Lord Ingall remove his household to London. When he received his mother's summons, informing him that Lord Ingall was urgently awaiting him at home for a private audience, he became alarmed that something had befallen Rebecca. He raced home, his annoyed guests following in his wake, to discover the earl had left in haste without a note of explanation. His efforts to follow Lord Ingall to his estate failed when Mr. Willoughby and Lady Miranda bombarded him with questions. It took him another good hour before he arrived at the Ingall Estate to learn the Ingalls were not in residence. What disturbed him more was that there was no message from his lordship or Rebecca. He did his best to question Palmer as to when the Ingalls would return, but the consummate butler revealed nothing of his master's intentions and he returned home, troubled over Rebecca's departure.

His concerns increased when Mr. Willoughby and Lady Raleigh attacked him with outlandish charges. Of all things, Mr. Willoughby accused Jonathan of dallying with Lady Miranda. Jonathan knew Arthur was besotted with the young debutante and had been part of her entourage since the "Little Season." He also knew that Arthur planned to offer for her hand in marriage which was why Jonathan agreed to invite Lady Raleigh and her daughter to Westfield Manor. Arthur hoped to soften Miranda's mother to his suit by establishing his connection to the Earl of Westfield. Jonathan thought Arthur's plan was working for he bore witness to his friend's cheerful and optimistic manner. However, within days of Arthur's arrival, his demeanor began to change from light and easy, to sulky and brooding. Before long, Arthur accused Jonathan of perfidy, plotting to usurp his good position with Miranda's mother, Lady Raleigh. It was common knowledge that title and wealth, like the face cards in a deck, trumped the suit of a man with only his lineage and a future inheritance to recommend him.

Unknown to Jonathan, Lady Raleigh refused Arthur's suit when he asked permission to pay his addresses to Miranda. The countess insulted him further by calling him blind. "Why do you think we are here!" she railed. Arthur was so shocked and angry at being deceived, he left Lady Raleigh to find and thrash Jonathan beyond recognition.

He found the earl in the rose garden with his hand coupling Lady Miranda's face. If he was an artist, the fetching scene of romance and innocence would have inspired him to paint it, but he was a man deceived and his jealously launched him to charge at Jonathan, physically yanking him away from his lady.

He yelled, "How dare you!"

Completely surprised, Jonathan barked, "What the deuce is wrong with you?"

Jonathan's affront took Arthur aback. He looked to Miranda to seek the truth. Miranda calmly spoke, "Arthur, dear, I have something in my eye. Lord Westfield has been unsuccessful in removing it. Please help me and then perhaps, you can tell me what is wrong."

Arthur dropped and shook his head in regret, "I am sorry." Miranda's endearments had instantly assuaged him. He realized he had let Lady Raleigh's remarks make more of what he saw when he came upon Miranda and Lord Westfield. He put aside his angst and lovingly took Miranda's face into his own hands to do her bidding. He looked into her troubled, reddened eye and chastised himself for doubting her devotion. He asked her to blink several times, hoping that whatever irritated her eye would come to the surface. He found an offending eyelash and carefully removed it with his linen square.

Miranda recovered immediately and took Arthur's hand to lead him to a nearby marble bench. She begged Jonathan to follow, knowing that he deserved an explanation for Arthur's behavior. She knew Arthur had spoken to her mother and suspected by Arthur's behavior, that all had not gone well. She hoped Jonathan could offer his assistance, or at least advice.

The earl listened to Arthur's tale and became enraged. "I have never made a promise to Lady Miranda," and then with an apologetic voice to the lady in question queried, "Have I?"

"No, my lord," responded Miranda. "Your behavior has been most proper and very obtuse, I must say. It was clear to me and all maidens in your company that your heart was not captivated, at least not by any one of us."

Miranda continued, "I fear my mama's skill in flushing out the servant's gossip has misled her. It seems that a rumor is being discussed, regarding your upcoming betrothal announcement at your ball. Since I am the only eligible lady in attendance and because of the speculation that occurred during the 'Little Season,' my mama misjudged the situation. Do not fault her too harshly. She is only doing what she thinks is best for me." Miranda looked at Arthur, "Give her time, she will come around, once she understands I love you and that I am not the object of Lord Westfield's affection."

Lady Raleigh did not come around. She insisted that Lord Westfield did allude to an offer and she expected a betrothal announcement to be made at the ball or else she would sue the earl for breach of promise. Witnessed by Mr. Willoughby and Miranda, Jonathan informed Lady Raleigh that he had every intention of making an announcement at his ball, but that his engagement was to Miss Stevens, not Lady Miranda.

Lady Raleigh inquired, "Who?"

Mr. Willoughby answered, "She is the vicar's daughter."

The countess shouted, "Do you mean to tell me that you will throw my daughter over for a little *chit*?!"

It took every ounce of Jonathan's strength to keep his composure. Lady Raleigh knew she had made a gross err in her heated remark and took a cautious step backward. Controlling his temper, Jonathan warned, "Be careful, Lady Raleigh, for an insult against Miss Stevens is an insult against me. Do not let my newly acquired earldom mislead you of the influence I own. I assure you, any attempt at slander towards ruining Miss Stevens and you alone will suffer the *ton's* abjuration. You know my connections too well to doubt it."

"But," she said, "I have already declared your intentions publicly. We will be humiliated."

In a imperious tone, he berated, "That was your folly. I suggest that in the future, you wait for an offer to be made for your daughter before you announce one."

Arthur thinking Lady Raleigh might reconsider his offer, asked her again, "Lady Raleigh. Will you permit me to pay my addresses to Lady Miranda?"

She bellowed, "Never!" and started to stomp away before Jonathan commanded her to stop.

"Who exactly did you communicate this false liaison with?" he asked.

Lady Raleigh stiffened her back and gave her answer while walking away, "Why with Lord Ingall, of course,"

Jonathan's breath left him as if he had been kicked in the stomach.

Impatiently, Jonathan greeted his guests for coming to his ball. He longed to see the Ingall family and had just given up hope that they would attend when he spied Lord Ingall enter the ballroom. His lordship approached him, greeting, "Good evening, Westfield. I hear an announcement is to be made tonight. I hope to offer you my felicitations."

Jonathan studied his lordship, anxiously trying to understand his comment. He asked him, "Are Lady Ingall, Mr. Stevens, and Miss Stevens here?"

Lord Ingall replied, "No, I removed them to London."

Concerned, Jonathan asked, "Are they ill?"

Jonathan's wretched face, softened the earl's manner. He said, "No, they are not ill only away on a visit."

"Then," offered Jonathan. "I am afraid, no announcement will be made this evening."

Roger found he could not keep from grinning. He said, "I think we need to talk."

Jonathan led the way to his private study where he unburdened his soul to a man his father once called, the "dearest of friend." They were just about to toast to his future betrothal when Lady Raleigh broke their celebration by barging into his study in hysteria. She was holding a note in her hand that she waved precariously, crying, "She is gone! Lord Westfield! She is Gone!"

"Who is gone?" he commanded.

"Why, Miranda," she bellowed. "And it is all your fault!"

Lord Westfield looked at Lord Ingall and then looked back to Lady Raleigh. He said, "What the devil are you talking about?"

Lady Raleigh took a deep breath and shoved the note into Jonathan's hand. He read it, summarizing for Lord Ingall, "Lady Miranda and Mr. Willoughby appear to have eloped." The color drained from Lady Raleigh's face when she heard the word elopement and her body crumbled. Roger saw her ladyship swoon and reached her just in time to break her fall.

"She will be ruined," she sobbed.

Roger, the calm and decisive of the two said, "All is not lost, yet. Westfield you will pursue them and bring them to London. Lady Raleigh and I will meet you there. I will procure a special license, while you Lady Raleigh will do what you do best and spread the word of your daughter's betrothal to Mr. Arthur Willoughby, son of Sir Miles Willoughby of Bedale in North Yorkshire. No one will suspect they planned to elope, since they will have your blessing. You will give your blessing?"

"Yes, yes," agreed Lady Raleigh whose concern now rested on her child's reputation and not on Mr. Willoughby's station in Society.

Lord Ingall in earnest, suggested, "Why they could even get married in a church if we find them in time."

Lady Raleigh almost cheered with enthusiasm, remarking, "Oh, yes! And a marriage breakfast! Oh! We must hurry. There is much to be done." Jonathan pulled his bell cord, requesting his horse Apollo be made ready while Lord Ingall waited for Lady Raleigh to pack her belongings, so that he could escort her to London.

Chapter Nine

Lady Ingall and Rebecca were anxious for the evening to end and for Lord Ingall to bring news of what transpired between him and Jonathan. Tonight was the Westfield Ball. Everyone was on pins and needles waiting to hear whether Lord Westfield had played Rebecca false. It was dusk and the street lighter had just called out the hour when the doorknocker banged loudly. The noise brought everyone to their feet and Rebecca wondered if news from his lordship could already have made its way to them. The Ingall's town butler hustled into the parlour to announce to his mistress that Master Henry was being carried to his room. He informed his ladyship that Henry's attending nurse requested an audience with her and the earl.

The announcement so shocked Lady Ingall that she felt her vision falter. Rebecca saw her stumble and came to her aid, steadying her with her arms and words, whispering, "My, lady, do not fear, I am with you and soon Lord Ingall will be here too!"

Lady Ingall with Rebecca in her wake, hurried to Henry's room. The boy's face was almost white, devoid of color except for the splotches of crimson on his forehead, cheeks, and neck, marking his fever. His eyelids were closed, his mouth slightly ajar releasing his slow moans of pain. The nurse placed a cold rag on Henry's head, then walked over to the windows to close the heavy damask curtains. Only the light from the fire being built and a small candle would illuminate the room. The nurse advised that bright light was painful for the patient at this stage.

Lady Ingall asked, "What stage?"

The nurse informed her that Master Henry suffered from Scarlet Fever. He was brought home when his fever began to climb to an alarming rate. "While we did our best to sequester and care for your son, we thought you would want him with you, especially when he began to beg for his mother."

Lady Ingall sobbed, asking everyone's forgiveness for her unseemly display of emotion. While she drew from years of training to control her emotions, Rebecca did her best to console her mistress by assuring her that Master Henry would improve. She ordered a footman to fetch their own physician and then she sent a groom to ride with an urgent message for Lord Ingall, informing him of Henry's illness. Last, she spoke to the nurse at length, receiving instructions and medicines for his care, before she thanked the caretaker and bid her farewell.

Rebecca had helped to nurse Scarlet Fever patients before and knew that survival depended on reducing the patient's fever. Master Henry was warmly bundled. Rebecca ordered the layers of blankets removed and then ordered that a bowl of ice be brought to the room. At their country estate, the Ingall's kept a full icehouse filled with frozen blocks of ice, that their own servants chipped out of their wintry ponds each season. However, here in London, they purchased their ice from subscription and had blocks of ice delivered each week, storing them in their insulated cellar. The underground cold chamber kept the perishables, like milk and butter, fresh. The effective drainage system in the ice cellar allowed the Ingall's to maintain as much or as little ice they desired. Rebecca knew there would be enough to cool Henry's body.

She then ordered a poultice, made as quick as possible for Henry's neck. The nurse supplied an effective recipe that she said would reduce the swelling on Henry's tonsils. Lady Ingall took a seat near Henry. She spoke softly to him in assuring tones, telling him she was here, he was home, and he was going to be all right.

The large ceramic bowl of chipped ice arrived and Lady Ingall and Rebecca took a chunk and positioned themselves on each side of Henry. They each swabbed Henry's arms and forehead in an attempt to cool his body. Henry's fevered body melted the ice quickly and started to drip upon the mattress. Lady Ingall drew her laced handkerchief from her sleeve to sop up the water. Rebecca rose and went to collect the porcelain water pitcher and basin used for washing from Henry's console. She brought it back to Henry's bedside table and poured the tepid water into the bowl and then added ice to cool it. Rebecca took the rag the nurse had placed on Henry's head and moistened it in the icy water. Ringing out the excess water, she placed the cold cloth on Henry's burning chest. Lady Ingall immediately saw the logic behind her actions and sent the attending footman for more cloths. The next hours were spent moistening and replacing the linen squares on Henry's body when they lost their coolness. Lady Ingall and Rebecca worked without rest. The physician came and supported their ministrations, prescribing a potion that was efficacious in Scarlet Fever patients. Lady Ingall dosed the remedy. Henry's eyes filled with tears trying to swallow the medicine. His throat burned. Tenderly, Lady Ingall coaxed him to drink the elixir. She persevered, getting Henry to not only swallow his potion, but to sip the cool tea she herself thought therapeutic, a long standing herbal tea sweetened with honey, passed down from generation to generation.

Lady Ingall would not leave Henry's side, but ordered Rebecca to retire to her room and rest. After a much needed repose, Rebecca secured a trundle bed to be brought in for her mistress. Jane's exhaustion overwhelmed her and though she fought it, she finally agreed to a short nap if the bed was placed alongside her son and Rebecca kept vigil over Henry. While she slept,

Rebecca continued to replace the warm linen cloths with cool ones.

It was during one of his treatments that Henry opened his eyes. Seeing Rebecca, he struggled to speak. Rebecca came closer to his beseeching eyes and chapped lips. She asked, "What is it, dear?"

Henry with teary eyes rasped out a reply, "I am afraid."

Rebecca's heart wrenched and she used all her strength to compose herself, before she said, "Do not fear, Henry. You are on the path to wellness. I know you hurt, but have faith. The Lord hears our prayers and he is with you." After a pause, Rebecca unclasped the chain from around her neck that held her locket. "Henry," she said, "my mama's locket has brought me good luck. Hold on to it and it will do the same for you." Rebecca took Henry's hand and closed his fingers around the locket. Henry attempted a smile, but his body, weakened from the fever, fell limp. Rebecca gasped when she saw his eyes close and his body sink into the mattress. She urgently placed her ear on Henry's chest and felt profound relief when she could hear his heart, though rapid, beat.

An aggrieved Lord Ingall, brushed past the butler and headed straight to Henry's room. There he saw his son pale and immobile. The room was eerily dark and quiet. He made out that his wife napped on a trundle bed, next to Henry and that Rebecca, slept in a chair on the opposite side. Rebecca startled awake when Lord Ingall approached, asking, “How is he?”

Rebecca rose, took both of his hands, and said, “Much better, his fever is reduced.”

Roger allowed the breath he was holding to release. His body started to shiver and Rebecca said, “Truly, Lord Ingall, he will prevail. I do believe the worst is over. His fever is remarkably reduced.”

Lord Ingall hugged Rebecca fiercely, exclaiming, “Thank you!” Then, he surveyed Rebecca’s face and saw her fatigue. Her face was haggard, her eyelids heavy, her voice husky, her hair and dress disheveled. He ordered her to rest, saying, “You have done enough, child. I want you to see Cook and have her prepare you something to eat and then get some sleep. I will see to Henry.”

Rebecca did not argue. She could use the reprieve, so she began to depart. Before leaving, she remarked, “I will return after I take a small respite, but do not hesitate to send for me if I can be of assistance.”

He nodded and replied, “Thank you, Rebecca. You may also ask Cook to send some tea and biscuits to break my wife’s fast.”

Two days passed. Henry was weak, but feeling much better. His throat still hurt and the rash across his body was starting to scab, but overall, knowing that he was getting better, cheered him. He still held onto

Rebecca's locket and felt quite sentimental, knowing how much she must care for him to let him borrow it.

Henry reclined against his pillows and played with Rebecca's locket. The latch opened and out fell a square of yellowed material, embroidered with a pattern. He guessed the linen was quite old and wondered if Rebecca knew it was inside the locket. After all, he thought, *"The locket once belonged to her mother, maybe she is unaware of it. I shall show her when I see her."*

Lady Ingall walked into the room, leading a maid carrying a tray of broth for Henry. Her entrance broke Henry's reverie and when he saw her, he returned her smile, saying, "I must be feeling better if I am getting sick of consommé." His mother instructed the maid to set the tray down on the nightstand next to Henry's bed. She picked up the *serviette*, unfolded it, and placed the napkin under Henry's chin. It was then that she noticed Rebecca's locket, and asked, "Henry, is that Rebecca's locket?"

"Yes," he replied.

"You know," she said. "I do not think I have ever seen her without it. She treasures it, dearly."

"I know," said Henry. "I am quite moved that she entrusted it to me. She said it has always brought her good luck and it would do the same for me. It has given me great comfort."

"I am so glad," she said. Then, she spied the unclasped locket and exclaimed, "Please, tell me that you have not broken it!"

Henry's eyes gleamed at his mother's outburst. He knew he deserved her exclamation for he had a habit of touching things he ought not. He braced himself for her reprimand and expressed his anxiety in laughter. He complained, "Ow! Don't make me laugh, Mama, it hurts my throat."

Lady Ingall retorted, "I did no such thing."

Henry attempted to control his giggling by whispering, "I accidentally opened the locket, Mama, and found a small piece of material. You know the locket once belonged to Rebecca's mother. Do you think she knows about it?"

"I do not know, Henry," she replied. "But give me the linen and I will replace it in the locket. I do not want anything to happen to it." Henry obeyed and handed his mother the small piece of cloth with Rebecca's locket. She felt the embroidery stitching and opened the linen for view.

Henry noticed immediately the change in his mother's demeanor. Her face paled, her eyes widened, seeming to explode from their sockets. She swayed and accidentally dropped the locket when she reached for the bedpost to steady herself. Henry cried out, "Mama, what is it?"

Jane hysterically ran to the bell cord and pulled it again and again. Then, she ran into the hallway, shouting her husband's name."Roger! Roger! Come quickly!" she called.

Rebecca was reading in her private suite when she heard Lady Ingall shouting. She flew into the hallway and ran to her mistress who turned anxiously from side to side, searching for her husband, Roger. Henry, with a barely audible voice, called from his bed, "Mama, are you all right?"

Holding onto Lady Ingall's shoulders, Rebecca tried to get her attention. When she finally gained eye contact, she asked her "My lady, what is it? What is wrong? Is it Henry?" Rebecca did not know whether to stay with Lady Ingall or run to see Henry. Jane looked at Rebecca and called her name.

She started crying, exclaiming, "Oh, Rebecca! My dear child."

It was at this moment that Lord Ingall spied his wife and Rebecca. He nearly collapsed when he saw his wife's hysteria. He ran into Henry's room expecting to see his worst fears realized. What he saw surprised him. Henry was trying to get out of bed. While, it was upsetting that Henry should tax himself, it did not warrant the emotion that his wife exhibited.

Lord Ingall halted Henry's rise and aided him back to bed. Henry whispered, "Is mama all right?"

He responded, "I shall see to her immediately. Do you know what has distressed her?"

Henry replied, "I do not know. I found a piece of cloth in Rebecca's locket and showed it to her. When she saw it, she went pale and started calling for you."

He responded, "Do not worry. I shall see to her. Pray, get some rest. I need to see you recovered. I will return later after I have tended to your mother." Roger hurried to his sobbing wife and wrapped his arms around her.

Rebecca did not know what to do. Lord Ingall asked her to have Cook send up some tea and brandy to his wife's suite. Then, he asked her to sit with Henry until he could return. Jane's sobs quieted, but her body continued to shake when Roger lifted her, carrying her to her bed. She babbled Rebecca's name over and over again. Roger could not fathom what befell his poor wife.

He gently placed Jane on her bed. Roger noted her rapid breath was making her lightheaded, seeing her eyes roll back in her head. He feared she would swoon and quickly opened her nightstand to find the smelling salts she kept there. He placed the opened bottle under her nose and after a few moments, he saw her eyes pop open.

Jane's abigail entered at that moment with the tea tray. Roger poured a small portion of brandy into a Sevres cup and filled the china with warm tea. He cradled his wife, brought the rim to her mouth and commanded her to take a sip. Jane obeyed. Roger demanded she take another sip and she obliged him again. Her eyes were bloodshot from crying and her cheeks were stained with tears, but after a couple of swallows of the fortified tea and having her husband's strength to lean on, her breathing finally regulated. Within minutes, her composure returned enough for her husband to ask, "Dear Jane, tell me, what ails you?"

In a stutter, Jane said, "R-Roger, look wh-what Rebecca had in her locket." Jane handed the cloth to Roger and then dropped her face into both her hands. Her tears flowed once more.

Henry, overcome with fear, wanted to know what was wrong with his mother. Rebecca did her best to pacify him. She did not know what to say to him, other than his mother was overcome and his father was seeing to her. Rebecca asked Henry if he knew what had troubled his mother. Henry instead of an answer posed his own question. "Rebecca, did you know there was a piece of cloth inside your locket?"

She answered, "Yes, dear. Did you find it?"

He replied, "Yes. It looked rather old. Was it your mama's?"

Rebecca said, "I do not know for sure. I only know that it is a part of my favorite blanket that I had as a child. When the blanket became too tattered, my mama cut a piece and put it in my locket for a keepsake." Rebecca thought for a moment, then asked, "Is that what upset your mama?"

Henry dropped his head and soberly answered, "Yes."

Roger took the cloth from Jane and recognized the embroidered family crest immediately. He looked at his wife and said, "Where did you say you found it?"

Jane answered, "It was in Rebecca's locket. Oh, Roger! What does it mean? Is fate playing a cruel joke on us?"

"I do not know," he said. "But, we will discover how something that once cradled our first born is nothing more than a remnant in a locket." Roger closed his eyes and fingered the embroidered stitching. After a moment of silence, he looked at his wife and said, "When you are ready, I will gather Mr. Stevens into my private study. He will have the answers to our questions, I am sure."

Both the Earl and Countess of Ingall fidgeted waiting for Mr. Stevens to arrive. Jane had quieted herself and had agreed to let Roger handle the interview. She was afraid her emotions would get the better of her. She was finding it difficult to compose herself. A concerned Mr. Stevens entered the highly tensed atmosphere and knew instantly that something was wrong. He hoped that Master Henry had not taken a turn for the worse. He had no other explanation for why the noon meal was interrupted or why he received the urgent summons.

He noted Lady Ingall pacing, wrenching a laced handkerchief in her hand. Lord Ingall stood stiff as a board with his hands clasped behind his back, staring out his window in apparent reflection. His only feature marking his anxiety was a nervous eye twitch. Lord Ingall turned around when Mr. Stevens called out his greeting and Lady Ingall stopped abruptly in her track. The vicar wondered at Lady Ingall's pleading look and his sympathy grew for the worried lady.

Lord Ingall pointed toward the settee and requested Mr. Stevens to sit. The vicar obeyed and waited to be enlightened. Lord and Lady Ingall sat opposite him and then Roger began the interview. "Mr. Stevens, I am sorry to summon you before we break our fast, but I have a few questions that necessitate asking. Please forgive the impropriety of them, but I beg that you be forthcoming for much rests on your answers. I will explain at the end of our discourse, the reason for them."

Astounded, Mr. Stevens replied, "I am at your service, my lord. You have been most generous to my daughter and me. You have called us family. I am more than happy to help you and Lady Ingall, if I can."

Roger continued, "Let us begin then. Mr. Stevens, is Rebecca, the daughter of your blood?"

Mr. Stevens jaw dropped. His head snapped when he looked at Lord Ingall, Lady Ingall, and then returned to look back at his lordship. He didn't know what to expect from their meeting, but surely this question was not it. His first reaction was to explicitly say, *"Yes, Rebecca is indeed my daughter,"* and while in his heart it was true, he knew that was not what Lord Ingall meant. He had always protected his wife and daughter from slander. He recalled, *"Isn't that why I married her in the first place?"* However,

Lord Ingall's question was driven from something else, for there was no way that he could have known that his wife was pregnant when they wed. The look on the earl's face compelled him to be completely honest.

Mr. Stevens belatedly answered, "No, she is not." Jane's gasp left her lips as though she had been holding her breath awaiting his answer. The rasping sound broke the interview and before Roger could query more, Mr. Stevens began his tale. "As you know, Rebecca has often spoken that I saved her mother from an uncomfortable position. She believes that I rescued her from an unhappy and hard-pressed service to the then baron. In a way, that was true. The baron took a great advantage of her. She came to me when she discovered she was with child. She was afraid that the baron would take the child's life if he knew. He was a wicked man, she said, and did not put it past him to kill her just to keep his good name. She exclaimed, 'Who would care about the untimely death of a maid? My life may be over, but I must save my child!' She begged me for sanctuary: to finish her term and give birth to her child. She asked me to find a proper home for her baby."

Mr. Stevens continued, "I was five and thirty at the time I met Rebecca's mother. I never thought I would wed. While I am most proficient on the lectern, I am quite speechless and awkward in the company of an eligible woman. No one ever looked twice at me until Mary. She had the most beautiful hair and could laugh like a song that you could never hear enough. I was very attracted to her and compelled out of true affection to help and protect her. To this day, I count my blessings that she said, yes, when I proposed. I had ten loving years with her. What joy!"

Rebecca grew just as worried as Henry about Lady Ingall when Lord Ingall did not return as promised. She told him once again not to fret, that she would seek out his father and ask about his mother. Henry relaxed. In a strained voice, he said, "Thank you, but do not forget to come back and tell me about my mama."

She smiled, tucked the blankets around Henry's body, kissed him on the forehead while assuring him, "I will not."

Rebecca searched the private suites of both Lord and Lady Ingall. When they could not be found, she proceeded to the earl's private study where he spent many hours tending to business. She knocked on the door, but did not wait to be summoned. Lord Ingall had always allowed her this liberty for she was considered family. She peered in and was surprised to see her father, Mr. Stevens, in conference with the earl and countess. Rebecca pushed the door open and overheard Lord Ingall say, "I understand. Can you tell me how this piece of linen came to be in Rebecca's locket?"

Rebecca made her presence known with her greeting, "Papa, is everything all right?" Lord Ingall, Lady Ingall, and Mr. Stevens all rose to greet Rebecca. She saw immediately that she had interrupted a serious conference. She asked, "What is wrong? I know it has something to do with the piece of my favorite baby blanket I kept in my locket. Please, tell me."

Lady Ingall sobbed and asked, "You used it as a baby?"

Rebecca came to her, placed her arms around her and consoled, "My lady, please tell me, what is wrong? Have I offended you in some way?"

Jane's knees buckled at Rebecca's kindness. Roger helped his wife to her seat, assuring Rebecca, "No, dear child, you have done nothing wrong. I fear some old wounds have resurfaced."

Roger asked again, "Please, Mr. Stevens, how did Rebecca come by the blanket, she used as a child?"

Mr. Stevens looked at Rebecca. He did not want to hurt her, but he knew it was time the truth was exposed. He said most sorrowfully, "My dear child, I guess I should have told you years ago, but a good enough reason never compelled me to do so. I have always loved you as my own. Your mother and I did not know who your parents were, so it seemed insignificant to say anything. We thought we were doing what was best for you."

In unison, Lord Ingall, Lady Ingall, and Rebecca queried, "What did you say?" Rebecca started to talk, but Lord Ingall held up his hand to quiet her.

"Allow me please," he said with unbelievable restraint. "Mr. Stevens, please explain. I thought you said that though you did not sire Rebecca, your wife was her mother."

Mr. Stevens continued, "I am afraid you have been misled. Rebecca entered before I could finish my tale. Rebecca's mother was with child when we wed. We were quite happy and were looking forward to Rebecca's arrival."

Jane interrupted, "When was Rebecca born?"

Mr. Stevens was surprised at Lady Ingall's question, but found an easy reply. "My dear wife," he smiled, "went into labor on a most horrendous night. Although the storm was relentless, her dear sweet humor prevailed until we learned the child was stillborn. It was a difficult birth and the midwife that attended, had no explanation other than it was God's will. We were both heartbroken and sequestered ourselves for the next two days. We probably would have stayed hidden in grief longer, if not for the miracle that God bestowed upon us. A wee baby girl, bundled in what came to be her favorite blanket, lay in a wicker basket outside our front door."

Jane took another sharp breath. Her wide eyes mirrored Rebecca's who looked completely stunned. Within seconds, Lord Ingall and his wife went to her and together, they wrapped her up in their arms, crying, "Oh! Elinor!"

Rebecca did not know what to think. She was confused herself, so she allowed them their moment. Before she knew it, Rebecca found herself in a tug of war when Lady Ingall turned her face to look into her eyes. She saw her smile. Then, Lord Ingall copied his wife's action and with pride, announced, "They are mine."

The joy in their eyes pleased Rebecca, but she wanted to know what had happened to cause this overflow of emotion. She disengaged herself, asking, "Please, will someone explain what has happened?"

Mr. Stevens stated, "I am afraid, my dear child. I do not know."

Lord Ingall with utmost glee said, "We are celebrating. A child that we thought was lost is now found."

Rebecca said, "You called me Elinor."

Jane looked at her husband and smiled. Then to Rebecca, she said, "Yes, we did, and indeed, you are."

In the next hour, Lord and Lady Ingall told their own story of joy and sorrow. How they gave birth to a beautiful daughter whom they named Elinor after Lord Ingall's mother. How Lord Ingall wrapped Elinor in the family ancestral blanket. They spoke of the terrible storm, the collapsed bridge they thought stole their child and they remembered their grief, one that was so all encompassing, that it took a young girl with a huge heart named Rebecca, to show them how to heal.

Chapter Ten

Mr. Willoughby and Lady Miranda proved to be terrible elopers. Their spontaneous departure for Gretna Green, a small city across the border in Scotland where one could marry without the reading of the banns, seemed simple, but was fraught with hindrances. Their elopement was plagued from the beginning, especially since they had no plans other than getting to Gretna Green.

Only their stealthy departure was discussed in detail. They decided they would each pack a small valise and hide it in the rose garden the day of the Westfield Ball. They agreed to attend the gala and then exit through a ballroom door like other couples taking the air, so their absence would not be remarked upon. Their plan was to retrieve their luggage and make their way to the stable where Arthur would confiscate Westfield's curricle. As his lordship's guest, one already permitted to ride the earl's horses at will, he did not expect anyone, stable boy or other to stop him. He had no qualms taking the curricle believing he was entitled, since Jonathan caused all the brouhaha to start. Both he and Miranda agreed, the earl owed them for not correcting the misconception that she was the one he planned to wed.

Besides, Arthur had nothing to lose. He knew once they returned to London for the Season that Lady Raleigh would dismiss his company. She would not want him discouraging any eligible suitors from seeking Lady Miranda's favor. After all, as she had informed him, "Lord Westfield is not the only eligible nobleman of rank worthy of my Miranda."

While it was possible for one of the grooms to summon the earl to verify Mr. Willoughby's right to take the curricle, Arthur was confident they would not. It was common practice on the night of a ball for extra stable boys to be hired to care for the guests' horses and carriages. These temporary ostlers rarely questioned their betters. They were too afraid to lose their job and too ashamed of their speech to question nobility. Arthur was sure that he and Miranda would escape without notice.

Arthur's plan was to drive non-stop to Gretna Green, acquiring fresh horses at each posting inn and stopping for respites of nourishment. He would not damage Miranda's reputation by staying overnight at an inn, but he began to worry that Lady Raleigh might find the note they left, too early, *"What if she sends someone after us?"* He berated himself, *"You ninny, of course she will send someone after us!"* Concern turned to fear at the idea of losing Miranda and he began to despair.

By the second posting inn, the eloping couple's exhaustion proved to get the better of them. Sitting inside at a table waiting for their tea, Arthur worried that he might not have enough money to get them to Gretna Green. The costs of acquiring fresh horses was quickly draining his funds and if that wasn't enough to make him fret, all he had to do was look at Miranda's downcast expression. She had been as excited as he, when they first began their journey to Scotland, but as they moved farther away from Westfield Manor, Miranda's demeanor changed. He grew concerned that she regretted her decision to elope and found his worst fear realized when she queried, "What have we done?"

"Do you still love me?" he asked.

Miranda could not bear Arthur doubting her love. She tried to keep from crying, but her eyes overflowed with tears. "You know I do, but mama will never forgive me. She will give me the *cut direct*, now that I am ruined. The *ton* will despise me, thinking I am wanton for eloping and more terrible than that, my mama will pay the price as I am sure they will abjure her, as well. I am a wicked daughter."

Arthur placed his hand over hers and asked, "Do you want to go back?"

Miranda replied, "I do not want to lose you or be forced into a marriage of convenience. I want to be your wife, only not at the sacrifice of my mama. She has loved me most dearly."

Arthur looked at Miranda and declared, "I am a fool to let your mother make me think less of myself than what I am. I am a most respectable and eligible bachelor. We will marry, but with proper banns and with friends in attendance." Bubbling a guffaw, he mischievously added, "And we will enjoy a most prodigious marriage breakfast at your mother's expense."

Miranda rejoiced. Her eyes gleamed and she added her own hearty laugh to Arthur's. Still smiling, Arthur proffered his hand to help her rise, saying, "Let's go see your mother."

Forgetting propriety, Miranda placed her arms around Arthur's neck and gave him a fierce hug, "Oh, Arthur! I love you, so much. Thank you!"

The ride back was cheerful. Both of them found peace in their decision to win over Lady Raleigh's approval, rather than estrange her through an elopement. They spent the ride discussing all of Lady Raleigh's favorite things. Miranda picked her brain to remember her mother's favorite flower, food, book, sonata, play, and holiday. Arthur was intent on wooing Lady Raleigh until she gave them her blessing. He told Miranda that he would request his parents' help, declaring, "with the Willoughby charm to help us, our marriage is inevitable."

Miranda felt giddy, freed from the guilt that had subconsciously weighed on her since their departure from Westfield Manor and she joined Arthur in laughter.

They had nearly returned to their first posting inn when a black steed came racing towards them. When the stallion passed their carriage, Arthur and Miranda heard the rider yell, "Whoa!!"

Jonathan rode Apollo alongside the curricle that Arthur had absconded from the Westfield stable, escorting the love birds back to Westfield Manor. He decided for decorum's sake, they should change the curricle for the Westfield carriage and have his mother join them on their trip to London. Jonathan hoped to quell any gossip regarding an elopement between Lady Miranda and Mr. Willoughby, by explaining the reason Lady Miranda did not return to Town with her own mother was because she offered herself as companion to travel with Lady Westfield. No one would question the need of Lady Westfield requiring company, since it was common knowledge that the countess had been in mourning the past year and had not been to London since her husband's death.

Amelia was more than ready to depart. She wanted to remove herself from the speculation that was already spreading throughout the manor about a possible elopement after Jonathan made a hasty departure to locate his absent guests of honor.

Arthur learned on the trip to London that Lady Raleigh was ready to permit him to pay his addresses to Miranda. He was thankful he did not need to become a sycophant to his future mother-in-law and Miranda was happy that an anticipated and heated battle, between two people she loved, would be no more.

Aside from Lady Westfield, everyone was exhausted when they reached London. Jonathan, Arthur, and Miranda had been awake for over twenty-four hours, except for the slumber they were lulled into from the rocking of the carriage. Ready to relinquish his guests, Jonathan instructed his coachman to take them all to the Raleigh town home where he expected Lord Ingall awaited with a special license. Though Arthur and Miranda had hopes of a proper marriage, they still did not know if any news of them making a midnight run to Gretna Green, was circulating among the *crème of society*.

The Westfield carriage stopped in front of the Raleigh town home and the passengers were shocked to see a flurry of activity. Hordes of tradesmen were coming and going. Both the earl and Mr. Willoughby had to create a path for Miranda to make her way to her front door. Arthur was about to take the doorknocker in hand when the door opened and they came face to face with Miranda's modiste. The woman made her curtsey and then hastily worked her way through the crowd to exit. Miranda saw she had an arm full of fashion plates and color swatches. She wanted to inquire what business her dressmaker had at her home when an exclamation called her to attention. She turned her head to find her butler greeting, "Ah! My lady, you have come at last. The countess will be quite pleased to see you." Miranda walked in receiving all the welcome her butler could bestow, while the earl and Arthur received nothing but disdain from the servant.

The trio entered the parlour and saw bolts of fabric, fashion plates, assorted flowers, cakes and invitations covering every piece of furniture. Lady Raleigh, with her back to the door, did not know of their arrival until her daughter timorously called, "Mama?"

Lady Raleigh turned. Emotion poured from her as she ran to her daughter with open arms, "My dear, dear, girl, how could you?"

"Oh, Mama!" Miranda cried. "I am so sorry. I did not mean to hurt you. It is only that I love Arthur so much and do not wish to marry another. He is all that is good and kind. It is because of him that I have returned, though I return most happily."

The countess was surprised. She thought the Earl of Westfield had caught them and forced them to return. Arthur, in her mind, was nothing more than a thief who had stolen an heirloom, so when she heard Miranda's outburst, she demanded, "Explain yourself, daughter."

Miranda continued, "Though I am very sorry for hurting you, I was most prepared to continue on to Gretna Green. Arthur saw I was unhappy and commanded we return. Oh, Mama! You should have seen him roar. It was truly romantic. He publicly exclaimed, 'I am a most respectable and eligible suitor. I will prove it to your mother.' Oh, Mama! Please say, 'yes.' He will make me most happy and you know, he is truly respectable."

Lady Raleigh was thankful that Mr. Willoughby was indeed a gentleman. To her daughter's delight, she said, "If he makes you happy, then I will relent. Why do you think this mess is in our parlour? Nothing but the best for my daughter." Miranda hugged her mother.

Arthur thought it safe to approach his future mother-in-law. He extended his hand to her and said, "Thank you."

Lady Raleigh took his proffered hand, shook it, and with candor replied, "I shall expect many grandchildren."

Arthur did not know how to respond to such a scandalous remark and looked to Miranda for help. He found her giggling, so he searched his brain for a proper response, returning his gaze to his future mother-in-law, only to find her grinning, ready to burst in laughter. The hilarity of the situation did not elude him. He felt his own chuckles surfacing. Before his guffaw exploded, he replied with glee, "It will be my pleasure, my lady."

Seemed to be forgotten, Jonathan felt extremely uncomfortable bearing witness to a private matter. He made his presence known with a cough. He asked, "Was Lord Ingall able to procure a special license?"

Lady Raleigh informed him, "We were met on our way to Town with an urgent summons for his lordship. It appeared that someone in his family was at death's door."

Jonathan panicked. Before Lady Raleigh could inform him that a special license was not necessary since there was no inkling of a scandal, he raced to his carriage and commanded his coachman to take him to the Ingalls.

Five long days passed since Jonathan burst out his carriage door to race up the steps of the Ingall town home, only to be halted by a "quarantine" sign. He was thankful it was not a black wreath. Worrying, he wondered, "*Who is ill and with what?*" He knew the front door would not be answered until the quarantine was lifted, so he took his card and slid it under the door. He left his footman to watch the service door to find out any information he could by interviewing the delivery boys or anyone else that had communication with the servants. He searched his mind, trying to remember the name of the Ingall's London physician. When his mind came up blank, he returned to his carriage hoping his mother would know.

To Jonathan's relief, Lady Westfield provided him with the physician's name and the earl immediately summoned the doctor to his town home. By the time the doctor came, Jonathan and his mother had worked themselves into a frenzy. They were quite relieved to learn that Master Henry survived a bout of Scarlet Fever and that the quarantine would be lifted in three days.

Jonathan made his way to the Ingall home the moment his spying footman sent the message that the quarantine sign was removed. He was shocked when

Palmer informed him that the family was not receiving callers. With no other option, he left his calling card expecting Lord Ingall to return his visit later in the afternoon. Jonathan waited. When the social hour passed and it became evident that Lord Ingall was not coming, he summoned the Ingall physician. Again, the doctor came to assure the earl that Master Henry was indeed well, aside from some scabs he acquired and that no one else in the family was ill.

The next day, Jonathan allowed his valet to fuss over his attire. He was quite confident that he would see Rebecca. He wanted to look his best. He planned to make his intentions of marrying Rebecca known to her father and the Ingall household. He purchased a small bouquet of flowers on his way to the Ingall home and with enthusiasm, knocked on their front door. A smiling Palmer opened the door and Jonathan thought the butler's demeanor quite jolly. His cheerfulness matched Jonathan's good mood and the feeling made him want to laugh. The nervous sensation of a racing heart and exuberance, reminded him of the time when he was about to be presented at court. He was so excited that he did not see the butler's composure change from mirth to hauteur, until the servant blocked his entrance. Palmer announced, “I am truly, sorry, My Lord Westfield, the family is not receiving visitors.”

Concerned, he asked, “Is someone else ill?”

Palmer grinned, “Oh, no, my lord! Everyone else is well, but have sequestered themselves for a period."

Without recourse, other than pushing the loyal servant out of the way, the earl handed over his calling card, the bouquet of flowers, and said, "Please let Lord Ingall know I request a private audience with him and give the bouquet to Miss Stevens with my felicitations."

Palmer replied, "Very good, my lord."

Frustrated beyond belief, Jonathan turned and swore a curse as he descended the steps of the Ingall town home. He returned home where he asked his mother if she had any insight to why the Ingall's, were not receiving visitors, especially him. The countess had no idea, but charged Jonathan to be patient. She took the opportunity to ask him to explain his fixed interest with the Ingalls. "So, tell me, Son. Do you have news or am I expected to learn your intentions, the same as the *ton*?"

"Why, Mother!" exclaimed Jonathan. "I thought you knew my heart."

"Yes," rebounded his mother. "I know where your heart lies. It is your intentions, I am unaware."

Jonathan looked at his mother seriously and bent down on his knee in front of where she sat. He looked her straight in the eyes, and said, "I love Rebecca dearly, and have been trying since my ball to offer for her. Please, tell me you approve."

Lady Westfield took both her hands and coupled Jonathan's face. She said, "My dear boy, I approve of anything that brings you joy, but I ask you, have you considered Rebecca's happiness and whether she is up to managing an earldom and the Society it brings?"

Jonathan answered, "She loves me, Mother. That I know. And she is very competent and resourceful. I know that she has inner strength and fortitude. Hasn't she already captured the hearts of not only our tenants, but Lord Ingall's?"

"Yes," she agreed. "But will her strength carry over when the *ton* mocks her lack of noble blood or shuns her society?"

Jonathan strongly retorted, "They would not dare!"

Lady Westfield continued, "They can be a cruel lot for their own amusement. Before you and Rebecca announce your engagement, be sure that she knows what may be in store for her."

Jonathan answered, "Mother, I cannot give her up. I would give up Society before her."

His mother smiled, showing her pride in her son. "Then you deserve her and I give you my blessing." Jonathan embraced his mother with much joy.

The following day, Jonathan returned home stomping his feet and cursing under his breath. Lady Westfield thought it quite a scene; reminding her of a tantrum he once threw as a child. When his temper failed to diminish, she exclaimed, "Enough!"

Jonathan looked at her and shouted, "They still will not receive me!" Lady Westfield thought this most odd and decided it was time for her to get to the bottom of things. Jane was her best friend. She knew sequestered or not, Jane would not turn her away without an explanation.

Jonathan could not thank his mother enough, and suggested, he accompany her. "Nonsense," she said. "They will surely refuse to admit us. I must impose on Jane's friendship and that I must do alone." Jonathan finally conceded, but commanded his mother to leave at once.

Propriety required Lady Westfield to wait in her carriage while her footman presented her calling card to the Ingall butler. Palmer recognized the Westfield livery and did not hesitate to admit the countess. He escorted her into the parlour, before seeking out his mistress to inform her of her visitor. He knew that Lady Westfield was an intimate friend of Lady Ingall and decided to err on the side of caution. He would let his mistress be the one to determine, whether or not, she wished to receive Lady Westfield.

Jane cheerfully called out her greeting when she entered the parlour. "My dear Amelia, it is so good of you to come. How did you find out?"

Amelia answered as she rose from her seat to greet her friend, "That is exactly why I have come, Jane. To find out, why you are all sequestered and not receiving callers. My son, is fraught with worry."

Jane laughed, "Was Jonathan here?"

Amelia squinted her eyes, taking in Jane's gleeful countenance. She saw her friend ecstatic, joyful, content, and asked, "Tell me now, what makes you so gloriously happy?"

Smiling, Jane exclaimed, "Elinor has returned to us!"

The next three hours were spent in a delightful conference. Jane, Amelia, and the now Lady Elinor, (though she requested that she retain the name of Rebecca in private to honor Mr. Stevens) talked relentlessly of what transpired the past week.

The Earl and Countess of Ingall agreed to their daughter's request, but were anxious to introduce their first born to the *ton* as Lady Elinor. Mr. Stevens wholeheartedly supported her introduction into Society as Lady Elinor Ingall, emphasizing that it was the right thing to do and did his best to assure Rebecca he was not slighted by the use of her true birth name.

The past week was a flurry of activity. Lord Ingall urgently summoned his father, the Duke of Hartford, and his first-born son, William, to Town. Other than the frantic summons to come to London, neither of them knew what beckoned them, so it was with expedience that they made their way to the Ingall town home.

Jane recalled for her friend, "We have been celebrating since we learned of Rebecca's identity, spending hours talking. We wanted to know every detail of Rebecca's childhood." Jane paused and added in a more somber tone, "We also wanted to understand why we were unable to find her after the storm passed. You will remember we hired multiple inspectors to search and locate Elinor. When nothing prevailed, we grieved that she was lost to the river."

Rebecca moved closer to her mother, saying, "Do not blame yourself. I have a good and loving life. I find myself the luckiest of women to have two sets of parents, that give me nothing but love and support."

Jane dabbed her eyes, looked at Amelia, remarking, "Is she not the best of daughters?"

Amelia agreed and asked, "Did your interview with Mr. Stevens avail any answers?"

Jane said, "No, not really. Though we could surmise some conclusions. We believe the wicker basket kept our dear Elinor afloat and that the river transported her quite a distance downstream out of our domain. Someone must have found her and took her to the local vicar. Mr. Stevens thought that perhaps the midwife directed the baby to be left at his cottage, knowing they had just lost their child. Roger has an inspector trying to locate the midwife to find out if she has any knowledge, but it seems unnecessary."

Jane continued, "Mr. Stevens said that everyone in his community accepted Rebecca as their own. The midwife did not expose that their daughter had died. He explained they never heard of our tragedy, though they did believe one day they might be approached. Mr. Stevens also remarked that he wanted to relocate to another parish, but his wife refused. He said she understood why someone would entrust their baby to her husband and why over time, they might want to see her again. So they stayed ten years in the same location and he only moved after his wife's death. Mr. Stevens feared that he might lose his daughter as well, but to be fair, I think Mr. Stevens wanted to introduce Rebecca to a broader society and I count my blessings that Providence brought them to us."

Rebecca waited patiently for her mother and Lady Westfield to have their conference. She began to fidget after a couple of hours passed. Finally, she interrupted their tête-à-tête and asked, "Is Lord Westfield well?"

Lady Westfield burst out laughing, "Oh, dear, I forgot all about Jonathan. He is much worst for the wear I am afraid. Overwrought with concern for you and totally frustrated that he is unable to pay court."

Rebecca blushed and queried, "Then, we have your blessing?"

Lady Westfield answered, "My dear girl, you have more than that, for like my son you captured my heart eons ago. I am delighted that I too, will be able to call you daughter."

Jane exclaimed, "Oh, dear!"

Rebecca turned to look at her mother, "What is it?"

She replied, "I just realized. I no sooner found you, than I will lose you again in betrothal."

"Nonsense," replied Rebecca. "I will always be near and always be your daughter." She clutched her mother's hand, asking, "May I have permission to receive him?"

Before her mother could answer, Lady Westfield shouted to Rebecca's regret, "No! Not yet." Amelia went on to ask Jane when Rebecca was to be presented at court.

Jane replied that Rebecca would be presented in three days. Her father-in-law, the Duke of Hartford, would accompany Roger to St. James Palace where they would present Rebecca as Lady Elinor to Her Majesty, Queen Charlotte. Her presentation at court would mark her *come-out,* her formal entrance as a young woman into fashionable Society, a requirement for anyone that wanted to attend a courtly function. The whole family planned to be there to witness Rebecca make her deep and royal curtsey to the queen and her son, George, the Prince Regent, also known as Prinny to his close friends.

Rebecca would be regally dressed, wearing the required and dated pre-Georgian fashion that consisted of a hoop skirt with a full train, when introduced to her sovereign in the drawing room. Her Majesty held firm on the rules of court dress and Rebecca would comply with the standard, completing her attire with white ostrich feathers in her hair.

Rebecca had been practicing under her mother's tutelage, making deep curtsies to a recuperating Henry while he lounged on the gilt chair in his room. Jane told Amelia that she hoped the queen would acknowledge Rebecca's birth, by placing a kiss on her daughter's forehead when she made her curtsey. Jane confessed her worst fear, that the queen might harbor a prejudice against Rebecca for her common upbringing. Jane cried, "Oh! Amelia! If the queen does not recognize her peerage, then you know the *ton* will abjure her. I am quite beside myself with worry."

Amelia sympathized and tried to appease her friend's worst fears, "Nonsense! Prinny would have already taken counsel with his mother. He would not set up the duke's granddaughter to such an effrontery. Do not worry, Jane, or you, Rebecca. All will go well."

Rebecca had been sitting anxiously throughout the whole conversation and was calmed by Lady Westfield's words. Before she could thank her ladyship, her mother intervened, "You may be right, Amelia. The duke informed us that Prinny will host a ball at Carlton House. He will receive all the debutantes, but he will acknowledge Rebecca first. Though unknown to us, the duke says Prinny plans to bestow a special honor on her."

Amelia clasped her hands together and smiled. "Oh, I am so excited! I feel like a girl in her first bloom. We will have a wonderful story to share with our grandchildren!"

Jane asked, "Whatever do you mean, Amelia?"

Amelia confessed, "Just this evening, my son professed his love for Rebecca. This of course, was not news to me, but his faithfulness was profound. He loves her so much, if need be, he would choose her over what Society dictates for a man of his standing. Rebecca, he would sacrifice his place in Society to be with you. While I am most happy that my son has remarkable integrity and has found true love, I am equally pleased that neither of you will suffer from the union." Amelia continued, "I think it befitting that Jonathan learn of your true identity at Carlton House with the rest of the *ton*. How fun it will be to see his face!"

Rebecca interjected, "Do you not think it cruel to keep him waiting?"

"Nonsense," replied Lady Westfield. "I will tell him that you will see him at the Prince Regent's Ball and that the Ingalls have you occupied until then. He will manage."

Rebecca looked at her mother who simply shrugged her shoulders. "Very well," she said. "I trust you to know what is best."

Chapter Eleven

Jonathan pulled out his timepiece and looked at it again. He could not believe that three hours had passed since his mother left to visit the Ingall household. Rules for morning calls were quite explicit. A quarter of an hour was appropriate. A half hour was imposing. Three quarters of an hour was downright rude. “Three hours!” he shouted. “What the deuce could be going on that requires my mother’s attendance for three hours?” He pulled on the bell cord and when his butler arrived, he asked, “Has her ladyship returned?”

He was disappointed in his answer, “No, my lord, she has not.”

Jonathan was about to call for his carriage when he saw his mother making her way to ascend the staircase. He was happy that she had returned and then became annoyed realizing that she was about to retire to her room without seeking an audience with him. She knew very well that he anxiously awaited news of the Ingalls. He raced over to her, took her by the hand and pulled her into his private study. Shutting the door behind them, he sat her down on a settee, but not before noticing her amused expression. He took the seat beside her and asked, "What the devil is going on? And don't tell me you don't know, because you have had three hours to figure it out!"

Lady Westfield masked her mirth and replied, imperiously, "Don't be absurd, Jonathan. Nothing is going on other than a family reunion of sorts. Did you know that William is home and Lord Ingall's father is also visiting?"

Taken aback by his mother's less than sympathetic tone, he replied, "No, Mother, I did not. Need I remind you that I was not admitted into the Ingall home these past few days and therefore, am not privy to their family news!"

Lady Westfield giggled, then did her best to ameliorate her son's temper. She said, "Rebecca sends her greetings and looks forward to seeing you in a couple of days."

"A couple of days!" he shouted. "Why so long?"

She reminded him that the Ingalls were having a family reunion, the reason why they were not receiving visitors. "You know how it is reflecting on memories," she remarked, "they didn't want any interruptions."

"But," inquired Jonathan. "Why two more days? And why can't Rebecca receive me?"

"Well," replied his mother. "You know very well that Rebecca is considered family. Besides, they are all in a flurry trying to ready themselves for the Prince Regent's

Ball. Rebecca herself told me that Lady Ingall procured her a new dress. She hopes to see you there."

Jonathan's demeanor softened when he heard that Rebecca looked forward to seeing him, though he complained, "But two days, will I never be able to make my addresses known to her and her family. For heaven's sake, I am an aristocrat, an earl of noble blood and I can't believe the devil of a time I am having trying to get myself wed. Am I not a most eligible and sought after bachelor?"

Lady Westfield smiled and kissed her son's cheek before rising. She made her way to exit, but not before turning her head to agree with his assessment, "Yes, Son, a most exceptional bachelor, indeed."

Too wound up to distract himself with reading a good book, Jonathan headed to his club the minute evening arrived. He hoped a few drinks and discourse on hunting or racing horses with his friends would distract him. He would even settle for a little Town gossip, anything, to take his mind off his missing Rebecca.

White's was full of people and chatter. Jonathan remembered his father sponsoring his membership into the club reserved for the aristocracy. They spent many evenings here on St. James Street and recalling the memories made him pause to gather his composure. He seated himself at a corner table and ordered a drink. When the servant returned with his whiskey on a tray, he raised his glass without fanfare and made a quiet toast to his father. He had just finished his second glass when he spied Arthur. Surprised to see him, knowing that he was not a member of the club, he asked, "Who are you here with?"

Arthur answered, "No one. I imposed on your membership. I told the gatekeeper that you were expecting me. The chap seems to like me and let me come in unescorted."

Jonathan queried, "How did you know I was here?"

"Your butler informed me," he replied. "I told him that we were supposed to meet, but I forgot where."

Jonathan retorted, "I shall have to talk to him regarding discretion."

"Oh, don't be so hard, man," scolded Arthur. "Besides, I wanted to see you and thank you."

"What for?" he asked.

"What do you mean, what for?" exclaimed Arthur. "Do you not know that I am happily engaged to the most wonderful and beautiful Lady Miranda? She is going to have the big wedding after all. Both her and her mother, are happier than...oh, I don't know what, but they are very happy."

"Oh, that," said Jonathan. "I am glad one of us got the girl."

Arthur flared in indignation, "What the devil does that mean?"

Jonathan realized that Arthur misunderstood him and explained, "Oh, calm yourself, man. I am not referring to Lady Miranda. You know very well my attentions lay elsewhere."

"Oh, right," he responded. "I forgot. How goes it with Miss Stevens? Although I do not understand the problem, other than you are far above her station."

Jonathan did not wish to engage in any conversation regarding rank, so he simply said, "She is being sequestered because the Ingalls are having a reunion. I won't get to see her for two nights, hence."

"I see," remarked Arthur. "Say, why don't you have supper tomorrow with Miranda and me. My future mother-in-law will be delighted to know that my connection to you is still intact." Jonathan was happy for the invitation and accepted. He left Arthur to his drink and headed home.

The next day, Jonathan found his mother with her reticule in hand ready to exit the front door. Suspicious, Jonathan stopped her and asked, "Where are you going, Mother?"

She stuttered her reply, "I-I forgot I have an appointment this afternoon."

Jonathan's eyebrows arched. He could tell she was keeping something from him and he wanted to know what, so like the day before, he pulled her into his study to question her.

Lady Westfield knew her ruse was not convincing, so she explained, waving her hands in frustration. "Oh, all right. No reason not to tell you. It is just that I did not want your feelings hurt."

Dumbfounded, Jonathan asked, "What are you talking about?"

She said, "I am taking tea with Jane and Rebecca today."

Jonathan's face began to color from the anger that quickly overwhelmed him. He blurted, "What!?! Are you telling me, they will receive you, but not me?"

In an effort to soothe her son, she said, "Yes, well no, not exactly. You see, Jonathan, you would be a distraction, an interruption to their activities. I on the other hand, am there to offer my help."

"Oh, please, Mother," he retorted. "What can you do, that I possibly cannot?"

His mother wore a smug grin. She tightened the strings on her reticule and made her way to depart, but not before declaring, "I, dear boy, can supervise their gown fittings."

To Jonathan's chagrin, he watched his impertinent mother exit. He stood alone with his arms crossed, ready to laugh at her wit, before he became distracted with questions regarding his own wardrobe. He began to wonder what he was to wear to the Regent Ball and decided to search out his valet to inquire. He found Stuart in his suite, arranging his toilette table for his evening ablutions.

"Stuart!" called Jonathan. "What have you lined up for the Prince Regent's Ball tomorrow?"

"I have pressed and ready, your finest black silk breeches and coat, milord," he responded.

Jonathan applauded his selection with an approving nod and then he ordered, “Have my diamond stickpin ready to wear, as well. You know, the one father always used to wear when he wanted to look regal.”

Stuart exclaimed, “Very good, milord! I also have plenty of cravats starched. I thought we might try a new fold for the occasion.”

Jonathan queried, “Occasion, is it? What is all the excitement about Carlton House. The Ingall household seems to be in an uproar over it?”

Surprised, Stuart asked, “Why, milord, have you not heard?”

“Heard what?” he asked.

“Why, milord, the Duke of Hartford is to present his long-lost granddaughter to the Prince Regent. Everyone is talking about it and curious to make her acquaintance.”

Lord Westfield asked, “Isn’t the duke, Lord Ingall’s father?”

“Yes, milord, I believe he is,” he answered.

“Then, that must be the reunion my mother talked about. Very well. Make sure all my best jewels are available for tomorrow’s use. I would not want Prinny to think I am under snuff.”

“Very good, milord,” replied Stuart with a proper bow.

Jonathan spent the rest of the day shopping. He thought he might purchase something special for Rebecca to wear to the Regent Ball. It was her first *ton* gala and even though she attended in the role of companion, he wanted to make it memorable for her. He wished he knew the color of her dress. He wanted to buy her a grand necklace of diamonds, but knew he could not without creating a scandal. Since they were not formally engaged, diamonds were an inappropriate gift for a suitor to give a young lady. Such jewels implied an intimacy that could ruin a woman's reputation. Instead, he settled on buying her a ruby brooch. A heart shaped ruby, nested in the center of a heart shaped golden brooch. He deemed it the perfect symbol of how Rebecca had captured his heart. As soon as he arrived home, he penned a short note to Rebecca that read:

Rebecca,
I can hardly wait to see you. Here is my heart that belongs only to you.
Yours truly,
Jonathan

Before he readied himself to have supper with Lady Miranda and Arthur, he charged his butler to have the gift delivered to the Ingall home. His order required the footman to inform Rebecca that the gift was to be opened prior to the ball and commanded him to wait to learn if the lady wished to send a reply.

Jonathan enjoyed the sumptuous supper Lady Raleigh presented, but soon grew weary of the chatter that centered entirely on the long-lost daughter of the Duke of Hartford. The only woman he was interested in was Rebecca and he could care less about a woman that was already being dubbed this Season's *Incomparable.* There was plenty of discussion about her common upbringing and whether Society would embrace her. Jonathan guessed that was why the girl was the topic of everyone's conversation. There was little known about her, even though Arthur said White's was full of speculation.

Apparently, after Jonathan left his club, Arthur overheard many of the lords claim she was quite a beauty, though no one could describe her. Others, talked about the large dowry the Duke of Hartford established for her and how he is sponsoring her *come-out*.

Lady Raleigh said, "I know nothing about dowries, but the servants tell me she was raised by commoners, a farm girl I believe." On, and on, the gossip festered until finally Jonathan's head began to hurt. He proclaimed the meal and company outstanding, before extending a gracious goodbye to his hostess. He left without further ado and made his way home. He went straight to his room where Stuart attended to his discarded clothing. Minutes later, Jonathan fell into bed and quickly drifted into a deep sleep.

Jonathan slept late into the noon hours, breaking his fast in bed with a large meal that Stuart had brought him. As he bit into a currant scone slathered with butter, he was surprised to see his mother enter his private suite without permission to enter. "Really, Mother," he scolded. "You might have knocked. I might have been indisposed."

"Ridiculous," she retorted. "You have nothing that I have not seen before."

Jonathan choked on the biscuit he was about to swallow. He quickly held up his hand, as if to ward off anything else she might say to embarrass him. When he finally managed to swallow his food and find his voice, he shouted, "Stop!"

She laughed and teased further, "Well, not since the nursery, anyway."

Truly, mortified, Jonathan begged, "Really, Mother! You must desist!"

Lady Westfield waited for her son to regain his composure before she asked the question that brought her to his room in the first place. "Now, tell me, do we ride together to the Regent's Ball? Or do you have other plans?"

"I wish I had other plans, Mother," he replied. "But I do not. I would be happy and must say proud, to escort you to your first public Town appearance since father's death."

His words, stirred her emotions bringing forth her own endearments, "You are a good son, Jonathan. Now, do we arrive early or fashionably late?"

"As you know, I always prefer fashionably late, but I am so anxious to see Rebecca, I would rather pace at Carlton House than here. Do you terribly mind?"

"Not at all," she replied. "I will meet you at eight o'clock downstairs. And Jonathan, do your best to look dashing. I do not wish to outshine you." Jonathan smirked and waved her off while taking another bite of his scone.

Awaiting his mother in the entry hall, Jonathan remembered her comment for him to look "dashing." He took another moment to inspect his reflection again in the hall mirror. He expected he would have to raise Stuart's salary for the man always dressed him to be an arbiter of fashion. His mother would not be disappointed in his style. As he looked at himself, a small cough interrupted his perusal. He turned to see his mother splendidly dressed.

Lady Westfield, wore a fine lilac cambric high-waist gown that was overlaid with a lilac laced skirt. Flowers made of silver silk thread and seeded pearls were embroidered into her bodice, complimenting the ancestral jewels she wore around her neck. She timorously handed Jonathan her laced shawl, wondering if he approved of her appearance. She turned around and waited for him to drape her shawl over her shoulders. Jonathan told her she looked radiant and then he did her bidding. He wished it was his father, rather than him, who had the honor to assist and escort his mother to the ball. He gently squeezed her shoulder and when she turned around, she saw the melancholy she felt in his eyes.

She consoled, "I miss him, too. He would have enjoyed tonight's festivities and would have loved to see his son decked out in such finery."

Jonathan let out a chuckle, before saying, "Then he, and not I, would be wearing these fine jewels, for I do not think he would let me out shine him." Both Jonathan and his mother gave in to their laughter and were still chuckling when their butler opened the front door to announce their carriage was ready.

The Regent's Ball was already a crush by the time the Westfields arrived at Carlton House. Apparently, the *ton* had come early in order to get a glimpse of the Duke of Hartford's long-lost granddaughter. Many of the nobility, had already procured a place from where they could observe the debutantes making their way to the regent's throne. The curious began forming a perimeter as if they awaited to see a parade. The relentless chatter, "Have you seen her yet?" echoed throughout the chamber. Jonathan maneuvered his mother through the crowd to the chaperone section, where most of the mothers of the debutantes sat. Lady Westfield informed Jonathan she would be most happy to sit there, as it provided a front row view of the ballroom.

Jonathan relinquished his mother to a most titled company, bowed and took his leave. He began searching the room for the Ingall family, hoping to find Rebecca amongst them. The hour passed and Jonathan became concerned that perhaps they had changed their mind to attend, when Mr. Willoughby and Lady Miranda greeted him. It took a second salutation before Jonathan's concentration broke and he acknowledged them.

Arthur began, "I say, Westfield, Are you all right?"

Jonathan replied curtly, "Yes!" and then softened his tone to say, "I am sorry, Willoughby, but I cannot locate the Ingall family and I was told they would be present."

Miranda interjected, "My Lord Westfield, I believe they are sequestered with the Duke of Hartford until his presentation of his granddaughter. We are now on our way to see the debut expected this coming hour. Why don't you join us, perhaps you will spy your Miss Stevens."

Jonathan reprimanded her, "While I would gladly call her *My Miss Stevens*, I fear I have no right and beg you not to impugn her good name with slander."

Miranda blushed, begging, "Forgive me, my lord. I did not think."

Arthur and Miranda led the way with Jonathan trailing. He was not interested in the Duke of Hartford's long-lost granddaughter, but if Rebecca was among his entourage, then he would suffer the crush to find her.

The reverberating sound of a gong hushed the room. Jonathan was taller than the crowd in front of him, so he located the Ingall family immediately, as soon as they entered from a side door. Rebecca looked stunning. Her hair was pulled up in the latest Grecian fashion with curls framing her face. A string of pearls weaved through her locks making her look quite regal. She wore a simple Empire cut white sarsnet dress that glistened with silver thread laced through her skirt. Her bodice was cut remarkably low, revealing the woman she was and Jonathan found himself completely mesmerized. He saw nothing else but her beauty, so he missed the poetry when the Duke of Hartford bowed to Rebecca and threaded her arm through his. Not until Rebecca advanced down the aisle and the chatter around him accelerated, did he realize that Rebecca was being presented to the Prince Regent.

Paralyzed, Jonathan wondered, *"What does this mean?"*

Then, Arthur nudged him and all the pieces began to fit. Arthur remarked, "Why, Westfield, that is a mean trick you played on us! How long did you know that Rebecca was his grace's granddaughter?"

Jonathan looked at Arthur and then returned his gaze to Rebecca. *"His grace's granddaughter,"* the thought, played over and over in his mind. He watched the duke hand a card to the lord-in-waiting. The nobleman bellowed: "Lady Elinor Ingall." Rebecca made her deep and royal curtsy and then, the crowd hushed when the Prince Regent directed the long-lost debutante to take the seat next to him. The whispers echoed through the room, acknowledging the special honor the prince had bestowed on Lady Elinor. *"Rebecca, no, Lady Elinor,"* thought Jonathan, had just received her irrefutable entry into the *crème of society*. Jonathan watched Rebecca sit beside

England's reigning prince as he prepared to receive the other ladies, who were making their *come-out* this Season.

Rebecca sat, keeping her posture straight, her knees together and her ankles crossed. Her hands were clasped in her lap, while she did her best to keep from showing too much emotion on her face. She knew the prince was placing a special honor on her by having her take a seat next to him and she did not want any lack of decorum, on her part, to mar the momentous occasion. She saw her mother and father beaming and were glad to see them so happy. Her mother had worried incessantly, fearing the queen would not acknowledge her peerage, by placing a kiss on her forehead when she made her presentation earlier this morning at St. James Palace. It seemed as though hours had passed awaiting to be presented to the queen in the long St. James Gallery. Without windows to provide a breeze, the congested hallway added to the already heated waiting area, making everyone agitated. Lady Elinor Ingall, like every other debutant, had to stand while they listened for their name to be called to be presented to the queen. The required dress of hoop skirts were awkward to maneuver and did not allow any lady wearing them to sit. Rebecca remembered her overwhelming relief when she was finally summoned to the Queen's Drawing Room. Before she made her way to the throne, the lords-in-waiting prepared her entrance by spreading her train out behind her. Rebecca looked at her mother and thought she might be more nervous than herself. She gave her a timorous smile, releasing the breath she unknowingly held. Then, her mother returned her smile and the joy Rebecca saw on her face gave her the courage she needed. Taking a calming breath, she straightened her shoulders and took her first step forward. Her eyes never wavered from the queen as she made her way to her, though her nerves trembled knowing the Prince Regent also watched her approach to the throne. When she reached the queen she waited to be introduced. A card bearing her name was given to another lord-in-waiting who announced her. Then, she curtsied so deep she feared she might tumble to the floor, but sheer determination kept her balanced and awaiting the queen's pleasure. She did not know whether the queen would extend her hand to be kissed or whether she would acknowledge her peerage by kissing her forehead. She knew the kiss was important to take her place in Society and to be accepted by the *ton*. While she was not ashamed of her background or regretted her upbringing, she hated to cause Lord and Lady Ingall any disappointment.

Time seemed to drag while she waited. Then the queen rose and kissed her forehead. She lifted Rebecca's chin, commanding her to rise. To her further surprise, both her majesty and the Prince Regent offered their sincere felicitations on her family reunion. She experienced such profound relief that she almost giggled. She made her final curtsies to her majesty and the Prince Regent, then she skillfully backed out of the drawing room, never turning her face away from her queen.

Jonathan watched the Duke of Hartford proudly stand by his granddaughter's side. He could see that Rebecca was uncomfortable with the attention being placed on her, but he also saw that she carried herself royally. There seemed to be an inordinate number of debutantes being presented to the Prince Regent and Jonathan breathed a sigh of relief when the last one made her curtsy. Before Prinny could disband his court, a line of nobility formed in front of Rebecca. It seemed everyone wanted a chance to gain the prince's favor by being presented to Lady Elinor. Amused, the Prince Regent allowed the receiving line to continue. He watched the *ton* flatter the girl, knowing they did so to appease him, but he also knew there were many eligible bachelors among his guests. He had decided he wanted to champion this young girl for the Duke of Hartford, who was a loyal servant to him. His good humor prevailed throughout the introductions and he found he liked the way the young girl handled herself royally. *"Yes,"* he thought, *"We will make her a worthy match among one of these eligible bachelors."*

Jonathan waited until he was last in line to greet Rebecca. He hoped he could escort her into the ballroom. As he moved closer, he immediately realized his err when he heard Lady Elinor say, "I am sorry, Lord Crumb, but my dance card is full."

Jonathan could not believe his gaffe, *"Stupid, stupid, of course, they asked for a dance during their introduction. I will never get a private moment with her."*

When the Duke of Hartford finally made Jonathan's introduction known to the prince and Lady Elinor, he momentarily lost his voice. Beseechingly, he looked at Rebecca and she encouraged him with a smile.

"Lord Westfield and I are well acquainted," she said. "Our family estates border one another and I am sure, Grandpapa, that you know how much the Ingalls treasure their friendship."

The Duke of Hartford agreed, "Yes, I believe your family has just come out of mourning. How does your mother fare?"

Jonathan was touched by his inquiry and said, "Thank you, Duke, for your concern. Mother is well and in attendance. Just this evening, we laughed as we realized how much father would have enjoyed the festivities."

The Prince Regent sentimentally remarked, "He was a good old boy. He always made me laugh, too!" Then he commanded, "Enough introductions! Let the dancing commence." With a wave of his hand, he signaled the musicians to begin.

The Duke of Hartford assisted Lady Elinor's descent from the platform where she had sat and said, "I see Mr. Brentwood is on his way to claim his dance with you, Elinor."

Jonathan was about to take his leave when Rebecca remarked, "I believe, Lord Westfield, that you have the first waltz. I do hope you choose to claim it."

Astonished, he could not help but smile feeling relieved and happy that Rebecca had not forgotten to save him a dance. Jonathan bowed his head in acceptance. He proffered his arm to her and replied, "I most certainly will, my lady. May I have the honor of escorting you to Mr. Brentwood." Rebecca smiled and took his arm when her grandfather released her into the earl's protection.

Mr. Brentwood arched his brow when he saw the Duke of Hartford relinquish Lady Elinor to the Earl of Westfield. *"I wonder if she forgot this dance belongs to me?"*

While he pondered his next move, he watched the Earl of Westfield escort the lady to him. Rebecca, as rank dictated, introduced Mr. Brentwood to the Earl of Westfield. "My Lord Westfield, May I present Mr. Brentwood to you?"

Mr. Brentwood made his salutation, "Westfield," giving a stiff nod. Jonathan responded with his own haughty acknowledgement and reminded Mr. Brentwood that he believed this was his dance. Mr. Brentwood gave Jonathan a smirk before proffering his arm to Lady Elinor. Rebecca was not insensitive to Jonathan's annoyance of Mr. Brentwood's attention, so she tried to appease him by showing him that only he held her favor. As she walked away on Mr. Brentwood's arm to take her place on the dance floor, she looked over her shoulder and gave Jonathan a warm smile. Jonathan returned her smile and then did his best to control his happiness, for he feared he was about to make a spectacle of himself by skipping away like a schoolboy.

Jonathan found an advantageous spot near one of the Ionic columns that graced the palatial ballroom, from which to observe Rebecca. Carlton House was filled with magnificent architecture and art. The décor itself provided ample material for discussion. Usually, the guests' conversations were filled with posturing their cultural knowledge, but tonight the evening chatter centered on Lady Elinor.

Jonathan enjoyed watching Rebecca dance. She seemed to glide across the dance floor. Her lightness of step caused her dress to float around her and he marveled at her grace, though he took no pleasure in seeing Mr. Brentwood partner with her. Jonathan watched Rebecca so intently that he did not hear his mother approach him.

"Well, Son," said Lady Westfield. "Rebecca is quite a hit. How goes it with the two of you?"

Jonathan turned and looked squarely into his mother's eyes, chastising, "I think, Mother dear, that you have not been forthcoming with me. How long have you known that Rebecca was Lord and Lady Ingall's daughter?"

His mother smiled, "Oh, don't be angry with me, Son. I found out just recently. I thought it would make a great story if her identity was revealed at the Regent's Ball. I will confess that Rebecca wanted to tell you, but agreed with much persistence from me, to do my bidding, so do not be mad at her. I told her you would enjoy the surprise."

"I am quite happy for her and the Ingalls," he said. "How is Mr. Stevens taking the revelation?"

Lady Westfield exclaimed, "Oh! He is quite happy for Rebecca. He always knew the day would come that Rebecca would unite with her blood parents. It pleases him that it turned out to be a loving and prominent family like the Ingalls."

He asked, "Did he know the Ingalls were her parents?"

"Oh, no," she replied. "Apparently, Rebecca was left anonymously on his doorstep a couple of days after he and his wife lost their newborn. They were too far out of the Ingall domain to be aware of their tragic loss, so no connection was ever made."

Jonathan lost his concentration when he heard Rebecca's soft laughter ripple through the ballroom. He spied her and her partner enjoying a tête-à-tête. Jonathan looked back at his mother and asked, "What do you know about a Mr. Brentwood?"

Lady Westfield looked to find Rebecca. Then, returned her attention to her son, asking, "You are not possibly jealous, Son?"

"No, Mother," he answered. "But I am chary. I shall not have every eligible bachelor and rake plying his wares at Rebecca before our betrothal can be announced. Tell me, are you acquainted with him?"

"Well, I have not met him," said Lady Westfield, "but I am acquainted with his grandmother, the Dowager Duchess of Aubry."

Surprised, he asked, "Is he an heir apparent?"

His mother responded, "No, no. He is connected, wealthy, but he holds no title. His father was a third son who made plenty of money in trade. I believe Mr. Brentwood profits dearly from shipping and other interests abroad. He has a beautiful country estate, a town home, and is considered quite the Corinthian." Lady Westfield paused, then with a serious and somber tone, interjected, "Jonathan, I do believe he is a favorite among those the Duke of Hartford calls friend. I would not hesitate to offer for Rebecca if that is still your wish. It seems that she is most likely to be sought after, now that the duke has presented her with a large dowry."

Jonathan queried, "What dowry?"

Lady Westfield responded, "You did not know. Why Rebecca is quite the heiress with fifty thousand pounds attached to her. It is said that Lord Ingall is to add to the amount as well."

Jonathan's whole body slouched as though he carried the weight of the world on himself. He trusted Rebecca's love for him, but feared Society would think he was making a marriage of convenience to increase his wealth. He was a romantic fool to want everyone to know that he and Rebecca shared a remarkable love. The strings signaling the waltz broke his thoughts. He looked at his mother and said, "Excuse me, Mother, but I have a dance to claim."

His mother responded, "Cheer up, Son, for love truly does conquer all."

Jonathan pulled his shoulders back and tugged on his waistcoat. As he walked off to claim Rebecca, he responded with mirth, "Indubitably, Mother."

Mr. Brentwood was extremely enjoying Lady Elinor's company. He liked her directness and honesty. He found her very easy to converse with and concluded, *"She is a quite sensible and knowledgeable lady. Not a flirt or coy debutante. Plus, I find it most intriguing that she is not interested in seeking my favor."* He noted the waltz was about to begin and that no escort had yet to claim her. He was not one to let an opportunity pass him by so he remarked, "My lady, it seems your partner has failed you, pray, allow me to claim his loss."

Before Rebecca could reply, Jonathan bowed, proffered his arm and proclaimed, "This dance is mine, sir. No one with any sense could ever forget Lady Elinor." Rebecca blushed deeply and accepted Jonathan's escort. As he led her to the center of the floor, Mr. Brentwood noted that Lady Elinor's eyes were fixed on Lord Westfield. He was annoyed that the lady never glanced back to offer him a smile of encouragement. He watched along with the rest of the *ton* as the Earl of Westfield and Lady Elinor Ingall took center stage. They made quite a romantic picture, looking deeply into each other's eyes, unaware of the conjectures and wages being made amongst the gossips and dandies of the *ton*.

Jonathan drew Rebecca into his arms posturing her into a proper waltz stance. He felt a spark when he took hold of her right hand and wrapped his right arm around her waist. His body warmed at the intimacy. He could feel Rebecca's body relax into his hold and he wished they were not in such a public forum, for he wanted desperately to confess his love to her. He felt immensely proud that he would soon be able to call this beautiful woman his own. He cared not that all Society witnessed his affection, though he was chary to keep the proper distance between them. He did not want to cast aspersions on Rebecca's character, nor encourage other gentlemen to take liberties. The *ton* loved to find fault, especially targeting the Prince Regent's favorites and Jonathan was determined to protect Rebecca.

Jonathan spoke first, "So, tell me, what do I call you? Is it Rebecca or Lady Elinor?"

Rebecca replied, "I have agreed to be introduced and called Lady Elinor in polite society. Privately, I prefer the endearment of Rebecca from loved ones, though my parents call me nothing but Elinor. I cannot fault them as that is who I am to them. I expect over time, it will be who I become."

Jonathan whispered, "Do I fall into the category of loved one?"

With amusement in her eyes, Rebecca exclaimed, "Most definitely, yes!"

Jonathan could not hold back his ardor any longer, "Oh, Rebecca, how I have missed you. Tell me, whom do I speak to regarding my offer for your hand. Mr. Stevens or Lord Ingall? Whom do you regard as your father and legal guardian? Rebecca responded, "Why both, of course."

“Then," he answered. "I will request a private audience with them both tomorrow.”

Rebecca's lips pulled into a smile that hit Jonathan like a beam of light. He tightened his hold on her and twirled her around the dance floor. They finished their dance, giddy in their joy.

The waltz ended and Jonathan hated to relinquish Rebecca to her next suitor, but he became pacified when he learned that she had saved him the last waltz. She remarked, “You know I would have given you more dances if we were engaged, but the rules of Society would only allow you two.” Jonathan smiled, understanding the speculation that three dances with one suitor caused. When he took his bow to leave, he saw that Rebecca had worn the brooch he had given her over her heart and he smiled.

Chapter Twelve

Jonathan watched as suitor after suitor claimed their dance with Rebecca. He observed every gesture and movement they each made towards his lady and especially noted if Rebecca favored anyone particularly. He could tell that she was forming quite a group of admirers who were willing to fulfill her slightest request. Jonathan lost count of how many glasses of lemonade were delivered to her. He wondered if she drank any of them. Jonathan did not want to be a part of her throng, so he did not engage with her bevy of admirers. Instead, he watched her from afar, a distance where he conveniently escaped her crush, but was close enough to intervene should any of her suitors act ungentlemanly.

Once again, the resounding gong hushed the room and the guests heard the Prince Regent's majordomo call them to supper. Jonathan walked over to his mother and leant her his arm to escort her to her seat in the dining hall before taking his own. The whole time, he kept an eye out to see who had claimed Rebecca. A surge of relief overcame him when he saw the Duke of Hartford usher Rebecca into the dining hall, though his comfort was short lived. His stomach immediately tightened when he saw that Mr. Brentwood had joined the duke, taking Rebecca's other neighboring seat.

Jonathan had a clear view of Rebecca, but he was not close enough to hear her conversations. Good manners kept him from trying to engage with her from across the table. He did his best to talk with the person seated next to him, but found he was completely distracted by Rebecca. Every time he started to engage in a conversation with his neighbor, Rebecca's melodic laughter reached him and his eyes instinctively sought out her location. He looked to see which man entertained her, *"Is it the duke or Mr. Brentwood that amuses Rebecca or is she simply being coquettish for their attentions?"* Then, he argued with himself, *"No, Rebecca is no flirt. If she laughs, it is from good humor. How I wish I was at her side."* His thoughts made him realize that it was going to be a long evening.

The young lady sitting beside him interrupted his thoughts. He apologized for his *wool gathering,* his reverie, before realizing that she was attempting to engage him in friendly discourse. Protocol dictated that equal time be given to each neighbor at the dining table and Jonathan surmised that his time had arisen to chat with her.

The lady in question asked, "My lord, do you arrive for the Season?"

Jonathan hesitated, causing a noticeable pause. He could not reply in earnest to say, *"No, I have come to offer for Lady Elinor."* It did nothing to assuage his mood when he noted the lady was clearly amused at his expense. Before he had her laughing out loud, he promptly answered, "Yes, precisely. My mother and I have just come out of mourning. We thought we should make an appearance to allay the *ton's* concerns for our welfare."

The lady apologized with sincere remorse, "Forgive me for not extending my regrets. It has been a year, has it not?"

"Yes," he replied. "Were you acquainted with my father?"

"Not personally," replied the woman. "But I was in attendance, as was your father, at many of Prinny's fetes. His good humor always prevailed with the Prince Regent."

Jonathan smiled, saying. "Yes, Prinny said my father could always make him laugh." Jonathan turned his body to gain a better look at the lady sitting beside him. He continued, "Forgive me, madam, I do not believe we have formally met. You seem to know me, but I am at a loss for your name. Please, give me the honor of an introduction."

The lady in question smiled, acknowledging, "No, my lord, we have not met. I am a few years your senior and made my *come-out* years ago. I fear I am considered on the shelf, but I still enjoy the splendor of Prinny's balls. I come to amuse myself, since my lack of fortune makes me an undesirable candidate for matrimony. I am Lady Anne.

While I have a superb bloodline, my profligate father, may he rest in peace, left me without a dowry, thereby condemning me to spinsterhood. However," she laughed, "You must not pity me. I am a favorite of Prinny's and so he always extends an invitation to me. Unless the *ton* needs a fourth for a card game, I am sorry to say, my silver salver is usually thin on the invites."

Dumbfounded, Jonathan did not know what to say to this woman. In his estimation, she revealed too much personal history to a mere stranger and he wondered, *"Does she want my pity or my protection?"* He showed his disdain by arching his brow before announcing, "Really, my lady, I believe you are too forthcoming."

Lady Anne replied with candor, "Do not judge me harshly, my lord. I have only expressed to you, all that is spoken about me. I would rather be upfront and allow you to determine whether you choose to continue our society, rather than to receive a set down after we have enjoyed each other's company."

Again, Jonathan did not know what to say. He took another good look at the lady. He found her to be a handsome woman though her dress was a few seasons old. She had straw blond hair, arranged in the Grecian style with locks framing her face. Her blue eyes were not brilliant, but offered a soft hue emanating a warmness about her character. Her aquiline nose marked her aristocratic bloodline. Her lips, he realized, were smiling. Anne laughed, "Do I meet with your approval, my lord?"

Slowly, Jonathan grinned and begged her pardon. "Forgive me, My Lady Anne, for attempting to draw your character from your appearance."

She queried, "Pray, tell me. What have you discerned?"

"It is said that the eyes are the windows to the soul and you, my lady, have a good soul. You need not feel that I will abjure you unless my estimation is proven wrong."

Anne bowed her head in gratitude. She had meant to challenge his lordship to ascertain his prejudices against the penurious, instead she found herself overcome with his gallantry. "Thank you, my lord, you are too good."

Rebecca intently watched the beautiful blond woman flirting with Jonathan. Her focus kept her distracted from hearing what Mr. Brentwood said. She did not realize he had just asked her to take a drive with him the following afternoon. She was waiting for him to stop talking so she could make her own inquiry. She answered, "Yes, of course," with no thought to what she just agreed. "Whom is that beautiful woman sitting next to Lord Westfield?"

Mr. Brentwood took his eyes off his distracted lady and searched where Lord Westfield sat. He, then replied, "That, my lady, is one of the regent's favorites, the Lady Anne."

Rebecca looked into Mr. Brentwood's eyes and asked, "What do you mean, sir, by the regent's favorites?"

Mr. Brentwood smiled and answered, "I am surprised that you ask, as you are considered to be in that category. I simply imply that Prinny favors her and would champion her character, should anyone ever try to impugn it."

Jonathan was enjoying Lady Anne's company, immensely. He listened to her recall the many outlandish Prince Regent galas, warmly remembering his own father's tales of those same events. The memory evoked his emotions.

Even from her distance, Rebecca could see that Lady Anne enthralled Jonathan and she wanted to know what they were discussing. She tried to recall if she had ever captivated Jonathan's attention so intensely. Her anger rose when she witnessed the lady pat Jonathan's hand and she wondered, *"Did he smile at her or was that a grimace?"* Seeing Jonathan being consoled by another woman made Rebecca edgy. Her mood was written on her face and Mr. Brentwood noticed her restlessness. He asked, "Perhaps, Lady Elinor, a breath of fresh air would avail you?"

Not considering the propriety of such an offer, Rebecca agreed thinking some fresh air would pacify her needless fears. She whispered her leave to her grandfather, who, deep in conversation with his neighbor, did not notice her departure. Rebecca was well versed in how to conduct herself as a lady and considered her behavior above reproach. She saw nothing wrong in accompanying Mr. Brentwood *al fresco*. She had walked the garden alone at Westfield Manor and the Ingall Estate many times with both Mr. Willoughby and Jonathan, so she thought there was nothing improper in joining Mr. Brentwood for some night air. Her confidence stemmed from the years she spent as Lady Ingall's companion. She knew she could hold her own in carriage, dress, and conversation. She had a natural talent for the pianoforte, watercolors, horseback riding, and her common upbringing gave her aptitudes in other areas, like gardening, household management, and nursing. Unknown to her, none of these skills gave her the polish she desperately needed to protect herself from the rakes and dandies amongst the *ton*.

Tongues started wagging, speculating on the Duke of Hartford's granddaughter's character, the moment Rebecca and Mr. Brentwood left the dining table without a chaperone. Jonathan reacted immediately at the first matronly snigger. To Anne's amusement, he abruptly rose and asked, "My lady, would you please do me the honor of walking with me?"

Jonathan had mentioned Lady Elinor's name enough times during their conversation for Anne to recognize he carried a *tendress* for her. She had also been ensconced in Society long enough to know how a simple err in judgment, could damage a debutante's reputation. She deduced Lord Westfield wanted to mollify the gossip over Lady Elinor's exit. She thought his stratagem magnificent. One couple leaving without benefit of chaperone is easily remarked upon, two couples appears common.

In earnest she accepted his offer, admiring his gallantry. They quickly made their way to follow Lady

Elinor and Mr. Brentwood into the ballroom. As soon as they entered, they spied the train of Rebecca's gown leaving through one of the terrace doors that led into the magnificent Carlton Gardens. Jonathan noted there was enough of a crowd in the ballroom to instigate chatter about a couple disappearing into the night without a chaperone. He hoped to find and return Rebecca quickly to the ballroom before her reputation became tarnished. The fact that she was an innocent and that Mr. Brentwood was a known rake, made his mission to find her urgent.

Jonathan hurried Anne into the garden, hoping to spy a clue to which direction Rebecca may have taken. He was relieved to immediately recognize her laughter and rushed to her direction. He was rather pleased to see Rebecca at a notable distance from Mr. Brentwood. He overheard her say, "Please, sir, do not waste your compliments on me, for my affections are already engaged to another."

Jonathan and Lady Anne approached at that moment and made their salutations. Embarrassed, Rebecca beseechingly looked to Jonathan for assistance. She was glad to hear him say, "My lady, I was charged to inform you that your father, Lord Ingall, requests your presence. I hope you will allow me to escort you back, as I require an audience with him, as well."

Rebecca smiled and started to walk towards Jonathan when Mr. Brentwood stopped her progress with a hand to her shoulder. He argued, "I say, Westfield, I am more than capable of escorting Lady Elinor to her father. After all, I am keeping her company."

Rebecca's demeanor showed she was upset that Mr. Brentwood had taken a possessive air with her. She stepped aside of his reach. Anne relinquished Jonathan's arm so that he could retrieve her. Upon threading Rebecca's arm through his and offering his other arm to Anne, he admonished Mr. Brentwood, saying, "I suggest, sir, that you explain to the Duke of Hartford, why the *ton* are speculating on his granddaughter's character and beg his forgiveness for your part in initiating the gossip."

Standing akimbo, seething at his lordship's effrontery, Mr. Brentwood suddenly realized the damage his cavalier behavior almost caused Lady Elinor. His anger quickly subsided and regret set in. He confessed, "You are quite right, Westfield. I have been remiss. I only hope Lady Elinor will forgive me and still honor me with her company tomorrow, allowing me to make it up to her." He looked to Elinor for an answer.

Not wanting to offend her grandfather's friend, Rebecca replied, "In truth, sir, I would be more comfortable with a party. Perhaps, Lord Westfield and Lady Anne, would agree to join us."

Mr. Brentwood replied with a smirk, "As you wish." He made his bow and left.

Jonathan looked at Rebecca and said, "Why the devil did you agree to that?"

Rebecca meekly replied, "Mr. Brentwood is a good friend of my grandpapa. I did not wish to offend him as I was sure he was acting on his direction. You need not be jealous. He is a bit old for me, do you not think?"

Both Jonathan and Rebecca had forgotten about Lady Anne until she started laughing. "I see that I am in the company of young love."

Angry at the lady's impertinence, Rebecca asked, "Is that why you laugh at us?"

"Oh, no!" replied Anne. "If anything, I am in awe of true love. I only wish I could find it for myself. What I find humorous, is that one of England's most handsome and wealthy bachelors is not held in high esteem by you." Anne continued, "However, I would be careful. For what I know of Mr. Brentwood's character, your abjuration of his suit will only tempt him more, especially a Corinthian like himself."

Rebecca's solemn face bore the mark of her regret in the scene that just took place. She looked at Jonathan who was not quite ready to assuage her guilt. He said, "Come, we have given the *ton* enough fodder to gab about. Let us make our way to the ballroom where I hope to finally claim my last dance with you."

Rebecca asked, "What about my papa?"

"That," claimed Jonathan with an anger Rebecca rarely heard, "was simply a ruse to save you from whom Lady Anne reminded me was a *devilish rake*. You owe her a debt of gratitude for aiding my rescue of you. Otherwise, I fear I may have had to call the scoundrel out!"

"Oh, Jonathan!" exclaimed Rebecca. "I am so sorry. I did not think, but when I saw you and Lady Anne whispering, I was so disturbed by your intimacy that I had to take my leave."

"Oh, the perils of love," exclaimed Anne. "It seems like ages since I enjoyed such folly."

Rebecca was not amused by Lady Anne's comment, but was cheered to learn that the lady was older than what she looked. It seemed that Jonathan did not hold her in any special esteem. She realized, *"He would never have come to my aid, if he did not love me."* She began to feel immensely better.

Jonathan, on the other hand, felt frustrated. It amazed him that somehow it was his questionable behavior and not Rebecca's, that caused her to venture into the garden with Mr. Brentwood.

Rebecca stretched her arms over her head when she kicked her coverlet from her bed. She felt refreshed after a good night's sleep. She wiped the morning dew from her eyes and remembered how Jonathan had led her around the ballroom in a waltz. She returned home in the early morning hours and fell into a deep slumber with thoughts of him. Her dreams were filled of Jonathan and like a poem, words speaking of warmth, happiness, and love crowded her mind while she slept, evoking visions of ardor. She felt giddy. She sat up in bed, still recalling the evening when she suddenly bellowed a laugh that resounded in her suite. She covered her mouth to muffle her uncontrollable giggles, but the memory of Jonathan's surprised face when he learned she had saved him two dances kept her in high spirits. She sighed remembering how he had come to her rescue in the garden, saving her from becoming today's latest *on dit*.

The memory sobered Rebecca and reminded her of Jonathan's scold delivered to her during their last waltz. Unlike the first dance where they spent most of their time smiling at one another, the second dance was nothing more than a harangue.

"Rebecca," he berated. "You must be more circumspect of your conduct in Society. There are men who would easily take advantage of you. Even when the interlude is of an innocent nature, the *ton* can be unforgiving, faulting and punishing the lady unfairly." Jonathan whispered, "The slightest lapse in decorum can bring ruin to your reputation and disgrace to your family."

Rebecca eyes watered. She feared she had fallen in Jonathan's esteem and asked, "And to you, Jonathan?"

Jonathan felt immediate remorse. He did not want to hurt Rebecca, but he felt it was imperative that she understand the risks in Society. Even so, looking at her teary eyes his composure softened and he pledged, "Never. You have my love, my trust, and my esteem. I may not always be around to protect you, so I beg you to be more circumspect."

Rebecca nodded in agreement which seemed to appease Jonathan. They were able to finish the waltz with more felicitation. Then, Jonathan returned Rebecca to Lord and Lady Ingall who until recently, were surrounded by well-wishers and sycophants. The Ingalls were always sought after by the *ton*. The news that they had been reunited with their long-lost daughter only added to their popularity. Their admirers wanted to know all the details regarding Elinor's life and the Ingalls found themselves besieged with questions during the entire ball. It was not until the end of the evening that Jonathan was finally able to seek out Lord Ingall. He requested a private audience with him and Mr. Stevens for the following afternoon. Lord Ingall granted the interview much to Jonathan's delight and he walked away content.

The Duke of Hartford overhead Jonathan's request for an interview, deduced his intention, and intervened. He asked his son, "Roger, does Westfield plan to offer for Elinor?"

Roger replied, "Yes, I believe so. He made his intentions known before Elinor's identity was realized. Elinor favors him. His character and prospects are exceptional. It will be a fine match."

"That may be so," remarked the duke. "However, I beg you to require him to wait until the Season finishes. Prinny has decided to champion Rebecca and he has already comprised a list of suitable bachelors to court her. He is quite enthusiastic about finding her an exceptional match and I fear that if we cut his game short, the repercussions will be unpleasant."

Shocked, Lord Ingall railed, "You cannot be serious. Elinor is no game piece and I will not throw her into a path where her reputation or heart could be at risk."

"Nonsense," retorted the duke. "She is my blood as well and I would never support anything that would bring her harm. You should be honored that Prinny favors her and is trying to secure her future. He does not know she is already settled. What could it hurt to let him play matchmaker? Let her enjoy her one and only Season as a debutante. Imagine, she will be the *Toast of London* and by the end of the Season everyone will be happy. Prinny will feel magnanimous and Elinor will be betrothed to Westfield."

Jonathan had just finished his breakfast when his mother entered the parlour. He set his cup down, looked at her quizzically and then asked, "What my dear mother has brought that smile to your face?"

His mother answered, "You make quite a pretty picture. Cannot a mother beam with pride to see her son in the *pink of fashion*? May I ask, do you call on Rebecca- excuse me, Lady Elinor today?"

Jonathan was wearing a blue superfine, double-breasted coat that hugged his shoulders. In an era where pads were worn by many of the Town dandies to improve their physique, Lord Westfield's figure was more than adequate and necessitated no such amenities. He complimented his coat with a pair of cream-colored pantaloons that accentuated his muscular legs, a product of his athleticism. He finished his attire with a square-cut sapphire in his cravat, a fob watch, and shiny black Hessian boots.

"Actually," he stated. "I have a private audience with Lord Ingall and Mr. Stevens at noonday. I hope to be able to pay my addresses to Rebecca afterwards. If all goes well, I shall stop by the Gazette and place an advertisement announcing our engagement. I do hope all goes smoothly, for I cannot fathom what else may occur to hinder you from offering your felicitations on our betrothal."

Lady Westfield responded, "I pray you are right, Son, though I must warn you that I heard rumblings last night. It seems that Prinny has taken an interest in Rebecca and it might make paying your addresses a challenge."

Anxiously, Jonathan asked, "What are you talking about, Mother?"

She continued, "It may be nothing, Son, so do not get up in arms until you speak to Lord Ingall, but it would not surprise me if his lordship does not grant his permission until Rebecca has finished her Season."

"If that is all," retorted Jonathan, "then it is nothing to signify, for I myself would want Rebecca to enjoy her Season."

"Very well," she added. "Remember, Jonathan, if you keep your senses about you, then I will see you happy in three months, if not before."

"Thank you, Mother," replied Jonathan. "I will keep your advice close at hand. Wish me luck!"

"My good wishes are always with you, Son," his mother confessed and with her blessing Jonathan made his exit.

Jonathan expected Rebecca to have company this morning. Protocol required a gentleman who gave remarkable attention to a lady at a social event to either visit the lady the next day or to send her a bouquet of flowers. After Rebecca's success at the Regent's Ball, Jonathan knew her admirers would settle for nothing less than seeing her again. Like a flower that draws bees to its nectar, Rebecca's sweet disposition and beauty beckoned gentlemen to her side. However, nothing prepared Jonathan for the frenzy he saw when he approached the Ingall town home. Curricles formed a row down Berkeley Street with grooms minding their hacks. Dandies holding bouquets of flowers lined the steps from the Ingall door down the sidewalk. Palmer did his best to regulate the mob and give each gentleman a modicum of propriety before admitting them to be received. He controlled the crowd in the parlour by allowing a gentlemen to enter only when one departed.

Lord Westfield walked past the line of Rebecca's suitors and to the chagrin of them, he entered the Ingall town home as though he lived there. He feared Palmer was going to stop him, but the efficient butler greeted him with aplomb, assuring the Earl of Westfield that his lordship awaited him in his study. Jonathan expressed his due appreciation with a compliment. “Thank you, Palmer. You are most prodigious in owning Lord Ingall’s appointments.”

Palmer bowed, proffered a smile, and led the way to Lord Ingall’s private study. The butler announced Lord Westfield to the Earl of Ingall and then returned to the throng of impatient admirers, waiting their turn to drop off their flowers and calling cards.

When Jonathan followed Palmer to Lord Ingall’s study, he spied Rebecca seated in the parlour surrounded by a bevy of suitors. She looked like a deer trapped by hunters without a place to run. Thankfully, Lady Ingall was there to run interference. Rebecca looked up just before Jonathan was about to leave her sight. A wave of relief crossed her face. He wanted to walk over and take her away from the throng of admirers that were overwhelming her. Instead, he offered her a warm smile that seemed to ease her mood and he continued to Lord Ingall’s study.

He was surprised not to see Mr. Stevens and asked, “Is Mr. Stevens not to join us, Ingall?”

Lord Ingall shook his head in the negative and pointed to a chair opposite his desk, asking Lord Westfield to take a seat. The earl's serious tone worried Jonathan. Then he remembered his mother’s warning and he cautioned himself to stay calm. Having risen to greet his guest, Roger returned to his seat behind his desk and informed Jonathan, “I fear Mr. Stevens is not comfortable discussing marriage settlements, but you must know that he favors you immensely and has no objection to your offer for our daughter."

Jonathan beamed, "Thank you, Ingall. You must know that I ask nothing of Rebecca other than her hand in marriage. You can rest assured that I will care and provide for her most faithfully."

"Yes, of course," he replied. "I know your character and your affections to be true, but I will do my duty as her father and ensure that Elinor is settled with a future that is intact."

He asked, "Then I have permission to pay my addresses to Rebecca, excuse me, I mean Elinor?"

Pausing, Lord Ingall answered, "I have no objection to your offer, Westfield. However, I must require you to wait until the end of the Season to pay your addresses. You must agree that my daughter has led a sheltered life and her circle of society has been limited. This is her first Season and while I trust her feelings for you to be genuine, I want her to have the opportunity to explore them. If at the end of the Season, she still favors your offer, I will grant my permission."

Jonathan thought the earl's tone suspect and asked, "Is there more to the situation that I am not aware? My mother informs me that Prinny may have a hand in Elinor's future."

Lord Ingall's eyes steeled when he looked at Jonathan. He said, "It is true that the Prince Regent has decided to take an interest in Elinor's prospects, but you can be assured that it will be I who decides her welfare. I will choose the man that is most worthy of her affections."

"Very good, Ingall," he retorted. "I meant no disrespect, but it seems that I am having a devil of a time securing the hand of the one who has captured my heart most dearly. Any advice you can give me would be most welcome, for as you know I do not have my own dear father for which to turn."

Roger relaxed. He said, "Do not fret, Westfield. For I know that Elinor cares for no other but you. If the truth be told, had Prinny not decided to champion my daughter, we would have begun the banns this Sunday. However, I will admit that I would probably still have required you to wait to marry until the end of the Season for the reasons I just mentioned."

The earl picked up a paper from his desk and handed it to Jonathan, "Can you believe that Prinny created a list of eligible candidates for Elinor and has charged each one of them to call on her and do their best to win her affections?" Jonathan's mouth dropped open when he took the paper and started to peruse the names. "Cheer up," said Roger. "Prinny placed your name on the list. It seems he found you a most exceptional candidate. I am surprised you have not been summoned to meet him." After a pause, Roger stated, "You realize, when you and Elinor finally make your announcement that Prinny will take full credit for it." Jonathan looked at Lord Ingall and saw that the corners of his mouth started to twitch and gave in to his own laughter when he realized the hilarity of the situation.

Chapter Thirteen

Lady Ingall escorted the last of Elinor's callers to the door, much to her exhausted daughter's relief. Being the center of attention for a group of admirers had mentally and physically sapped Rebecca's energy. Her back ached from sitting with perfect posture and her face felt scored with lines from having to smile throughout the day. She found it hard to believe that young ladies in Society relished this type of attention.

There was only one person's interest she craved and she was beginning to fear that something had gone terribly wrong. Every time Palmer entered the parlour to make an announcement, she was sorely disappointed to learn it was not a summons from the earl, but another suitor arriving.

She expected her father to call her into his office so that Jonathan could pay his addresses to her. She worried what could have caused him to leave without seeing her and before long, her head began to throb, relentlessly.

Most of Elinor's admirers had left early to tidy themselves for the late afternoon jaunt through Hyde Park. Members of the *ton*, in what was considered the height of fashion during the Season, dressed in their finest walking clothes to promenade in their extravagant curricles and carriages along the dirt track known as *Rotten Row*. Rebecca, or the newly introduced Lady Elinor, would be one of them for she agreed to ride with Mr. Brentwood. The gentleman was expected to arrive within the hour and Rebecca's headache was growing worse by the minute. Lady Ingall insisted her daughter take a small repose and helped Rebecca up the stairs, begging her to lie down. She promised she would learn what transpired between her father and Lord Westfield and then she would return with news to allay her daughter's worst concerns. Rebecca submitted to her care, allowing her mother to help her to her bed. She stretched out on top of her counterpane while her mother went to pull the bell cord to call for a maid. Rebecca could not hear her mother's instructions, but before long, she felt a dampened cloth smelling of lilac being swabbed across her forehead. The aroma soothed her senses and she let out a deep breath. Lady Ingall placed the square of linen on her daughter's eyes and told her not to worry that she would return soon.

Rebecca wondered if Jonathan had changed his mind. Though of noble stock, she still considered herself a commoner, not belonging to the sphere she now lived. She was a girl that knew how to work with her hands and serve others. She was not comfortable in an idle life. As others pampered her to distraction, applying obsequious adoration upon her, she was not sure that she could be the countess that Jonathan deserved. She had thought she was capable of assuming the title of countess when she was merely the vicar's daughter because she was already accepted among the gentry who neighbored the Ingalls. She did not fear the elevated position with both the Countess of Westfield's and the Countess of Ingall's support. However, here in London, among the *ton,* her confidence faltered on whether she was up to the task of adapting to this aristocratic society. She shuddered when she wondered if Jonathan had the same concerns.

Jane anxiously knocked on the door of her husband's private study before opening it to peer inside. Roger looked up from his desk and bid his wife to enter. Jane rushed in closing the door behind her, asking, "Roger, what has prevailed between you and Lord Westfield? Elinor is overwrought with concern. Pray, tell me, did you refuse his suit?"

Roger took a deep breath and exhaled slowly before walking around his desk to take both of his wife's hands in his. He said, "Calm yourself, my love. It is not as bad as all that, though I fear the next three months will try everyone's patience."

Jane begged, "Roger, please do not be so circumspect and tell me what has happened?"

Roger sat his wife down on the chair that Lord Westfield had recently vacated. He kneeled to bring himself to her eye level. "It appears," he explained, "that Prinny has decided to champion our Elinor by finding her a suitable husband. For this reason, but primarily for the concerns we previously discussed regarding Elinor's lack of society, I have told Lord Westfield that he may not offer for Elinor until the end of the Season."

Worried, Jane further asked, "What do you mean when you say that the Prince Regent is set in finding Elinor a husband?"

Laughing, Roger stood, grabbed a piece of paper off his desk and handed her the list of suitors the Prince Regent created, as candidates for Lady Elinor's hand in marriage.

Jane perused the list, asking, "What is this?"

Roger explained, "That my dear, are the noble few that Prinny thinks suitable for our Elinor. He has charged each one of them to try their suit. He is determined to secure her future."

Jane gasped, "Why Lord Fife is as old as you, surely you would never countenance his offer?"

Roger walked around his desk and took his seat. He then clasped both of his hands together and placed them on his desk. His manner was serious and Jane collected herself to listen. She waited to hear what her husband had to say.

Roger proceeded, "I have talked in depth with my father regarding this folly. As you can understand, I was quite disturbed when he told me of Prinny's intentions. I must say I balked at his interference, but was persuaded to see it as the compliment it is intended to be. More than that, I fear that if we reject Prinny's assistance, which I am sure is a token of his affection, we could cause irrevocable damage to our daughter's acceptance by the *ton*. For while Prinny can be all fun and games, he can easily hold a grudge and his abjurations would have a rippling effect through the upper echelons of Society that could only harm Elinor. If you review the list again, you will see that Prinny was fortuitous enough to place Lord Westfield on the list. When all is said and done, Prinny will compliment himself on securing the prominent match."

Jane asked, "But, what do I tell our daughter?"

He replied, "Tell her to enjoy her Season and the attention of her admirers. If at the end of it all, she still desires Lord Westfield, then I will consent to their marriage."

She said, "She will not like it, Roger. She is a sensible girl and knows her heart. She is not one to play games. Her suitors will find that their romantic trifles are not returned. If anything, she will chide them for their flirtations."

Roger remarked, "Then, she will be labeled an *Original*. I do not think with our connections, any harm will come of it."

"Very well," she said. "I will assuage our daughter's worst fears and tell her that Lord Westfield has not given up his suit for her. I will inform her that she has a bevy of admirers that hope to call her their own. You know, Roger, she will think this is all quite silly."

Roger rose from his chair and walked around his desk to collect his wife. He ushered Jane to the door, agreeing with her assessment, "As do I, my dear."

She made her way to Elinor's bedroom. She had promised to bring her news regarding Jonathan's interview with her father and was anxious to relieve her worries. She knew Elinor was scared that Jonathan had changed his mind regarding a union with her and wanted to assure her that it was not the case.

Jane entered her daughter's private suite and thought she slept, seeing her lay prostrate with her eyes closed and her breathing regulated. She carefully took a seat on the edge of the bed near Elinor's head. Taking the lilac fragranced cloth that she had dampened earlier, she stroked her daughter's forehead as she had done before. Rebecca opened her eyes, grabbed her mother's wrist to halt her ministrations. She exclaimed, "Does Jonathan still wish to offer for me?!"

"Yes, yes," she calmed. "I fear he is just as disconcerted as yourself, having not only to wait to offer for you, but to have to compete with other suitors for your favor."

Rebecca sat up and asked, "What do you mean?"

Lady Ingall explained the circumstances as she knew them.

"Why, this is simply ridiculous!" Rebecca shouted. "How can I allow someone to woo me when I have already been wooed? Plus, It seems very unladylike to play with a gentleman's affection like that. For heaven's sake, I know Jonathan would not like it at all."

Lady Ingall replied, "Your father and I are not suggesting that you engage in any wanton behavior. We just want you to enjoy the Season. Just because your feelings are attached to Lord Westfield, does not mean that you cannot enlarge your circle of society and enjoy some amusement while you are in London. Should you discover at the end of the Season that your feelings are not what they should be for Lord Westfield, then the wait will be well served. If you find that your feelings for Lord Westfield have not changed and you still desire a match with him, then the town polish you acquire will also be well served."

"Really, Mama," retorted Rebecca. "I am no dazzling debutante. You saw how uncomfortable I was today with the gentlemen that flirted with me. I think the only reason Jonathan and I found our way to one another is because our stations were so beyond a suitable match that we never considered a liaison. It is really ironic how an unsuitable match like ours, bloomed into a companionship and ardor that will last us a lifetime. I cannot imagine loving any man other than Jonathan and I have no idea how I am to deal with these suitors that the Prince Regent has cast upon me."

Her mother replied, “I beg to remind you that you are a daughter of an earl and the granddaughter of a duke. You are of noble blood and are far from unsuitable, regardless of your upbringing, or what you lack in the art of coquetry.” She continued, “You know, Elinor, you did quite well with your bevy of admirers at the Regent’s Ball. Why do you think you are incapable of continuing to do so?”

Rebecca answered, “First of all, Mama, I was in quite a stupor as you must know. My nerves were so wound up that I barely remember my introduction to the prince. Besides, those bevy of admirers that you so like to refer, conversed among themselves and required no banter from me other than to reply, “Yes, thank you. I very much would desire a refreshment.” Rebecca laughed, “I do not think I have ever drank so much lemonade in my life.” How am I to manage knowing that they are after my favor? It seems so disingenuous when my heart is otherwise engaged.”

Her mother responded, “You are too hard on yourself. You will deal with these suitors the same way you have always responded with everyone you meet. You will treat them with compassion and friendship. Elinor, you have enough sense to waylay their admirations while respecting their feelings.”

“Very well, Mama,” relented Rebecca. “Please ring for Hannah. We shall put my senses to the test as I believe Mr. Brentwood should be calling soon. You did say he was on the list, did you not?”

Lord Westfield found a summons from the Prince Regent, the future King George IV of England, waiting for him when he returned to his town home. The summons ordered him to appear at Carlton House the next morning. The command did not surprise him as Lord Ingall had already alerted him to the Prince Regent's plans. However, the regal summons petrified his mother. She had no idea why the realm's fickle future king demanded an audience with her son. She kept vigil in the parlour, waiting for him to return home, worrying incessantly.

When Jonathan finally entered the room where she anxiously sat, his mother was too overcome to wait to be greeted, she cried, “Why does Prinny demand an audience with you?”

Jonathan smiled, walked over to his aggrieved mother, kissed her on her cheek before answering, “It appears that Prinny has designated himself matchmaker, deciding to find a most suitable and prominent match for Rebecca.”

“Why?” his mother exclaimed, “When she has one with you!”

“Indeed,” he responded. “Unfortunately, he is unaware of it. Lord Ingall warns me to appease Prinny’s penchant for amusement. He further counsels me not to incite Prinny's temper for fear that Rebecca's standing in Society would be compromised.”

"If not you," inquired his mother, "then who may I ask does Prinny have in mind for Rebecca, I mean Elinor? Am I to assume that you gladly relinquish your claim?"

Jonathan finally lost his temper, "No, Mother, you may not! I have no such intention of releasing Rebecca, Elinor, or any other name given to her, though I will play the Prince Regent's game. It seems Prinny has created a list of eligible bachelors and I find it most fortuitous that I am on the list. Otherwise, I would be having a most difficult time keeping Prinny's suitors for Rebecca at bay."

"Who is on the list?" asked his mother.

"Well, besides myself," replied Jonathan, I counted nine. Most of them are lords, but there were two untitled gentlemen: our infamous Mr. Brentwood and a Mr. Walker."

She asked, "Who are the lords?"

Jonathan answered as he ticked off their names on his fingers, "Rushton, Crumb, Riverdale, Mansfield, Fife, Trenton, and Brenner."

Lady Westfield reflected, then said, "Lord Fife is too old and Lord Crumb is too shy. Riverdale, Mansfield, and Trenton are your friends, aren't they? You were all at Cambridge together. They will play, but are not ready to settle down. Their fathers still hold the titles and those young bucks have too many oats to sow. They have ample siblings in line to succeed, so there is no rush for them to marry. Rushton and Brenner will give you a run for your money. They are older and may take Prinny's command more seriously. I am told that they are in the market this

Season for a wife as they are looking to set up their nurseries. They will be looking to make an exceptional connection, not a love match. As you know Jonathan, a love match is rare in our sphere. I expect Rushton and Brenner will enjoy the competition and use all their charm to seduce Rebecca. I would hate to see her fall for their suits. They are most accomplished flirts, as you know."

Jonathan remarked, "You are too kind in your assessment, Mother. Rushton and Brenner are devilish rakes and you know it. Rebecca is no fool. She will not be interested in their empty compliments."

"Perhaps, Son," said his mother. "She will not find them empty."

Jonathan grimaced, asking, "What do you know about Mr. Walker?"

She answered, "Nothing, but I would keep an eye on Mr. Brentwood. I hear he has been shopping for a title and Prinny may grant him one if Rebecca chooses his favor. Prinny would do so to honor the Duke of Hartford, who you know is a particular favorite of his, and to ensure her future in Society."

"It is of no consequence," he retorted. "Rebecca loves me."

"I have no doubt, Son," replied his mother. "But many a love match has gone asunder due to complacency. I would not relent, but pursue your suit with alacrity. Otherwise, I am concerned that an innocent like Rebecca might turn to your rivals for comfort."

"You put the fear in me, Mother, but I hear your advice and shall yield to it. Rebecca will find no truer gallant than me. Try as my rivals might, they will not succeed. I must now beg your leave for the games begin this afternoon. I make up a party with Mr. Brentwood, Lady Anne, and Rebecca. I do not risk being late, so I shall see you later."

His mother wished him good luck.

Mr. Edward Brentwood applauded his strategy in picking up Lady Elinor in his sporty two-seater curricle. He knew she wished their excursion to include the Earl of Westfield and Lady Anne, but he thought it ludicrous to share his time with a known rival. His grace, the Duke of Hartford, was a long standing friend. He had warned Edward that Lord Westfield had an advantage over all of Lady Elinor's suitors. His grace cautioned him that his granddaughter's heart was already secured by Westfield. However, the duke encouraged him to court Elinor, reminding him the gesture would place him in a favorable light with the Prince Regent.

Mr. Brentwood had not considered matrimony since a youthful infatuation. He was quite happy enjoying his bachelorhood, though he had to admit he had moments where he yearned for something more than the attentions of a widow or paramour. On most accounts he was content with his life. His only regret was that he lacked the respect that a title provided. He grew up at the fringes of Society. His grandfather was an aristocrat, but his father, a third son, had ended up marrying the daughter of a tradesman. It was a fortuitous match in terms of fortune, but the connection or lack thereof, severed his father's ties with the noble *ton*.

Through the years, his father's business savvy had added an incredible *largesse* to his inheritance. His father hoped that wealth would one day open for his son those doors that his marriage to his mother regrettably closed. Edward's grandmother, the now Dowager Duchess of Aubry, was always sympathetic to her grandson's plight. She loved him dearly and did her best to champion him into Society, but the *ton* held firm on their prejudice towards wealth acquired from trade. She found herself less than tolerable with the lot, choosing to abjure them when possible.

Edward's greatest asset was his friendship with the Duke of Hartford cultivated by his grandmother. His grace, upon the dowager's encouragement, sponsored Edward whenever possible into Society and became quite fond of him. Edward's own business savvy, his athleticism, and stellar character placed him in a favorable light with the duke and eventually, the Prince Regent. Over time, his handsome features and innate charm made it easy for the *cream of society* to tolerate his company.

It was his grace who convinced Edward to court his granddaughter when he learned the prince intended to bestow a title on any untitled gentleman who secured Elinor's hand in marriage. Edward was not at all happy about engaging in such a jejune competition. He definitely was not in the market for a wife, particularly a country girl that lacked the town polish and hauteur to reckon with the *ton*. However, upon further reflection he agreed with his grace. He could see how his unwillingness to court Lady Elinor could be misconstrued as a snub. He did not need to give the *cream of society* another reason to abjure him. Word of Prinny's matchmaking scheme was spreading like wildfire through the *ton* grapevine. Edward shuddered, thinking of the gossip he would bestir, if he did not play his part in the prince's magnanimity.

Besides, Prinny liked him and he wanted to keep it that way. It had taken him a long time to gain the Prince Regent's favor. He was not going to throw it all away by refusing his request. Edward resigned himself to the inevitable. After all, he was thirty years old and probably should consider setting up his nursery. *"If I can finagle a great connection, a large dowry, and my own title, then I would be a fool to throw away the opportunity."* On this final thought, he pulled his curricle to a stop in front of the Ingall town home on Berkeley Square. His *tiger*, the groom wearing a yellow and black waistcoat employed to ride on the back of his curricle, hopped off and came to take the reins from him. Edward commanded him to walk his matched greys, up and down the street until he collected Lady Elinor.

It surprised Edward to find Elinor still entertaining a trio of suitors. He grimaced at the three young bucks fawning over her. His entrance drew the gentlemen to stand when Elinor rose to greet him. Introductions were not necessary for the rakish reputations of Lords Riverdale, Mansfield, and Trenton preceded them. However, Edward submitted to Elinor's introductions, first to her mother, then to the lords. He waited patiently for the salutations to end. It was clear to Edward, upon seeing the lords' grins, that they knew he was on Prinny's list. The game was on. Edward recognized Prinny's penchant for mischief. He thought Prinny must have amused himself greatly to put together a set of Corinthians to compete for Elinor's hand. *"I will need all my wits to stay in this game."*

Lord Trenton interrupted his reverie, "I see you have beat us to the punch, Brentwood. I understand you have the honor of accompanying Lady Elinor on her first jaunt through Hyde Park."

Edward looked at Elinor, asking, "Is that true, my lady? Have you never been to our venerable Hyde Park?"

She answered, "Yes it is true. This is my first time to Town. Until now, I have been either sequestered with Henry or preparing for the Prince Regent's Ball. I have not had any opportunity to tour London."

Lord Riverdale interjected, "My dear girl, were you ill?"

"No, no," said Rebecca. "Only Henry suffered, but I feared for him greatly and found I could not leave him."

"I say," asked Lord Mansfield, "Are you telling us that you nursed him?" Mansfield was stunned as were Elinor's other guests. It was *beyond the pale,* for a lady of quality to personally administer to her own children. Chores were delegated to servants and taking care of a child was a task assigned to nurses, nannies, and governesses. Among the aristocracy, children were rarely seen until they became an age where they served a purpose. Such as, increasing wealth and alliances through marriage. Until then, they were cared for by the servants and finally sent to boarding schools. A lady's employment was not to her children, but to her lord by first producing an heir and then to overseeing his household. Ladies primarily concerned themselves with fashion and gossip. Taking care of an ill child would be farthest from their mind, so Elinor's response had all the gentlemen gaping when she replied, "Well yes, myself, and my mama."

Lady Ingall blushed at the attention drawn to her by her daughter's remark. She said, "Now, this discussion has turned tedious. Are you not expecting Lord Westfield and Lady Anne to join you for your excursion?"

Rebecca smiled, "Yes, I expect they are running a little late."

Trenton announced, "It is time we took our leave, but we look forward to making up our party with you for Vauxhall Gardens."

Riverdale asked, "Do you ride, my lady?"

Rebecca beamed, and said, "Oh, yes!"

He then queried, “Then, may I ask for your company tomorrow morning, so that you may see Hyde Park when it is less crowded?”

Rebecca looked to her mother for permission. Upon seeing her affirmative nod, she replied, “Yes, thank you. I would enjoy that very much.”

“Until tomorrow, then,” he said with a final bow. Rebecca watched her three suitors take their leave and then took her seat.

“I am afraid I must make my apologies, my lady." remarked Edward. "I was so excited to show you my new curricle that I forgot that you had invited Lord Westfield and Lady Anne to join our party. I fear, I only have room for two.”

Her bottom lip was beginning to protrude in a pout when she heard Palmer announce the arrival of Lord Westfield and Lady Anne. Jonathan entered the room escorting Anne on his arm and having heard Edward's comment, he announced, “How fortuitous, Brentwood, that I have brought my own carriage, for it will accompany us all.”

Rebecca revealed a full set of teeth in a very wide smile. Lady Ingall was glad no one of consequence was there to acknowledge her daughter's gaffe. Aspiring debutantes were coy and presented modest smiles. Lady Ingall, though pleased to see her daughter happy at Jonathan's arrival, shivered when she thought of the cruel remarks the *marriage mart* mothers would be happy to exploit in order to diminish Elinor's popularity. *"I say, does she think she is a horse up for auction showing all her teeth like that."* She looked at the party before her, sighing a relief. She was sure no one here would comment upon anything to cause her daughter harm.

Jonathan disengaged Anne's arm and made an appropriate bow to Lady Ingall before making his way to Rebecca. He kissed Rebecca's hand and smiled into her eyes. He then turned, brought forth Anne, introducing her, "I trust you remember, Lady Anne?"

"Oh, of course," said Rebecca. "You look quite stunning."

Anne's countenance faltered when she looked at her dress. She was disappointed. She had thought Lady Elinor to have a generous spirit. It surprised her that the young debutante should mock her out of season dress. She was used to being ridiculed by the *ton* for her penury, but she thought Elinor was different: a kinder, compassionate lady. One who did not value a person by her style of dress. Anne's pride peaked and she stiffened her spine. She drew from her own noble upbringing and presented Lady Elinor with a haughty facade, preparing herself for a long and uncomfortable outing.

Rebecca immediately sensed her blunder when she saw the embarrassment in Anne's pallor, Jonathan's scowl, and her mother's crimson face. Jonathan was about to make amends when Rebecca intervened. She explained, "Forgive me, Lady Anne, you misinterpret my praise. I compliment your inner beauty, it radiates a warmth that illuminates you. Truly, I am most honored to have made your acquaintance and hope to call you friend."

Anne relaxed. Elinor's words were a balm to her pride. She responded, "Thank you. I would be honored to call you friend, as well."

Rebecca proffered her hand to Anne, "Let me introduce you to my mama, the Countess of Ingall."

Jonathan followed in their wake as Rebecca introduced Anne to her mother. While he stood next to Rebecca, he took her hand in his and began to thread it through his arm. Edward took notice and exception to Jonathan's proprietary behavior. He remarked, in a curt and intervening manner, "I believe, Westfield, that today I am Lady Elinor's escort."

Jonathan acknowledged Edward's claim with a stiff nod. He made a brief apology, while begrudgingly relinquishing Rebecca to him. He then proffered his arm to Anne who offered him a sympathetic smile. The couples bid a proper adieu to Lady Ingall and exited the parlour. The Westfield's carriage was parked in front of Edward's curricle. Edward's *tiger* was holding the reins to his greys, waiting for his master to make his way to him.

Edward did his best to check his temper at having to instruct his own groom to drive his curricle home and to return in two hours with his horse. Jonathan overheard his commands and remarked, "There is no need for a mount, Brentwood. I would be happy to carry you home."

Edward balked. He liked being the benefactor not the recipient of someone's generosity. He preferred for gentlemen to owe him favors, not the other way around, so it was with tight lips that he responded, "You are too generous, Westfield." Reluctantly, Edward dismissed his groom and then continued his escort of Elinor to the Westfield carriage. With precision, the Westfield groom opened the carriage door and set down the carriage step. Rebecca allowed Anne to precede her. She then entered and sat next to her. Smirking, Jonathan gestured for Edward to enter next. Edward could not refuse his benevolence, since Westfield owned the carriage and it was his right to enter last. Much to his dismay, Edward found himself sitting opposite Anne with Jonathan sitting across from Elinor. He noted that everyone, aside from himself, seemed quite amenable with the seating arrangements.

Edward was too upset at being outmaneuvered by Westfield to initiate a conversation. Instead, he let his thoughts ponder the enigma of Elinor. She was a nobleman's daughter raised as a commoner. She had a noble dignity about her, yet she presented a friendly open nature. Normally, the *ton* would shun someone with brute honesty and frankness, but her regal bloodline gave her *carte blanche.* Her uncommon behavior simply marked her an *Original*, someone untouchable by Society's strict decorum.

Edward's first doubts about courting the young debutante were being diminished by his blossoming attraction. He had to admit that he liked her. He liked the way she cared for her sick brother and he liked her hospitable nature where she saw to her guests' comfort. It was a rare occurrence for a lady of quality to personally administer to her family's needs and even more rare to see a lady compliment another woman. His reflections made him realize that he wished to earnestly court Elinor. *"I think she would make an exceptional wife, if I can derail this puppy love of hers with Westfield. I believe we might be very well suited."*

His mind meandered with visions of pleasant interludes when suddenly, Anne's voice interrupted him, "Are you *wool gathering*, Mr. Brentwood?"

Edward could not believe he had disengaged himself so thoroughly, that he allowed himself to come under scrutiny. Taking in the view from the open carriage, he saw they had traveled the length of Berkeley Street. It seemed that Westfield was going to take Mount Street to enter Hyde Park through the Grosvenor Gate.

Edward was saved from having to respond to Anne when Jonathan pointed out The Duke of Devonshire's home. The earl explained he dispatched his coachman with directions to take the Grosvenor Gate to Hyde Park so he could show Lady Elinor the prominent Mayfair district. He continued his role as docent, noting the homes of his acquaintances who lived on Berkeley and Grosvenor Square. He promised Lady Elinor the next time she took tea at his own prominent Mayfair town home that he would give her a tour. Edward frowned realizing the connection between the Westfields and Ingalls would be a difficult hindrance to overcome. His mind immediately began to strategize. He had a competitive nature and he thought he had an ace or two that he could play to even the odds. More specifically, he thought it was time to bring his grandmother, the Dowager Duchess of Aubry, to London for a visit. Perhaps, she could help level the playing field of his noble competitors. He found himself smiling and to his chagrin, came under the scrutiny of Lady Anne again. When he caught her eyes, he said, "I seem to amuse you, my lady. Perhaps, you would like to share the thoughts that occupy your mind?"

"Actually," she replied. "It is your bemusement that interests me. What, pray tell, is responsible for your jovial countenance?"

Edward answered, "It would be ungentlemanly for me to disagree with you, my lady, but I hardly find myself laughing."

"No, indeed," she retorted. "But, I do believe you and you alone, are privy to some humor that escapes the rest of us."

Anne smiled and Edward found himself stifling a short cough that could easily be mistaken for a laugh. Before their tête-à-tête could continue, they heard Elinor exclaim, "Oh, Jonathan, I mean, My Lord Westfield. Do you think we might stop at Gunter's for some ice? I hear it is quite the thing to do."

Jonathan smiled, responding, "Of course, if Mr. Brentwood and Lady Anne have no objections. We will stop on our return trip when perhaps the crowd has thinned. Let us continue to Hyde Park and take our refreshments afterwards." Edward frowned at Elinor's use of Westfield's Christian name. It reminded him of his greatest hurdle: her already engaged heart. He wasn't about to let something like *puppy love*, dissuade him, now that he considered her the perfect wife. He had time and he would begin by being agreeable. He nodded his approval to stop at Gunter's on their return route.

They entered the Grosvenor Gate and immediately their procession slowed, the promenade of carriages controlling their pace. Rebecca exclaimed, "I have never seen anything like it! There are so many carriages and everyone is quite in their splendor. It is true then what they say, that our mission is to see and to be seen."

Jonathan laughed, remarking, "You are too forthcoming, my lady, but, yes. The nobility do like to flaunt their fashion like peacocks. They strut their plumage to draw attention to themselves. Look over yonder, I believe that Lady Miranda and Mr. Willoughby are doing their best to bring their curricle alongside us."

Rebecca asked Anne, "Are you acquainted with Lady Miranda and Mr. Willoughby?"

Anne replied, "I know of Lady Miranda but we have not been introduced. I believe this is her first season. As for Mr. Willoughby, I think it would be difficult to find someone who had not made his acquaintance."

Jonathan laughed, saying, "Yes, you are quite right. He is a most obliging sort of fellow and not too long ago, carried quite a bit of a reputation. I think he was on his way towards becoming a devilish rake, but Lady Miranda changed his path to both their satisfactions.

Edward smiled at the term *devilish rake*, knowing the misnomer had more than once been applied to him. Anne caught his eyes and smiled, as well. He responded, "I believe it is said, the love of a good woman can make the man."

Surprised, Rebecca remarked, "You surprise me, Mr. Brentwood, I would not have thought you would allow your heart to dictate you."

Awestruck at Elinor's impertinence, he inquired, "And why, my lady, would you think that?"

"Because," she answered with candor. "You are on the list!"

Stunned at her directness, Jonathan, Edward, and Anne looked at each other, neither knowing what to say. Slowly, they saw a flicker of amusement in each other's eyes and gave in to the moment by laughing wholeheartedly. When their high spirits subsided, they saw a very perplexed Elinor with inquiring eyes. Innately protective of her, Jonathan took it upon himself to explain to her their very uncharitable outburst. He calmly said, "My lady, you must take care and not mention the list. As improper as it was for Prinny to create it, I fear it is your reputation that will be tarnished if you speak so cavalierly and publicly about it. I implore you, for your sake, be chary."

Rebecca's eyes started to tear and Jonathan took her hand. He consoled, "Do not feel as though you behaved badly for you are beyond reproach." He gave her hand a loving squeeze before releasing it. He saw her force a smile in response.

Stiffening her back, she addressed Edward, "I do beg your pardon, sir. I meant no harm."

"There is no need, my lady," he replied. "I do believe we all found your candor most amusing, but I agree with Westfield that the less said about Prinny's list, the better. I beg that you not judge me too harshly, for truly, it is your sweet countenance and not the list that entices my admiration." Rebecca blushed to Edward's delight, Jonathan's displeasure and Anne's amusement.

Mr. Willoughby managed to maneuver his cattle to bring his two-seater alongside the Westfield's carriage. He and his lady chimed in unison, "Good Day!" Sitting forward, Miranda added, "Are you enjoying yourself, Lady Elinor?"

Rebecca was happy to see that Arthur and Miranda were happily betrothed and that all the misconceptions about a possible union between Jonathan and Miranda resolved. She earnestly wanted to embrace Arthur's fiancée as a friend. She answered, "Yes, very much so. There is so much to see. May I present, Mr. Brentwood and Lady Anne to you?" Both Mr. Brentwood and Lady Anne nodded.

Arthur said, "We are acquainted with one another, but I do not believe they have been introduced to my intended, Lady Miranda." Edward gave a most charming smile, saying, "It is my pleasure to meet you, Lady Miranda."

Anne smiled and added, "And I am pleased as well, to make your acquaintance."

Rebecca interjected, "Lady Miranda and Mr. Willoughby are friends of Lord Westfield and myself." Jonathan beamed when Rebecca coupled their names together. Edward's scowl intimated that he also noticed the connection, adding to Jonathan's further amusement.

Chapter Fourteen

Jane lounged in her bed enjoying her morning repast of dried toast and tea, when she heard a soft tattoo on her bedroom door. She beckoned, "enter" and was surprised to see her daughter come into her suite wearing one of her fashionable riding habits. She thought Elinor looked exquisite in her shako hat and scarlet military-style ensemble, featuring epaulettes, frogs, and gold braiding ornamentation on her jacket. She asked, "Why are you up so early and dressed?"

Rebecca answered, "Oh, Mama, did you forget that I am to ride this morning with Lord Riverdale? I cannot begin to tell you how much I am looking forward to this ride. I must confess that I have been feeling hemmed in, so I am doubly glad that papa brought my mare to Town."

Her mother queried, "But, Elinor, I thought you said you enjoyed your ride yesterday?"

Rebecca gleefully responded, "Yes, it was great fun seeing Society in its glory and I loved the sweet confections at Gunter's, but the propriety of Society can be so tedious. I miss spending time outdoors where I can feel the sun on my face and the solitude of peace."

"Elinor," she reprimanded, "you do take your abigail to chaperone?"

Rebecca gave an affirmative nod when she left, grinning at her mother's concern. She was anxious to ride her mare and briskly made her way to the parlour where she waited for Lord Riverdale to call.

Riding alongside Riverdale, Rebecca felt the brush of the cool wind on her face. She loved the crisp air, breathing in a heavy dose like a hungry child stuffing his mouth with food, though her nostrils flared at having detected an odd fragrance. It was a strange blend of scents. Rebecca could discern the smell of sweet dewy grass and the woody fragrance of the oak and birch trees, but she also detected a pungent stench. The perverse smell, unknown to her, rose from the filthy Thames and areas around the city where waste was left to pollute the London air. Rebecca twitched her nose as if she wanted to sneeze. Riverdale having spied her contortions, laughed, remarking, "The park is nicely laid out, but it is not the country. You will not find the pastoral smells that are familiar to you."

"No," smiled Rebecca. "I fear, I was not bred for city life. While London is full of amusements that I have yet to see, my heart longs for the peace and solace of my ancestral home. Plus, I miss my employment."

Riverdale caught himself stammering, "D-Do not tell me that you work, my lady? I find it very hard to believe that the Earl of Ingall has apprenticed his daughter of all things."

Rebecca laughed. "Your wit is most exceptional, my lord, but you forget that I was raised the daughter of a clergyman and I am inclined to making myself useful. I do not know how to be idle."

He reflected, inquiring, "May I ask, my lady, what type of employment you seek when you are at home?"

"I assure you, my lord," she answered, "it is nothing scandalous or demeaning, but if I was at home, I would be visiting our tenants and seeing if I might be of service to them."

Riverdale checked his horse and looked at Lady Elinor with much astonishment. He was unsure of what he felt. Her behavior would be abhorred by the *ton*, why, he at the least should abjure her, but he found he could not. He could easily imagine, how the *cream of society,* would disparage her for "working" and communing with the lower classes. If not for her noble connections and her champion, the Prince Regent, the *ton* would likely give her the *cut direct*. Her behavior, for a lady of quality, was clearly outrageous, but somehow he found her endearing. It would seem that Lady Elinor was an *Original* and he was happy to own her acquaintance.

Rebecca and Riverdale turned their heads at the sound of hooves hitting the hard ground. They saw two galloping hacks making their way to them. Rebecca laughed recognizing Lords Mansfield and Trenton. Riverdale responded to their arrival with a scold, “What the devil brought you out this early? I have never known either of you to rise before noontime.”

Smiling, Lord Mansfield replied, “You did not think we would give you the advantage? Nay, Riverdale, you must consider us duty bound to keep you company.”

Laughter filled the air, giving Rebecca's and Riverdale's mounts a start. Rebecca brought her horse under control immediately and her skill was noted by all the lords. Their horses were getting antsy, so they each gave a heel to them, riding abreast of each other and chatting with good humor. Rebecca exclaimed, “Oh! How I envy you, Lord Mansfield and Lord Trenton. What I would give to race and have the wind in my face. My mare has not had an exceptional run in quite awhile.”

Riverdale asked, “Is there no end to your surprises, my lady?”

“Pray, what do you mean?” she inquired.

He asked, “Perhaps, you could explain what you mean. Am I to understand that you are accustomed to gallop when you ride?”

“Oh, yes!” she exclaimed. “Why if I was on Apollo, I doubt if anyone could catch me!”

Trenton interjected, "You cannot be serious. Are you telling me that Westfield grants you permission to ride Apollo? Why he doesn't allow anyone to ride him."

Riverdale chuckled, "To be precise, you mean that Westfield does not allow *you* to ride him."

Rebecca added with a mischievous taunt, "Perhaps, my lord, you are unable to maintain a good seat."

A cacophony of snorts, guffaws, and giggles erupted and Mansfield pressed, "I declare Trenton, that is a challenge if ever I heard one. You must respond. Does anyone know if Westfield has brought Apollo to Town?"

"How fortuitous!" exclaimed Trenton who relished the opportunity to prove them wrong. "Is that not him approaching from the east?"

It did not take long for Lord Westfield to surmise what all the frenzy was about. He was not particularly pleased that Rebecca had somehow become the center of a wager and hoped he could squash the challenge before the London clubs started to place bets. This was the kind of folly that gentlemen loved to wager. Jonathan feared that Rebecca's reputation would be tarnished if he could not rein in the increasing enthusiasm. He said, "Gentlemen, it is well known that Apollo can outride all your mounts. And while I will vouch for Lady Elinor's equestrian skills, I am sure that you can all see the impropriety of a competitive jaunt between Lady Elinor and yourselves. I beg you all to desist."

Riverdale was quick to concur, "You are quite right, Westfield, but I must say the idea of Lady Elinor on Apollo outracing us does enchant me."

"May I ask," he queried. "Who initiated the idea in the first place?"

Rebecca was first to reply. "I am afraid that I was brooding at not being able to take a good run. You know how much I enjoy the exercise."

Trenton added, "She is being demure, Westfield. The honest answer is she impugned my riding skills and lucky for you, I am an obliging fellow and took no offense. By the way, why are you out and about this morning?"

Westfield answered, "I expect for the same reason you and Mansfield are here. I wish to join Lady Elinor's party."

Riverdale rebuffed, "Well, it wasn't supposed to be a party, Westfield. In fact, you all have become a nuisance, interrupting Lady Elinor and myself."

Rebecca smiled at Riverdale, exclaiming, "Fustian! They did no such thing. I am enjoying everyone's company and it would make me quite happy if I could call you all friend."

He retorted, "Does that include Westfield, as well?"

Rebecca swept her eyelashes down, inhaled a long breath and did her best to keep her color from rising. Westfield gave a severe look to Riverdale who offered, "Very well, my lady, friend it is, but if you should change your mind, I would be more than happy to take our friendship to another level."

Rebecca looked at Riverdale and did not know what to say, so she simply looked at Jonathan. Much to her other suitors' chagrin, she gave him an endearing smile. Jonathan wanted to declare that Rebecca belonged to him. He was tired of competing for her attention and hoped that when he met with the Prince Regent, he would be able to do so.

Jonathan was so wound up after meeting with Prinny that he decided to stop by White's for a stiff drink. He needed the elixir to calm his frustration and prepare him for the barrage of questions his mother would throw at him the minute he returned home. His interview had not gone as he hoped it would. He needed to get his own anger under control before he could assuage his mother's temper, which was sure to explode, when she learned the prince was determined for Rebecca to be courted by his list of suitors.

He managed to enter White's and circumvent his peers to find a quiet corner where he could reflect on his and the prince's conversation. He was surprised the prince was genuinely concerned for Rebecca's future. He had thought that Prinny created the list of suitors for Rebecca as a way to amuse himself, but after their tête-à-tête, he realized that the prince had Rebecca's best interest at heart. The story of the Ingall's loss of Elinor as an infant and how she was raised and worked as a commoner affected him greatly. He wanted to recompense Elinor for what he thought was a tragic upbringing and ensure her future in the *ton* by arranging a wedding with a nobleman. He thought marriage to a peer was adequate compensation for a lady separated at birth from her rightful sphere. Jonathan admired the prince's sincerity, but cursed his interference. Prinny had thought it was wonderful that the earl loved Lady Elinor. He himself was a romantic. Did not all the world know he favored the infamous Mrs. Fitzherbert? The prince was happy that Lady Elinor welcomed Westfield's suit, but he also thought it only fair that everyone be given an equitable shot at her admiration. Yes, he understood that Jonathan had offered for Lady Elinor prior to her identity being known. "But don't you see, Westfield," said Prinny. "That is why it is even more important for her to gain the attention of multiple suitors of superior rank. She should be courted with all the 'pomp and circumstance' as someone of her station is due. You must acknowledge that at the time she accepted your offer, it was her only advantageous one. A lady of her rank should be sought after, not merely grateful. I have solicited appropriate suitors for her consideration. I am amused that you are thoroughly engaged in the competition for her hand, but do not trespass on my good humor to suggest I deter from what I feel is my most magnanimous behavior."

Jonathan tried not to take offense that Prinny thought Rebecca only accepted his offer because it was her most advantageous one. He knew to continue to argue with him would only cause more injury to his case, so he bowed in obedience and left Carlton House. He realized he was back where he started, vying with countless other suitors for Rebecca's hand in marriage. A sharp slap to his back propelled his mind to the present to see Riverdale smiling down at him.

"And what?" remarked Westfield, "Do you find so amusing?"

"Well," he responded. "I would never have guessed that you were ready to relinquish your bachelorhood. But after today's jaunt, it is clear that you are quite smitten. Why don't you just offer for the lady?"

"I have," announced Westfield.

"No!" he exclaimed. "Do not tell me she refused your offer. I thought it obvious that she returned your affection. Surely, Lord Ingall can have no objection."

"None in the least," responded Jonathan. "No, it is all Prinny's interference. I must wait until the end of the Season to declare myself and I am finding it most tedious, competing for the attention of my betrothed."

"Is she really?" asked Riverdale.

"Well," replied Jonathan. "Not technically, but unless her feelings change for me within the next three months, I expect to receive your most heartfelt congratulations."

"I felicitate you now for finding a most remarkable lady, Westfield. I do not know how you will constrain her independence though, for she appears to have a mind of her own on what constitutes proper behavior. It seems to be a conglomeration of both the stations she has held in her life. She is a beauty and an *Original*. Your children will find their upbringing quite different from ours I would hazard to guess. Could you imagine our mothers nursing us themselves?" Riverdale started to laugh.

Jonathan's memory stirred, recalling a time when he was a young boy in bed with a fever. *Yes, I can more than imagine my mother nursing me when I was sick. Perhaps, Rebecca's love of family is what draws me to her."*

"Well, you don't have to worry about Mansfield, Trenton, or me," he remarked. "We like Lady Elinor extremely well, but have no plans to dally with her affection. Especially, since you are serious about her. Take no offense, but I think she is too independent-minded for any of us. She is not the demure debutante that we are used to, even if she is on the quiet side. While she appears more comfortable listening than talking, her eyes reveal an intellect uncommon with our Society debutantes. Say, she isn't a *bluestocking* is she?"

Jonathan replied, "No, not a *bluestocking*, but she is very learned. As for her quiet tendencies in Society, that comes from being invisible as Lady Ingall's companion. Once you spend more time with her, you might change your mind about your intentions. Lady Elinor is a *diamond of the first water*. Besides her beauty and intellect, she is warm and compassionate and will make me a most exceptional countess. I cannot imagine anyone else with whom I would rather spend my life."

"I am happy for you," he said. "I hear that the odds are looking good for Brentwood. Any concerns there?"

"I do not trust him," answered Jonathan. "Prinny has promised him a title if he is successful. I would not put anything past him to make the connection, so I would be indebted to you to help me keep Lady Elinor safe."

"You need not ask," replied Riverdale. "It is obvious Lady Elinor is new to the machinations of Society. I can speak for Mansfield and Trenton when I say, we like her too much to let her fall into danger."

"Thank you, Riverdale," said Jonathan. "I must take my leave. The Ingalls join me and my mother for the opera this evening."

"How odd," he stated. "Don't they keep their own box?"

"Their visits to London are few, so they choose not to keep one, especially since the duke does and it is always at their disposal if they wish," responded Jonathan.

"How providential for you, Westfield, that they do not wish. I bid you a good evening," he concluded.

Jonathan smiled, replying "Thank you, Riverdale, I shall. By the way, have you made up your party for Vauxhall. Lady Elinor tells me that you go tomorrow?"

Riverdale grinned, explaining, "Yes, Trenton and Mansfield go. I have also included Willoughby and his betrothed, Lady Miranda. I suppose you wish to be included?"

"Precisely," answered Jonathan smothering a chuckle. Then somberly, he inquired, "Whom have you asked to chaperone?"

Riverdale replied, "I thought I would invite Lady Anne, since she has been on the shelf these past years. I thought she would be adequate. I know Lady Elinor is pleased to call her friend."

Jonathan countered, "Yes. Lady Elinor does indeed own her for an acquaintance, but you are too harsh to invite her to fill the chaperone role. Lady Anne is far from being a spinster. Her lack of dowry seems to place her in that light, but she still has a number of years before she is considered ineligible. It would be ungentlemanly of us to do so, and a disservice to her. For her sake, ask Lady Ingall to accompany us, if she is unable, advise me and I will ask my mother to attend."

"Very well, until tomorrow," he replied.

Mr. Edward Brentwood could not keep himself from glancing at the Westfield's Box to observe Lord Westfield and Lady Elinor in what appeared to be an ongoing conversation. Not once did their heads separate. It was clear they had no interest in the opera for their eyes never wavered from one another. Their profound intimacy was vexing Edward to distraction, feeling his chances for winning the lady's hand in marriage dwindle. He sat next to the Duke of Hartford in his opera box growing increasingly mad at his rival's success. He thought the duke seemed unaware of his angst since his eyes focused on the stage listening to the aria being sung, undoubtedly with uncommon feeling. He regrettably let out a "hmmrph" when he saw Elinor's hand cover her mouth in an attempt to smother a chuckle from something that Westfield said.

The duke, without turning his head, commented, "You will gain nothing by brooding. Either promote your own interests or desist and offer your felicitations to Westfield."

Edward grimaced, replying, "I am not brooding. My mood for a better lack of description is contemplation. I am simply planning my next move."

"And pray, what may that be?" queried the duke.

Edward answered, "I leave in the morning for Aubry. I seek my grandmother's aid in leveling the intimacy between the Ingalls and the Westfields.

The Duke of Hartford commented, "I think that is wise. I will endeavor to request that my daughter-in-law oblige herself to any invitation the dowager presents. I wish you good fortune, but I remind you that my granddaughter's happiness outweighs all else."

Chapter Fifteen

Lord Riverdale hired a barge to take his party across the Thames to Vauxhall. The pleasure garden located on the Surry side of the river was a regular amusement for the *bon ton*. The idle rich liked to host small dinner parties in the fashionable booths and then promenade through the elm lined avenues in their finery. Riverdale arranged for his family's steward to turn their transport for the evening into a soiree, complete with spirits and music. The proficient servant selected their finest champagne and freshest strawberries from the Riverdale cellars and kitchens. He also secured a solo violinist to play for the trip to Vauxhall. Rebecca was in awe of the splendor of it all. Although she had lived among the Ingalls for the past few years and was used to the accoutrements of wealth, she was unfamiliar with the extravagancies the *bon ton* engaged in to secure their amusements. To her, everything was new and delightful. Her eyes widened taking in all the sights.

Rebecca, with Jonathan at her side, scanned the evening delights, from twinkling lights from other barges on the water to listening to the music that resounded around her. From the corner of her eye, she saw Miranda and Arthur standing together in conversation with the lords. Miranda's lofty posture and Arthur's relaxed pose created a stark contrast between them and Rebecca thought the picture was reflective of their characters. Rebecca liked Arthur who was far from pretentious. His manners were impeccable and he had a friendly presence that put everyone at ease, unlike Miranda, who demanded what was due her station.

Miranda acted as though the extravagant transport was a common occurrence for her and ignored the sights, preferring to engage the lords in conversation. She reveled being the center of attention having no other debutante present who wanted to challenge her position. While she played at coquetry, Rebecca and Jonathan meandered along the edge of the barge. Her head turned in time to see Miranda swat Lord Riverdale's arm with her fan when she heard the lady chime a forced giggle. Miranda's eyes were bright, gleaming, and she looked like she was enjoying herself immensely. It seemed the gentlemen also took great pleasure in her manner. If anything, they all participated like actors in a theatre performing a play, tossing witticisms back and forth in a discourse that seemed scripted.

The scene mesmerized Rebecca so much that she could not stop watching the interplay. She heard Miranda say, "Really, My Lord Riverdale, a single violinist. I thought you worthy of a quartet. Don't you find the single string a bit tedious?"

Rebecca saw Riverdale transform in the blink of an eye from a cheery gentleman to a haughty lord. She thought of the mimes who with a wave of their hand could change the expression of their smile into a frown. Everything about Riverdale changed: his posture, manner, and expression. When his lordship pulled out a spyglass from his waistcoat, she was reminded of those aristocrats who used the accoutrement to insult an inferior person of class. She feared he was about to give Miranda a set down, but instead, he simply arched a single brow, extended his leg, sweeping his arm in a full arc, while bending deep from his waist to perform a courtly bow. He said, "My apologies, my lady, that the music does not meet your standards, I am all regrets."

Miranda laughed, carelessly unaware she had affronted his lordship. She said, "You are forgiven, my lord, but I shall expect you to exceed my expectations the next time I agree to join a party of yours."

Rebecca thought Arthur was as uncomfortable as she was regarding Miranda's remark, but she was not sure. Lords Trenton and Mansfield revealed nothing other than stoic faces, as though the remark was never made. She watched them walk away to the opposite side of the barge, giving the affected members their privacy. One thing she had learned living among the upper class, was that the aristocracy was a duplicitous group. Often times, what seemed to Rebecca as rude was considered witty. She was not sure of Miranda's intention or if she had one. Before she could turn to beseech Jonathan for guidance, she was interrupted by Riverdale's question. Looking pointedly at her, he asked, "What do you say, Lady Elinor. Have I failed to please you?"

Rebecca blushed. She did not like being put in a position to be contrary, but his earnest question compelled her to answer with her known frankness. Her own manner reflectively stiffened, when it seemed everyone waited for her to respond. She thought she saw Trenton and Mansfield offer her an encouraging smile. She clasped her hands in front of her body and took a breath before she replied, "No, my lord, you have not failed me. Allow me to offer my heartfelt appreciation to you for inviting me to share in such a remarkable evening. I am very much enjoying the ambiance that you have created and find the melodies that the violinist plays, much to my liking. He is a virtuoso is he not?"

Riverdale's proud posture broke upon hearing her answer. He replied, "You have an impeccable ear, my lady, and are quite correct in your findings. I am pleased to have someone in my party who recognizes exceptional talent. Mr. Louis Spohr is a renowned violinist and a composer. He is a guest of my mother's and plays as a favor to her."

Riverdale grinned. He walked over to Rebecca and placed a light kiss on the back of her hand. Then he bowed to her and commanded his servants, "More champagne for everyone. We must not diminish the ambiance that Lady

Elinor praises." Trenton and Mansfield rose their glasses to toast her, cheering, "Hear! Hear!"

Rebecca smiled in relief that her remarks were well received until Jonathan stepped in front of her. He whispered, "I compliment your honesty, Rebecca, but I fear though unintentional, you have caused Lady Miranda injury."

Rebecca looked over Jonathan's shoulder to see Miranda sulking. She caught the lady's eye only to see her return a scowl and turn her back on her. She looked at Jonathan, softly exclaiming, "Goodness! Should I apologize to her?"

"Perhaps, later," he replied in a low voice. For now, drink your champagne and tell me how you knew Mr. Spohr was a virtuoso?"

Speaking softly, she replied, "Really, Jonathan, how could I not? I have heard enough ill music to know when I have heard something remarkable."

"You do yourself a disservice, Rebecca, for I cannot claim the same aptitude and believe me, I have heard plenty of ill music to last a lifetime. I believe Riverdale is right and that you have an impeccable ear. You are quite accomplished on the piano forte to my recollection."

Rebecca blushed, replying, "You are too generous." She then took the smallest of sips from her champagne glass.

Jonathan noticed her small sampling of the sparkling wine and remarked, "Do you not enjoy your champagne?"

"Oh, yes!" she practically shouted. "It is sweet and the tiny bubbles tickle my nose."

He countered, "But you only appear to let the liquid gold touch your lips. Do you swallow anything?"

Rebecca giggled, "I am not sure. My mama cautioned me quite extensively not to indulge in too many spirits or else I could fall into a stupor and find myself acting scandalously."

Jonathan laughed, saying, "One glass will not hurt you and I am here to protect your virtue. Let us enjoy ourselves, for I am happy not to have to compete with Mr. Brentwood this evening for your favor."

Her eyes widened, exclaiming, "Jonathan, you cannot be jealous! Besides, there is no competition. You and you alone, own my heart. Do not mistrust my affections. They are honest and good!"

Jonathan's eyes beamed with ardor. He wished he could take Rebecca into his arms. He settled instead for taking a large gulp of champagne. His only response was a silent prayer, "Lord, give me patience."

The barge docked at the Vauxhall steps and Jonathan helped Rebecca to disembark. He was happy that he and Rebecca could finally enjoy each other's company without a bevy of suitors or family members to check their behavior. Riverdale acquired a spinster aunt, Mrs. Jenkins, to act as chaperone for the unmarried ladies in the party. Riverdale's aunt was used to being pulled into service by her relatives and was extraordinarily intuitive to understand, she served best when she became inconspicuous.

Smiling, Riverdale generously paid the shilling for each of his guests and led them into the grove. Jonathan watched Rebecca turn her head side to side to take in the central area of the gardens. Riverdale pointed out the exotic supper boxes where they would dine later and pointed to how they overlooked the Gothic orchestra area where the band performed. Rebecca stopped when she saw the great life-size marble stature of Handel. The sculptor carved the composer in a relaxed state with him sitting in his evening gown and slippers.

Jonathan was happy Rebecca was enjoying herself. He explained, "Did you know, my lady, that Handel was a frequent performer here at the garden and that this statue of him was unveiled while he lived. I believe at the time, it was the first full-size statue of a commoner exhibited. It created quite a stir, in regards to its propriety, in both his common class and dress."

Rebecca enthusiastically stated, "Oh, my lord, I am overcome with all the beauty that surrounds me."

The lords smiled at her sheer exuberance. Riverdale remarked, "I say, my lady, do I not deserve your praise, since it is indeed my invitation that brought you here?"

Both Jonathan and Rebecca laughed. She replied, "Indeed you do, My Lord Riverdale. You have my sincere appreciation for planning such a marvelous excursion for me."

Rebecca saw Miranda's affronted face and quickly added, "Forgive me, I meant to say for planning for me and all your guests." She then asked Miranda, "Have you ever seen anything like it?"

Arthur found Elinor's cheerfulness infectious and with a hearty smile turned to see what Miranda would add. He was sorely disappointed to see his betrothed, stiff and proud. He guessed she was still put out being upstaged by Elinor in regards to her earlier uncouth remarks regarding Mr. Sphor. Arthur knew that Miranda's remarks were typical of all debutantes engaging in harmless flirtations. There was an art to coquetry and until Miranda criticized Riverdale's generosity, she had been successful in entertaining the lords. Arthur placed her gaffe on her youth and believed the rest of the gentlemen had already forgotten the incident, but it was clear to him that Miranda took Elinor's remarks as an affront and it seemed she would not easily forgive her. He wished Miranda realized that Elinor meant no insult to her, she just simply did not subscribe to anything other than frankness.

Miranda replied flatly, "I have been here before, Lady Elinor, but will admit to always finding it congenial."

Miranda was used to her peers backing her up when she made a cutting remark and expected nothing less from the lords in her party. Since Elinor's enthusiastic outburst reflected a trait associated with the common, she thought the other members of her party would lend their own austere remarks. Such gawking that Lady Elinor engaged in was considered gauche, so she was both surprised and disappointed to find herself, the center of mockery.

Her face blushed crimson when Westfield and Riverdale chuckled, “Congenial, indeed!” Feeling herself the spectacle she meant to make of Elinor, she was glad when Arthur took her hand, threaded it through his arm and patted it with affection. She did not care to be the object of mirth and felt genuine fear when she thought she might be further ridiculed. Only when Riverdale made his announcement, drawing everyone's attention away from her, did she find a modicum of relief.

“We have a good hour before supper is served. Shall we take the Grand Walk and let Lady Elinor discover the hidden delights that Vauxhall offers?”

Rebecca's eyes widened with genuine interest, she asked, “There are delights?”

Riverdale answered, “You must explore the lanes, but there are indeed hidden temples, sculptures, and other architectural wonders that I am sure you will find enchanting.”

“I am already enchanted,” replied Rebecca with awe. Jonathan proffered his arm and escorted Rebecca down the three hundred yard avenue known as the Grand Walk. The gravel crunched beneath their shoes and Jonathan watched Rebecca take in the sights, sounds, and smells of the garden. The elm, lime, and sycamore trees gave off a distinct smell. Jonathan could tell that Rebecca was keenly aware of her surroundings, so he was not surprised when she exclaimed, "Oh, listen! It is the nightingale. How charming."

Jonathan leaned into Rebecca and whispered, "Not as charming as you, my lady. I confess I am seeing the gardens for the first time, for never before have I marveled at their wonder. You bring everything to life, Rebecca."

Rebecca blushed at Jonathan's praise and then looked to see if anyone took note of his comments. If they did hear him, she was happy they were discreet enough not to allude to it. Their party grew and shrank through the evening as friends, of Jonathan's and the lords', joined and left their group. Rebecca could not remember, aside from the Regent's Ball, ever meeting so many fashionable people in one evening. As dusk fell, they made their way back to the supper booths to enjoy the transparently thin sliced ham, made legendary by Vauxhall.

That night, settled into her feather bed, Rebecca found the excitement she owned kept her from sleep. She was exhausted, but her mind was too active recalling the splendor of the evening, to fall into slumber. She remembered the rows and rows of immaculately groomed tall trees that lined the gravel walks and the multiple treasures she found when a path terminated. She released a small giggle recalling the antics of the lords. In jest, they tried to mimic some of the sculpture poses and they made up ridiculous legends about them. Trenton informed her that one particular Buddha was feared because a person with an impure mind would be struck dead if they touched the stature. Before Rebecca could remark, "Fustian," Trenton touched the stature and acted as though he had an apoplexy. He had everyone in stitches.

Supper was even more of a marvel. They enjoyed a feast of thinly sliced ham, fresh fruits, cheeses, custards, tarts, and other delicacies. As the sun set, she heard a whistle blow. Then to her surprise, the lighting of over a thousand oil lamps bathed the garden with warm light. The sight was a wonder. Servants placed in strategic places throughout the garden, lit a fuse when they heard the whistle and like magic, hundreds of lights ignited. The event was even more special because Jonathan was by her side every minute. The lights seemed to dance while the orchestra's music permeated the air. Rebecca could still hear the music in her mind. She would never forget the magic and romance of walking the tree-lined avenues with Jonathan. She would always remember how he never left her side or took his eyes off of her, not even to watch the fireworks. Rebecca grinned remembering how she had told Jonathan that he was missing the beauty of the night and he said, “Hardly.”

She turned to grab her spare pillow and hugged it, trying to soothe her restlessness. She flopped unto her back again, squirming around to find a comfortable position. She sighed and then expelled a deep breath. She let out another relaxing breath and before long, exhaustion set in. Her eyelids closed and pulled her into slumber, but not before whispering, “I love you, Jonathan.”

Chapter Sixteen

Edward spent his whole trip trying to determine how best to explain the circumstances surrounding Lady Elinor to his grandmother. He was still trying to figure out exactly what to say to her, when her salutation deemed it unnecessary. "So, Edward, you have come for my help? I wondered how long it would take before you realized how useful I can be. Tell me, is she worthy of your affections?"

"I see my business precedes me," he responded. "And yes. She is worthy of my affections. Her lineage is exceptional and to my benefit, her common upbringing prevents her from owning the hauteur that you aristocrats seem to breed into your children."

The dowager lifted her left brow, grimly staring at her grandson. She chided, "Really, Edward, you must not be so vulgar."

Ignoring his grandmother's comment, he added, "I do not think she finds me repulsive because I am in trade. If not for an ardor she claims to have for Lord Westfield, I do believe she might take a liking to me. I have been the cause of more than one of her smiles."

"Well," began the dowager. "I know all about it. You know us *bon ton* have the best network for relaying information. I understand that Westfield is considered the favorite in winning her hand, though White's, that renowned gentleman's club of yours, is giving odds in your favor. Apparently, you have many more conquests than Westfield. I do not think they consider age in that area to be a factor, do you?"

Edward grinned, "You are quite impertinent, Grandmother, and no, I do not believe they factored in age. Tell me, do you approve of Lady Elinor for my wife?"

The dowager exclaimed, "Since when have you ever asked for my approval?" Edward began to respond when the dowager raised her hand, exclaiming, "Wait! Do not answer that."

"Well, Grandmother?" he queried.

"I am well aware of the title that Prinny has offered should you be successful with Lady Elinor. I am not so *high in the instep* to abjure her upbringing. You know very well that the Duke of Hartford is a cherished friend of mine. A connection between our families would be exceptional. And though you reek of trade, it does not demean you in my eyes or my heart. You are of noble ancestry. You have my blood in your veins. Do not let any aristocrat let you think you are less than you are. And since you often refer to us noble few as a smug group, I will concur that we do not look for love to make a respectable union. Title, wealth, connections, those are the important elements in securing a noble marriage, so yes, I would approve of a union with Lady Elinor. She will bring you a title, a large dowry, and excellent connections. However, I caution you to make sure that Lady Elinor's heart is not truly engaged to Westfield. You are not the type of man who could live with a woman who is in love with another man. You are too proud and even more sentimental. The only reason your father survived being cast from Society was because he truly loved your mother. She was his world and he never had any regrets about quitting his sphere, until he saw how it impacted you. It hurt him to see the children of his brothers and his friends, mock you for your inferior station. As much as you want a title to legitimize your place in the *ton*, I know that you could not stand to be cuckolded. Are you sure that Lady Elinor and Westfield are too young to know their hearts?"

"I have rarely been bested in the pursuit of a woman. As you so brazenly noted, I have quite a number of conquests, but you are right to caution me. Lady Elinor is not your typical debutante. She is not looking to find an eligible match. She is looking for love and believes to have found it. I confess, I envy Westfield for being the object of her ardor. She truly is beautiful. If it were possible to usurp Westfield's place in her heart, I would truly prosper. Do you have any suggestions? Will you come to London and develop a relationship with Lady Ingall?"

"I do not believe I will be of use in London," she said. "I suggest I invite a party to visit Aubry and include the Ingalls."

"Oh!" exclaimed Edward. "That is an excellent idea to separate Westfield from Lady Elinor. I applaud your stratagem."

"Don't be silly, Edward," she admonished. "You know the saying about absence making the heart grow fonder. No, we will not separate them. I intend to invite the Westfields, as well."

"Then," pursued an annoyed Edward. "How is that supposed to help me?"

"We will test the strength of their ardor," she explained. "Lady Elinor is receiving much attention. Why not garner some for Westfield? Let us see how secure is their relationship. Was not your cousin Catherine once on intimate terms with Westfield?"

Edward laughed, remarking, "I do believe you are right, Grandmother, though their intimacy was during their nursery days. If I remember correctly, they were both disciplined for contriving a mock wedding ceremony."

The dowager laughed, "Yes, I remember. Aubry was mortified, though the Earl of Westfield had a way to make everyone end up laughing over their scandalous behavior."

"Really, Grandmother," queried Edward. "Hardly scandalous, neither of them had reached six years of age."

"Regardless," she countered. "They always tended to be drawn towards one another. Perhaps history will repeat itself."

"You are quite the tactician, Grandmother," he complimented. "I am happy to have you in my corner. Tell me, who else makes up your house party?"

Lady Ingall entered her husband's study bringing the dowager's invitation to Aubry to show to him. She was not surprised to receive the request for their company. Her father-in-law had paid a particular visit to them just to request his son and wife to oblige his dear friend, the Dowager Duchess of Aubry, should any invitations prevail. Jane had expected an invitation to tea, not a request to join a party to sojourn at Aubry for a fortnight. Jane handed Roger the invitation and after he read it, he said, "We cannot decline without seeking my father's disapproval. He rarely asks that we extend ourselves in this way. We must go."

She sniffed in disgust. "I am sure this all Mr. Brentwood's doing. She is his grandmother, is she not?"

Roger answered, "I believe she is, but remember we honor my father by attending. Do not let the quest for Elinor's hand concern you. We will be there and according to the dowager's invitation, we may make up our own party to attend. If it makes you feel better, you may invite the Westfields and anyone else that Elinor wants."

Her heart lightened at his words, "Thank you, Roger. I so worry for our daughter with all these machinations in pursuit of her favor. She is not prepared to deal with the Mr. Brentwoods of the world."

"Jane," argued Roger, "you do Mr. Brentwood a disservice. He is an honorable man. True, he is tainted by trade and considered a rake, but it is not uncommon for a man to be called such who has escaped matrimony for as many years as he has. I know him to be of stellar character. He is an intimate friend of my father's who I know champions him whenever possible. Do you think my father would encourage a union if he was not worthy?"

Jane's mouth dropped and barely exclaimed her shock, when she asked, "What are you saying, Roger? Do you not support Jonathan's suit?"

My interests and support are for Elinor and Elinor alone," he retorted."I have no issues with Westfield's suit and if Elinor accepts his offer at the end of the Season, I will complete the marriage settlements that will secure our daughter's welfare and happiness. Until then, I will allow Elinor the Society that a lady of her standing deserves. Do you not agree, Jane?"

"Very well, Roger," she relented. "I see your point. I am making 'a mountain out of a molehill.' That is the saying, is it not? I believe Fox used the expression in his 'Book of Martyrs' in reference to exaggerating a trifling difficulty."

Roger's eyes twinkled with amusement. Grinning, he said, "Really, Jane, You need not solicit compliments for your wit. You forget, my dear, that I am well aware of your incomparable intellect. It has served me well through our marriage and I always applaud your proficiency."

She smiled, extended her hand to her husband to kiss, saying, "Thank you, Roger. I am glad you know to appreciate me. As for our daughter, I will trust in her to know her heart and will accept the dowager's invitation with the grace that it was offered." She began to leave and then stopped short of the door, turning, she inquired, "Roger, you will stay the whole fortnight at Aubry and not leave me alone to guard our daughter?"

Her husband laughed, remarking, "I do not think you will need me to guard Elinor with Jonathan there, but rest assured, unless an emergency calls me away, I will be in attendance as you see fit."

"Thank you, dear," replied Jane, leaving with a smile.

Jonathan could not contain his grin looking at Rebecca who sat across from him in the Ingall carriage. He could tell she wanted to laugh at her mother's rant. It was not her first diatribe since they left London, making their way to the Aubry Estate.

"Honestly," she complained. "I cannot fathom why Roger insisted on attending to our tenants' problems personally. Is that not why we have a steward? I think he never planned on going with us to Aubry and I am quite put out, Elinor, especially since we present ourselves to the dowager, so as not to offend his papa."

The Dowager Duchess of Aubry lived at Aubry, while her son, the present Duke of Aubry and his family resided in Town during the Season. Parliament brought the lords to London, while the galas and balls of the *marriage mart* tempted everyone else. Lady Ingall, having learned that Jonathan's mother was to join the party, had begun to look forward to the visit, but then the Westfield tenants presented their lord with issues from which only the earl could resolve. Jonathan was ready to make his regrets when his mother insisted she act in his stead. She was more than capable, so Jonathan agreed to her offer. While Rebecca was pleased with the outcome, her mother became further discontented.

Rebecca held her mirth in check watching Jonathan try again to ameliorate her mother. "I am sure your steward would not have messaged him if he was capable of solving the problem himself. I am positive Lord Ingall had every intention of accompanying you."

Jane responded miserably, "Of course, you are right. I am simply letting off steam, though I cannot but feel that Mr. Brentwood is behind the invitation that has us quite put out."

"You are probably right," agreed Jonathan. "However, the invitation, most definitely, is an honor to Rebecca. Though I hate to admit it, Mr. Brentwood would not solicit his grandmother's approval, if he was not serious about courting her. Unfortunately for him, Rebecca's heart is already engaged to me."

Rebecca beamed while her mother admonished Jonathan. "While that may be true, my lord, you must be circumspect. You are not yet engaged and any illusions to an alliance will only taint my daughter's character. I beg you to be chary and to remember to address Rebecca as Lady Elinor."

Jonathan grinned, replying, "Of course. While I look forward to announcing our betrothal in the future, I will abide with your wishes and make no claims on Lady Elinor until the end of the Season. For now, I will be content knowing that I am secure in her heart." And upon further reflection, Jonathan felt the doubts that were weighing heavy on him diminish. He had not realized how much Prinny's accusation that Rebecca accepted him because she had no others had troubled him. He no longer feared losing Rebecca to a suitor for he trusted in the love they shared. The epiphany was powerful and overwhelmed him with joy.

Jonathan was happy that he had the full length of the back facing seat to stretch out his legs. He preferred to ride when he traveled, but the regal well-sprung carriage with comfortable leather squabs, warming bricks, lamp lighting, and hidden compartments filled with wine and repasts, made the trip bearable. The best part of the long journey for Jonathan was looking at Rebecca and listening to her calming voice. He liked the sound of her lyrical speech and even better he liked that she had something to say. Rebecca never bored him. They had a lot in common to discuss: literature, music, horses, and especially the welfare of their combined tenants. He even liked that they didn't need to fill up every moment with speech. Just being with her was pleasant.

Lady Ingall seemed to feint sleep more often than not. Jonathan believed the ruse was so that he and Rebecca could speak without censure, but he was not fooled by Lady Ingalls's occasional snore. Neither was Rebecca. More than one time, Rebecca mischievously discussed a contrary topic just to watch her mother suddenly awaken. Lady Ingall was quick to ask what she missed and then with satisfaction added her opinion to the discussion.

As they neared the Duke of Aubry's vast estate, Jonathan remarked to Rebecca, "You will enjoy the properties. There are immense bowling greens and three ornamental ponds. The largest pond is more like a lake than not, for it has an island at its center. There are rowboats to provide recreation and access to the island. I came to visit with my father when I was a child and one of my fondest memories is visiting the island. Another of the ponds is stocked with trout and pike. I have fished there, but I expect you would prefer the lake, where I might glide you about so that you may take in the sun rather than cast a lure." Rebecca and her mother laughed in unison.

Lady Ingall was the first to comment, "Then, I fear, my lord, that you do not know our dear Elinor, as well as you think. She is quite proficient in casting a line as her brothers William and Henry can attest."

Rebecca interjected, "They have yet to beat my largest cache, a bounty of eight heads."

Jonathan laughed, remarking, "I shall have to make sure the Westfield Pond is properly stocked, so that I may delight in your bounty when we are married Lady Elinor."

Lady Ingall gasped and delivered a stern reprimand. "There you go again, Lord Westfield. You must not be saying such duplicitous remarks in polite society. I beg you to be chary."

A chagrined Jonathan begged forgiveness, "I do apologize, my lady, I promise from hence to be the most proper of gentleman."

The Earl of Westfield, the Countess of Ingall, and Lady Elinor followed the Aubry butler, Frenton, into the parlour referred to as the Sun Room. They took in their rich surroundings. On one side of the parlour were a number of tall arched windows, framed in white and dressed with gold damask drapes that were pulled back with golden tassels. The windows let in an abundance of light that made the room bright and cheerful. The yellow painted walls, gilt wood mirrors, and white chair rail added to the illumination. The walls were adorned with a multitude of Poussin, Rembrandt, and Gainsborough paintings. Intricately carved and gilded baroque furniture dotted the room. A profuse amount of vases filled with bunches of lilacs graced the tables. Rebecca breathed in the redolent sweetness and smiled in approval. Edward saw her expression and approached her with an explanation, "My grandmother loves lilacs and I would guess that they are a favorite of yours, as well."

Rebecca smiled and said, "Indeed, they are."

Edward extended a warm welcome to his guests. Lord Westfield immediately extended his hand to Edward. Edward looked to see if Westfield proffered two fingers in greeting or his hand in earnest before he offered his own. The *bon ton* liked to degrade those beneath them in station by barely making contact with them upon an introduction: the proffered two fingers, in lieu of a handshake. It was their haughty way of snubbing anyone outside their Society, especially those persons who acquired wealth through trade. Edward's vast fortune came from trade. He was the recipient of many two-finger introductions, so when Jonathan firmly took his hand in his to shake, he instantly took a liking to his rival.

Edward bowed to Lady Ingall and bestowed a kiss on her hand. Then, with what Jonathan deemed posturing, Edward took hold of Rebecca's hand. He brought her fingers to his lips and kissed them lightly, his eyes never wavering from hers. He smiled at her in a way that brightened his face, making him, Jonathan begrudgingly admitted, annoyingly attractive. Without missing a beat, Edward took possession of Rebecca by threading her hand through his arm and escorted her to the Dowager Duchess of Aubry to be introduced. Jonathan and Jane followed in their wake, but not before Jane raised an arched brow to Jonathan in warning.

The dowager looked quite regal in her gold frock trimmed with French lace, sitting on a red velveteen settee. The ostentatious hearth with a fire burning behind her provided a picturesque backdrop for the grand dame. The dowager rose to meet her guests. Edward said, "Grandmother, I believe you are acquainted with Lord Westfield and Lady Ingall, but have not yet been fortunate to meet the Earl of Ingall's daughter, Lady Elinor."

Edward released Elinor's arm and introduced the dowager, "Lady Elinor, may I present my grandmother, the Dowager Duchess of Aubry."

Rebecca made an impressive curtsey and when she rose, she found a set of warm eyes welcoming her. The dowager said, "Lady Elinor, I am happy to meet you. I have heard much about you and I am looking forward to our getting better acquainted." The dowager then bade welcome to Lord Westfield and Lady Ingall. She said, "My lord, it has been quite some time since you have visited. You must know that my son and I were greatly saddened by your loss. Aubry and your father were quite fond of one another."

Jonathan replied, "Yes, I know. I visited Aubry many times with my father when I was a child. He held the duke in high esteem. My mother and I were greatly touched by the sympathy letter you sent and thank you."

A bit overcome by Jonathan's comments, the dowager, took the lace handkerchief that she kept hidden in the cuff of her sleeve and dabbed her nose before she drew her attention to Lady Ingall. "I am glad to receive you, Lady Ingall. I rarely get to London and I am grateful to you for bringing such an amiable party for my enjoyment. I hope you find your stay pleasurable. I was sorry that Lady Westfield and Lord Ingall were called away on business."

Jane replied, "Both My Lord and Lady Westfield were sorry to send their regrets. It is gracious of you to invite us. Thank you. We are very much looking forward to enjoying your company and beautiful home."

The dowager responded, "You are too kind and most likely more than ready for a respite." The dowager looked at her grandson, commanding him, "Edward, please instruct Frenton to escort our guests to their rooms. Have him order tea and a cold collation that they can enjoy in their suite to assuage their hunger until we dine." She then looked at her guests, announcing, "Rest, we keep Town hours so as to accommodate all our guests. I will see you again at eight o'clock."

Lady Ingall remarked, "May I ask who else joins your party?"

The dowager replied, "My granddaughter, Lady Catherine, Mr. Willoughby, his betrothed Lady Miranda, and our own vicar Mr. Drake and his wife.

Chapter Seventeen

Jane was surprised that her daughter was given her own suite of rooms. She certainly had no need for two bedrooms joined by a private parlour and she wondered if her hostess did not assign the second bedroom to Elinor for some nefarious reason. Then, she remembered that Roger was expected to accompany her, so any thoughts of perfidy soon left her mind. While her abigail unpacked her luggage in her bedroom, she sat with Jonathan and Elinor in her sitting room to consume their repast. As promised, a pot of tea, some cucumber and salmon sandwiches, plus cheese and fruit tarts were delivered to their rooms to calm their hunger. The light luncheon was welcomed after a long day's journey. The snack rejuvenated Rebecca into conversation and she asked Jonathan how he knew the Duke of Aubry.

He explained, "My father and the duke were friends because they both loved to ride and hunt. My father would bring me with him when he visited Aubry, my mother preferring to remain at Westfield. In the beginning, I was too young to join him in the hunt, so I spent my days in the nursery with the duke's daughter, Lady Catherine. You will meet her later, if she indeed comes. I would not think a house party of elders is much to Lady Catherine's liking. She much prefers the accolades she receives in Town during the Season."

Rebecca chuckled, "I would not call us elderly, Jonathan."

"Well, I did not mean you and I," he retorted.

Lady Ingall in mock dismay, exclaimed, "Well, I hope you did not mean me, either."

Jonathan blushed, to both ladies pleasure.

Feeling sorry for embarrassing Jonathan, Rebecca tried to stop her mother's laughter by raising a serious topic. "Do you think Lady Miranda will still be miffed by my contradicting her censure of Mr. Spohr? She quite abjured me the entire night at Vauxhall, though I must admit my attentions were so diverted, I did not really care about the ire she so deftly directed at me."

Her mother remarked, "She is a silly girl. Imagine, criticizing the talent of a most renowned violinist. She should be happy that none of us spread her solecism among the *ton*. If Lady Riverdale had heard of her ill manners towards her guest, she would have banned her from this Season's musicales."

Jonathan interrupted, saying, "Lady Miranda is indeed a silly girl whose folly of trying to gain Lord Riverdale's good opinion failed miserably and put her to the blush. She is to be pitied and not admonished. Arthur is a good friend of mine and for his sake, let us do our best to ameliorate Lady Miranda's feelings."

"I do not understand, Jonathan," said Rebecca. "If Miranda loves Arthur, why did she desire Lord Riverdale's good opinion and are you saying she lied, when she said Mr. Spohr was tedious?"

Jonathan released a chuckle at Rebecca's forthright nature and took a moment to control his mirth before he answered her. "My dear, Rebecca. You are so good and I love you, but I will leave you to your mother's wisdom, who is better able than I, to elucidate why a woman engages in mendacity. Personally, I find such behavior unattractive, but some men like to engage as a matter of sport. I shall take my leave so that you may enjoy your mother's company in private. Shall I meet you in the drawing room at eight o'clock?"

"Yes, thank you," responded Rebecca and her mother in unison.

It was by sheer coincidence that Rebecca and her mother met Jonathan at the head of the stairs when they began their descent down the grand staircase to the drawing room. Lady Ingall stepped ahead of them so that they could have a moment to greet one another. Jonathan took in Rebecca's beauty, remarking, "You are a vision Rebecca. I will find it very difficult to hold attendance with anyone, but you."

She blushed, crediting her abigail for putting her in the *pink of fashion*.

Jonathan replied, "I must confess that I did not notice your fashionable dress, but now that you bring it to my attention, I applaud your abigail, most prodigiously."

Rebecca grinned. He was such a charmer and she loved him for it. She could not imagine anyone else thinking her as lovely as he did and she credited his outlandish remarks to the ardor he held for her. She found it incredulous at times, that a handsome and caring earl wanted her for his wife.

When they neared the drawing room, she stalled their entrance, so as to respond in kind to him. Before she could speak, she found herself forcefully disengaged from his person. Her arm was pried from his and she was rudely pushed aside by an unknown lady. She watched the interloper exuberantly greet and pull Jonathan away from her. She heard the lady whisper to him, "*Mari*."

Rebecca recognized the French language, but was unfamiliar with it. She moved into the drawing room, watching Jonathan attempt to disengage the blond beauty from his arm. Rebecca noticed that Jonathan's face initially expressed frustration and then changed to pure joy when he recognized his assailer. She heard him say, "Lady Catherine, why I did not expect the *Toast of London* to grace us with her presence when the Season is still in full swing. I am quite astonished and most pleased to see you."

Rebecca scowled, asking herself, *"Did he call her the Toast of London? Why did he not mention she was a beauty?"*

Catherine smiled and replied, "I could not refuse when grandmama told me you made up her party. I have only fond memories of our times together and since I have not seen you for ages, I found I could not stay away. My! How you have matured. I hardly recognize the boy I once knew. Tell me, how glad are you, that I am here?"

Rebecca heard Jonathan reply, "Very," right when Edward approached her. He asked, "Lady Elinor have you met my cousin, Lady Catherine, the Duke of Aubry's daughter?"

Rebecca, a bit distressed over the familiarity she just observed between Jonathan and Lady Catherine, said in a quiet, but tight voice, "No, I have not had that honor."

Edward proffered his arm, saying, "Allow me to make your introduction." Rebecca placed her hand on his arm and walked with him to where Jonathan and Catherine stood.

"My dear cousin," interrupted Edward, "Allow me to introduce Lady Elinor, the Earl of Ingall's daughter. Her mother, Lady Ingall, with whom you are acquainted, accompanies her. Lady Elinor, may I present Lady Catherine Brentwood."

Rebecca replied, "It is an honor to meet you, Lady Catherine."

"Oh, Edward!" exclaimed Catherine. "Why must you insist on dragging Lady Elinor over to meet me? How tedious you are. I beg your forgiveness, Lady Elinor, for I am sure you were engaged in some delightful conversation when my cousin, who is all propriety, interrupted you. I am pleased to meet you too, but pray, do enjoy yourself. Do not feel you must attend to me. We will have plenty of time to become better acquainted. I understand that Mr. Willoughby and Lady Miranda are acquaintances of yours. I am sure you are anxious to visit with them. My Lord Westfield and my visit can only bore you. You see we are old friends and have much to reminisce. Forgive me, are you acquainted with his lordship?"

Before Rebecca could reply, Jonathan exclaimed, "Yes, my lady, we are very well acquainted. Our estates neighbor one another and Society has brought us together on many occasions."

Catherine's face brightened. She said, "Oh! Wonderful! You are friends. Then, there will be no hard feelings when I monopolize your time to reacquaint myself with you."

Jonathan gave Rebecca a sympathetic smile. She realized he was powerless to rebuke her, since he could not publicly make his attachment to Rebecca known. In addition, he could not risk affronting his hostess's granddaughter, so with affability Jonathan remarked, "Yes, Lady Elinor's friendship is one I value."

Rebecca offered a warm smile and looked into his eyes hoping to express to him that she understood. She replied, "Thank you, my lord. Your friendship is most important to me, as well. Please excuse me while I make my greetings to Mr. Willoughby and Lady Miranda."

Rebecca made her way over to greet Arthur and Miranda. She was apprehensive, but hoped Miranda had forgiven her for any embarrassment she had caused her on the barge to Vauxhall. She was to be disappointed for no matter how she attempted to engage in conversation with the couple, all that she could solicit was a haughty nod from Miranda and a remorseful smile from Arthur. It was clear with the steely looks Miranda gave Arthur that she was not interested in his attempts of mediation. Rebecca resigned herself to the snub, excusing herself to join her mother.

Jonathan watched Rebecca walk away with Edward while Catherine tugged him by his arm to bring him over to a settee. He expected to be bombarded with questions by her, but before she could begin, Frenton entered the drawing room to announce dinner was served. As the highest-ranking male in the room, Lord Westfield was expected to escort the dowager into dinner, but she waved him off taking Lady Ingall's arm for an escort. Rebecca found that Lady Catherine, as the duke's daughter, outranked her, so she watched Jonathan proffer his arm to Catherine to escort her into the dining hall. She had no wish to separate Miranda from Arthur, so she found herself on the arm of Edward. Mr. and Mrs. Drake followed in rear. Everyone, except Rebecca and Jonathan, found themselves partnered agreeably when they sat down for supper.

Rebecca was seated at the far end of the table from Jonathan who sat next to the dowager and Catherine. The Dowager Duchess of Aubry sat at the head of the table while her grandson, Edward, sat at the other end with Rebecca sitting on his right side and Miranda sitting on his left. Rebecca, as much as she tried, could not hear any of Jonathan's conversation, but from his and Catherine's animated faces, she expected they were having quite a reunion.

No sooner were their seats taken than Miranda engaged Edward in conversation and held it throughout dinner. Rebecca thought he tried to extricate himself on a number of occasions, but the rise of Miranda's voice constrained him from ending their discourse. Rebecca tried to converse with Mrs. Drake, but she found the lady was more interested in her food than talking. That left Rebecca with only her thoughts to entertain her, since neither of her neighbors wished to converse with her. She was hurt at Miranda's blatant campaign to abjure her.

Protocol prevented Rebecca from chatting with someone that sat across the table from her. Even though she saw that Arthur suffered equitably. It seemed both of his neighbors, Miranda and Catherine, had little desire to speak to him. They were absorbed with their other neighbor. It was clear to Rebecca that Miranda was doing her best to injure her by monopolizing Edward's attention. However, Rebecca thought Arthur suffered more from

Miranda's actions. Catherine, on the other hand, only had eyes for Jonathan. There was no ulterior motive. She clearly was besotted with the earl. As much as the lady's adulation irked Rebecca, she knew it was up to Jonathan to squelch the lady's devotion. She only hoped he did it quickly. As for Miranda, she fretted, *"How am I to make amends to her when she is doing her best to shun me?"*

Dinner finally ended. The dowager stood, the sign for the ladies to remove themselves to the drawing room. The men, then made their exit to the duke's study where they would enjoy a glass of port, a cigar, and an engaging discourse on either politics or horseflesh.

Rebecca was the last one to enter the drawing room having lagged behind the other women. She saw that her mother was in deep discussion with the dowager and that Catherine and Miranda were having a private chat by the fireplace. Mrs. Drake sat alone sipping a cup of tea.

Catherine's and Miranda's giggling deterred Rebecca from intruding upon them, so she made her way to a seat near Mrs. Drake. Rebecca asked Mrs. Drake about her parish and listened for a greater part of an hour, how that lady was overtaxed with the duties of a clergy wife. Rebecca was quite wearied by the time the men entered. She further fatigued when Catherine claimed Jonathan the moment he entered the parlour. Her head ached. She wanted to retire and sought permission from her mother.

Lady Ingall became alarmed when she saw her daughter's pallor and begged the dowager's forgiveness for leaving her fine party. She confessed that she herself was quite weary from the day's travel and asked that they be excused. Lady Ingall escorted her daughter out of the drawing room. Neither of them looked back, for if they had, they would have seen solemn faces on Lord Westfield, Mr. Brentwood, and Mr. Willoughby.

Rebecca would have been much appeased, had she known what had delayed the men from joining the women in the parlour. Edward was quite severe with Arthur for allowing Miranda to dominate his attentions at dinner. Edward felt his neglect of Elinor greatly and he assailed Arthur for not checking his fiancée's behavior. He admonished, "Why did you not aid me when I tried to disengage from her company? Could you not see that she was using me to affront Lady Elinor?"

Arthur begged forgiveness, explaining that Lady Miranda had been in a temper since Vauxhall and that he had yet been able to squelch her ire. Jonathan, having heard how Rebecca was ill-treated, found himself lashing out at Arthur. He berated him and warned him, if he could not check and correct his fiancée's behavior towards Lady Elinor, that he would take it upon himself to do so. He railed, "I will do it if you cannot and I assure you, it will not be with an easy touch!"

Before Arthur could respond, Edward insisted on knowing what transpired at Vauxhall. The story of Miranda's solecism, her censure of a virtuoso, seemed to mollify everyone's temper to the point that they had felt some pity for Miranda. Even Arthur could not take offense when they referred to his betrothed, as a "silly girl." With tempers reduced, they all agreed that Arthur was to take Miranda aside when they returned to the drawing room, and remind her to behave as a lady of her station should. They sealed their resolution by enjoying another glass of port to toast to the sensibilities of men. They felt a comradeship and were quite pacified until they entered the drawing room where they found Elinor sequestered with the tedious Mrs. Drake. She looked pale and quite withdrawn, as someone who had resigned herself to her fate. The giggles of Catherine and Miranda penetrated the room. It was obvious that Elinor had not sat with Mrs. Drake by choice.

Before any of them could come to her aid, Catherine intercepted Jonathan on his way to Rebecca, the dowager chastised Edward for staying away so long, and Miranda captured Arthur keeping him by her side. Rebecca managed to excuse herself in all the commotion. With her mother accompanying her, she exited the drawing room before any of the gentlemen could ameliorate her.

The gentlemen were not the only ones who noticed Elinor's morose and fatigued state. The dowager was keen from the onset that something was amiss. Unlike Lady Ingall who held to protocol, conversing equally with her dinner partners, the dowager was anxiously watching the interplay or the lack it between

Edward and his partners at dinner. She knew that Edward was enthusiastic on fostering a relationship with Lady Elinor, so she was sure his neglect of her was not his doing but that of Lady Miranda. The dowager wondered what the silly *chit* was up to since her betrothed Mr. Willoughby was also being neglected. Not the actions of a young woman supposedly in love. That was the *on-dit* anyway, since Mr. Willoughby managed to secure her without an esteemed title, connections, or wealth. Plus, there was rumor of a rushed marriage. Why, the girl was betrothed before she even enjoyed the Season! Her beauty would surely have generated more than one offer. Aside from all that, wasn't Lady Miranda considered an acquaintance of Lady Elinor? Didn't Edward invite her to make their invitation more palpable to Lady Elinor? All was not well. The dowager had seen Lady Miranda take possession of her granddaughter when they entered the parlour. She surmised they wished to gossip about the latest scandal until she saw them disregard Lady Elinor. She watched them huddle together in some type of mischief, whispering, looking at Lady Elinor in jest, perhaps making an innuendo about her. Indeed, all was not well and the dowager decided that she needed to get to the bottom of the fiasco before her party suffered.

Upon Jane's and Rebecca's exit, the dowager rose and commanded, "I do believe that Lady Ingall has the right of it. It has been a long day. I suggest we all retire for we have some activities planned for tomorrow that require plenty of rest. Catherine, please escort Lady Miranda to her room and then attend to me in my suite. I bid you all good night."

Everyone rose and left to retire, except the gentlemen who stayed behind looking quite exasperated at having their best-laid plans crushed. Arthur was first to speak, "I say, I am sorry, Westfield. I had every intention of scolding Miranda for her ill treatment of Lady Elinor. You can count on me to speak with her tomorrow. I really do not know what has gotten into her. This is not the woman that captured my heart. Ever since we arrived in London her demeanor has changed. I almost feel she resents me at times, as if my presence is ruining her Season. You know, you are quite lucky that I did not see the prize in Lady Elinor when we first met and I do not mean her dowry. I always liked Rebecca, excuse me, Lady Elinor. In fact, we had some jolly good times, but I did not realize her kindness and compassion were unique unto her. I hope you know how lucky you are."

Edward interrupted him by saying, "I believe it fair to say, that both Westfield and myself are beholden to you, for your lack of foresight. May I suggest, Gentlemen, that we allow my grandmother to speak and guide Lady Miranda before her party becomes unsalvageable." Jonathan and Arthur nodded their heads in agreement and bid good evening as they each took their leave.

Edward did not retire to his room. Instead, he made his way to the dowager's suite of rooms where he expected to find his cousin, Catherine, in attendance with his grandmother. He knocked and was immediately bid enter by what he knew to be his grandmother's voice. Before he could shut the door, she asked, "Is it true that Lady Elinor made herself ridiculous with Lord Riverdale by not recognizing the talent of Mr. Sphor?"

Edward was astonished. Lord Westfield and Mr. Willoughby had just relayed the story only an hour ago. How could it have been confused in such a short period of time? He asked in distemper, "Who told you such slander?"

The dowager extended her arm to Catherine's direction. The girl smugly smiled, retorting, "Really, Edward, slander? Why I heard it straight from Lady Miranda, who unlike yourself, made up the party to Vauxhall. Apparently, Lady Elinor asked Lord Riverdale, "He is a virtuoso?" and to this Catherine chuckled.

Edward scowled. Then, he berated her, saying, "I fear, Cousin, you have been ill used. While you are correct that I did not make up the party to Vauxhall, Lord Westfield and Mr. Willoughby did. They have informed me this evening, that it was Lady Miranda who committed the solecism in affronting Mr. Spohr by calling his solo 'tedious.' Lord Riverdale put Lady Elinor to the blush by requesting her opinion. With grace, she acknowledged Mr. Spohr's talent and Lord Riverdale's generosity in sharing it. Lady Miranda failed to add, 'Is he not?' to her recall of Lady Elinor's statement regarding Mr. Spohr for her own malicious reasons." With a harsher tone, he continued, "You have chosen unwisely, Cousin, to align yourself with a family whose connections are inferior to the Ingalls.

Lady Miranda's mother holds only a courtesy title since her husband is deceased, while Lady Elinor's grandfather is a duke and her father an earl. Together, they have enough influence to make you and Lady Miranda look quite absurd. Lady Ingall's company is favored over your own mother's in Society. If she chose, she could abjure you from quite a number of this Season's events. Lucky for you, she is not of a malicious nature."

Catherine lost all color to her face. She became quite overwrought, listening to Edward's heated soliloquy. She looked beseechingly to her grandmother who exclaimed, "Edward! Enough! I understand the situation, and shall handle it. Tomorrow, I expect you both to extend undue attention to Lady Elinor. I do not want to see that child grieve while she is my guest. Is that understood?" Catherine and Edward looked towards each other before nodding in agreement.

The next few days, Rebecca found herself the center of attention. The marked decline in camaraderie between Catherine and Miranda did not go unnoticed by her. It seemed everyone, aside from Miranda, was concerned over her and were making sure that she was always with company. Unknown to Rebecca, the dowager had put Miranda to the blush delivering a proper set down for her behavior. The dowager told Miranda that had she kept her mouth shut, no one would have ever been aware of her stupidity. Her own ill behavior to thwart the blunder unto Elinor is what brought the ridiculous story public. She warned her to ameliorate her feelings towards

Lady Elinor or else she would send her home and she would be happy to share with the *ton* why she did. Lady Miranda made her abject apology, adding that she would improve her behavior. The party gathered the next day to play lawn games and each day thereafter to engage in other amusements. They went on garden walks, picnics, and horseback riding. On their sunniest day, they took the rowboats out on the lake.

As much as Rebecca enjoyed the company and the activities the dowager organized for her guests, watching Catherine's admiration of Jonathan stilted her happiness. Each day Catherine claimed Jonathan for her escort, leaving Edward to partner with Rebecca. She found Edward to be an agreeable and charming gentleman. She could not fault his attentions, since she believed his motivation came from being a good host and not an ardent suitor. However, watching Jonathan show interest in another woman brought out Rebecca's worst traits. She tried hard to be gracious and not think unkind thoughts of Catherine or hold Jonathan responsible for Catherine's admiration, but their daily pairing unnerved her. She thought Catherine bold. She could not remember one time when she fluttered her eyelashes at Jonathan. Check that. Maybe once, when she wanted to ride Apollo, but she couldn't remember a time when she made a spectacle of herself by mooning over him. Check that...drat. As angry as she got, she found it hard to blame Catherine for being attracted to Jonathan, thinking, *"who would not be?"*

Fearing her jealousy would fester like a splinter she tried to ignore the couple by letting Edward distract her with his undivided attention. Her self-control was tested more than once when she saw Catherine clutch Jonathan's arm to whisper him endearments and when the lady literally pulled him back to her whenever he tried to leave her side.

Her only consolation was that regardless of Catherine's actions, Jonathan with gentlemanly skill, found a way to escort her into Rebecca's and Edward's company. Rebecca noticed that Jonathan always seemed to keep her in his sight. She took great comfort knowing that he disliked seeing her paired with Edward as much as she disliked him being with Catherine. Arthur moved from couple to couple when he found himself without companion. Miranda had disengaged herself from the party after being chastised by the dowager for her bad behavior towards Elinor. Whether from guilt or embarrassment, she chose not to participate in any of the games or discussions, even lagging behind the rest of the group in their walks. Arthur tried to cheer her up but to no avail. He eventually left her to her own gloomy company and joined the others in merriment.

The cheerful party, minus one, decided to play a game of Pall Mall on the east lawn. They all headed across the green to set up the game, when Rebecca caught sight of Miranda trailing behind, veering towards the garden. She followed her and saw that Miranda had taken a seat on a stone bench, dropping her head into her hands.

Rebecca's heart wrenched for the unhappy lady. She walked over to where she sat and waited for Miranda to take notice of her. She knew the shadow she cast onto Miranda would force her to look up to see who blocked the comforting sun. Miranda stiffened her back when she saw Lady Elinor and was prepared to depart without offering a greeting when Rebecca spoke, "I am not mad at you, Miranda. I am sorry I caused you an injury with my appraisal of Mr. Spohr. I did not mean you any harm. Please, come join the party. You are greatly missed, especially by Mr. Willoughby."

Miranda's composure broke. Contrite, she stood, crying, "Oh! You are too good to apologize. I am the one who is sorry that I abused our friendship in such a malicious manner. I did it only because I feared humiliation. Please forgive me and say I have not done irreparable damage to our acquaintance."

Rebecca soothed, "What kind of friend would I be if I did not forgive you? Your friendship means too much to me. Say no more. Wipe your tears and let us rejoin our party."

Arm in arm, they made their way over to the bowling green where the others were setting up the frames for Pall Mall, a popular lawn game where mallets are used to hit balls through wire frames placed among a course. Rebecca immediately spied Jonathan walking towards her. He held a piece of paper in his right hand and he looked concerned. She relinquished Miranda's arm and hastened her steps to meet him. Miranda made her way across the lawn to greet Arthur who was relieved to see her smiling.

Rebecca asked, "Jonathan, is something wrong?"

Jonathan replied to her beseeching eyes, "I am afraid I must return to Westfield. My mother begs my attendance, post-haste, to settle a tenant disagreement."

Rebecca frowned. Jonathan smiled back at her. Taking her hand, he brought it to his lips for a light kiss. She flushed, returning his gaze. She always marveled how his slightest touch brightened her demeanor, igniting her nerves with anticipation. She was connected to this man and his departure saddened her. He released her hand, saying, "I will do my best to return, but I expect I will more than likely see you in London just as the Season ends. I cannot tell you how I await that day, so that I may speak with your father. Until then, I will see you in my dreams. Be good, Rebecca, while I am away. Do not fall for any gallantry."

Rebecca smiled, whispering, "I will miss you, dearly, and I hope your leave is short. I too, await the Season-end. Do not worry about my giving my heart away because I have already done so."

Jonathan replied, "As have I, my love."

He bowed to her and was about to take his leave when Catherine, making her way across the green, stopped him. "Is it true? Do you leave our party for Westfield Manor?"

He replied, "Yes, I only return to the house to bid adieu to your grandmother and Lady Ingall. It was a great pleasure to reacquaint myself with you and to fulfill the obligations of my youth. You are a beautiful lady. I wish you much felicity."

Jonathan bowed and left, but not before Catherine whispered to him, "*Adieu Mari*. It has been fun." Jonathan smiled and left.

Edward reached Rebecca a few seconds after Jonathan took his leave. He said, "It is a shame that Westfield had to take his leave, but pray do not let it dampen our party. Our game of Pall Mall is ready to begin. You have only to choose between the red or the yellow mallet that Catherine, in her nursery days, personalized with a design. What is your fancy, my lady? However, I beg you from leaving me with the mallet that looks like a daisy."

Rebecca laughed, easing Edward's mind by selecting the yellow mallet when they made their way back to join the rest of the party. The game seemed dull without Jonathan, but Rebecca did her best to be cheerful. She could not help but be distracted by Catherine's address to Jonathan. She knew "adieu" meant good-bye, so she figured "*mari*" must be a name, but what? She could just ask Catherine, but that would mean confessing to listening to a private conversation, a very unladylike behavior. She decided she would ask her mother later, what the French word "*mari*" meant. Her decision allowed her to relax and enjoy the game. Later, to her surprise, she realized she was having fun. Her spirits rose enough to smile at Edward for which he reciprocated in kind.

The amiable party continued through dinner. Afterwards, the group broke up into two tables of card players. Elinor and Edward partnered against Miranda and Arthur at one table and the dowager partnered with Lady Ingall against Mr. and Mrs. Drake at another table. Catherine sullenly walked amongst the tables, occasionally tapping her fingers behind the backs of chairs and tables while she languorously hovered.

Edward in grand spirits, suggested, "Let us take the curricles out tomorrow for a brisk ride over to Beacon Hill. We can have Cook pack us a basket of a cold collation and we may picnic after perusing the grounds. There are some fine rock formations that I am sure you will all enjoy, plus the vantage is quite spectacular." Edward paused, then laughed, "We will have to draw sticks to see who Lady Catherine rides with, now that Westfield is absent. But to her credit, she does not take up much room."

Catherine exhaled a guffaw, saying, "Do not put yourselves out on my behalf, Gentlemen. I leave tomorrow for London. I wish no affront, but I came to see Lord Westfield and now that he is gone, London and its Society beckon me. I do wish you all continued felicity on your sojourn and will be happy to see you again in Town." Catherine turned to the dowager and said, "Grandmama, I wish to leave early, so may I be excused to retire?"

The dowager replied, "Yes, Catherine. I am glad for the time that you graced us with your society. I shall see you after the Season ends with the duke, or do you travel with friends?"

Catherine responded with mirth, "You have not had enough of me, then?"

Smiling, the dowager replied, "Ah, yes. You are quite right. Do wait an appropriate time for me to rehabilitate before you return."

With a smirk, she retorted, "I always do, Grandmama." She then bid Lady Ingall and the others good evening and took her leave.

Rebecca found herself annoyed at Catherine's declaration over her preference for Jonathan's company. It reminded her of the French word "*mari*" that she needed to have translated. She looked at her mother who looked so exhausted that she would probably retire immediately at the end of the card game. She realized her question would have to wait another day.

Chapter Eighteen

The portico was filled with footmen carrying bags to the ducal carriage while Catherine excitedly took her leave the following morning. She offered hugs and endearments to her favorite cousin and friend. The early departure brought only the young guests of the household to bid farewell because the more advanced members still slept. Rebecca and Arthur did not want to intrude upon Catherine's intimate farewells with Edward and Miranda, so they watched the emotional parting from a respectable distance. Rebecca could not hear what was said, but as Catherine stepped over the threshold, she saw her wave goodbye and exclaim, *"Adieu, bon ami!"*

In response, Miranda waved back to her friend and then hearing Rebecca's outburst, replied, "*Oui, un peu.*"

Rebecca was surprised Miranda spoke to her in French. She did not realize she had spoken her thoughts out loud.

She asked, "What?!"

Miranda repeated, "You asked me, if I spoke French and I said a little."

Stunned, Rebecca tried to project a casualness about her interest in the French language. She asked her how long she studied and if she had ever seen Paris. When she felt assured that Miranda could have no idea of her motives, she queried, "I once heard a lady call a gentleman, 'maw-ree,' tell me, is it proper?"

Miranda laughed, "It is, if it is her husband. 'Mari' means husband, Lady Elinor."

Before Miranda could take notice of Rebecca's pallor, Edward and Arthur hustled the ladies into their awaiting racing curricles. The amassing grey clouds alarmed Edward enough to remark, "England is not known for its temperate weather, I suggest we begin our excursion while the weather is good." Edward assisted Elinor up into his carriage while behind them, Arthur helped Miranda to take her seat. Edward took the lead, since he knew their direction.

They had planned to leave for Beacon Hill as soon as they saw Catherine off. Making haste, Edward whipped his reins to start his matched chestnut bays into action. He smiled, thinking his horses would have an easy go of it, since he had no intention of cutting them loose. He relished the opportunity to singularly enjoy Lady Elinor's company. He thought the slow ride to Beacon Hill provided him the perfect opportunity to charm her and he began with an enthusiastic discourse about the landmark. "The rock formations are quite remarkable. They are remnants from a volcano, you know, and gives us the amusement of discerning their character. There is one particular set of rocks, when viewed by the side offers a profile of an old man."

Edward smiled at his knowledge of such trivia and clucked his mares. He glanced at Elinor who seemed deep in thought. Rebecca finally noticed her surroundings. She could not recall how she became seated next to Edward in his curricle. Her mind was totally focused on Miranda's words, *"mari means husband, Lady Elinor."*

Her head was pounding with questions, *"What could Catherine mean calling Jonathan, husband? Does he have a prior obligation with Lady Catherine that supersedes his offer to me? What did he say to her when he left? He said something about fulfilling an obligation of his youth?"*

Rebecca thought she was about to cast up her morning meal. She tried to gain some strength from knowing that Jonathan loved her, but then the nausea would overwhelm her again, especially when she remembered that Jonathan, being an honorable man, would respect a prior obligation. She felt her head spin and she raised her hands to press the sides of her temple like a vise, hoping to stop the vertigo. She felt her panic rising, a scream ready to be released until Edward's voice broke into her nightmare. His voice managed to soothe her, to bring her focus to the present. She dropped her hands to her lap and turned her head to him. Edward saw her pallor and the tears in her hazel eyes. He reacted without thinking and placed both ribbons in one hand.

He used his other hand to take hers. He felt her clammy palm and feared for her health. He asked, “What is it, my lady, what ails you?”

She beseeched, “Why does Lady Catherine refer to Jonathan as her husband?”

Confused, Edward asked, “My cousin told you that Westfield is her husband?”

Rebecca shook her head from side to side, saying, “No, of course not, but I heard on more than one occasion, Lady Catherine, call Lord Westfield, 'maw-ree.' What connection does she own with Lord Westfield? Please do not spare my feelings, I must know!”

Edward clucked the reins, maneuvering the chestnuts around a pothole. He paused in thought, then replied, “I am doing myself great injury, my lady, in responding honestly to you. I believe you are completely unaware of just how much I have grown attached to you and hold you in cherished admiration, to the point of losing my heart. You have provided me an opportunity of which I could easily take advantage of your trust to further my own intentions. However, it is your trust, I believe, that I shall ever be permitted to hold, so therefore I do not risk losing it. Even if I was tempted, I find I am more concerned with your happiness than my own. You need not fear of any connection between Lord Westfield and my cousin Catherine. Any assignation between them occurred when they were in the nursery room. I believe, as the family story is told, Westfield was barely six years old when my cousin insisted on becoming his bride. You would have to ask him how she got him to agree to her folly. At fours years old, she may have simply cried to coerce him to comply. All that I know for sure is that my uncle was quite outraged when his daughter announced that she would be going home with the young viscount, his title at the time, since they were recently wedded. From that day forward, Westfield and my cousin were properly chaperoned."

Rebecca's face beamed while she laughed. A hearty robust laugh, heard by Arthur and Miranda who raised their eyebrows in surprise.

Rebecca told Edward that he was a good and honorable man, and that she was happy to call him friend. She said she was sorry if she had misled him into thinking her heart was not engaged, but the truth was that she had given it to Lord Westfield long before she even knew her connection to the Ingalls. "I cannot receive your addresses, Mr. Brentwood," she said with sincerity, "but I will be your truest friend, especially when you need me, as well as My Lord Westfield. He will be grateful for the respect you have shown us by honoring our connection and he will be most thankful that you have spared me unnecessary grief."

Smiling, Rebecca sat up straight and said, "You have revived me, Mr. Brentwood. I am most joyous and am very interested on learning more about Beacon Hill. Do you mind retelling me about it? I fear I was quite distracted earlier." Edward bellowed a laugh. Arthur and Miranda looked at each other again, this time with concerned faces over the remarked intimacy of the pair riding before them.

Over the last days of their sojourn, Edward and Rebecca grew closer. Gone was the awkward tension that existed when Edward tried to seek her favor. Rebecca no longer worried over affronting him for his zealous pursuit of her hand. Their relaxed demeanor enabled them the comfort of being themselves and getting to know one another better. The solace of the Aubry Estate provided them the perfect sanctuary for their burgeoning friendship.

Arthur and Miranda grew troubled when they always saw them together. If they walked in the garden, they found Edward and Rebecca sitting quietly in repose. If they went to the library, they found them sharing a book. If they dared to tease Elinor, they found Edward quick to come to her rescue and through it all, Rebecca seemed relaxed as though Edward's admiration was nothing unusual.

With their visit at an end, both Arthur and Miranda decided that their friendship to Lord Westfield, dictated that they alert him to what might be a change of heart on Elinor's behalf. It was decided that Arthur would ride straight to Westfield Manor, while Miranda traveled with the Ingalls and Edward to return to London.

Arthur found Jonathan in his study. In his concern over the developing ardor between Edward and Elinor, he did not wait to be announced by the Westfield Butler. He followed in the servant's wake. It was the butler's duty to learn whether the lord or lady of the house was receiving guests. There were rules after all and while it was impertinent of Mr. Willoughby to breech etiquette, the butler thought it unwise not to admit him, since he was a known friend of his master. However, the butler lost all respect for the gentleman when he did not wait to be announced, entering his master's study, shouting, "Westfield!"

Jonathan looked up from his desk to see who called him. Delighted, he stood and walked over to greet Arthur. "Willoughby, it is good to see you. Are you alone, or have you managed to bring the Ingalls with you?"

"No, no," said Arthur. "Though I wish I would have thought of it. I am afraid the rest of the party proceeds to London. I have come to collect you. Why, in heaven's name, are you still here?"

"Well," he replied. "It was not my intention to stay this long, but to my exasperation, I find it was a cow that is the bane of my existence. Tell me, why do you look so rattled?"

Jonathan directed him to sit in the wing chair by his desk and then walked around and took his own seat. He leaned forward placing his clasped hands on his desk and inquired, "This looks serious, Willoughby, tell me what troubles you?"

Arthur answered, "I am concerned, yes, but it is for your interests and not mine. I fear Mr. Brentwood is making headway with Elinor and I have come to warn you of their growing affection towards one another."

Jonathan sat back seeming to consider what Arthur just revealed. Arthur could not believe Jonathan's lack of concern and urgency. He expected him to rise, rant, and demand their immediate departure. He did not expect him to say, "You must be famished after your ride. I shall see to it that a room is made up for you, so that you may refresh yourself before supper."

Arthur stood, asking, "But, Westfield, what about Elinor?"

Jonathan responded with equanimity, "I thank you for making this trip to see me. I do not doubt that Brentwood has doubled his efforts to win Elinor's heart in my absence; however, I am not concerned. You see, I am in possession of her heart. She once told me that she could not give it to anyone else because she had already given it to me. I trust in what she has told me, so I am not concerned about Brentwood. Relax, Willoughby. Let us get you settled and then over supper, I will tell you a story about the cow that has caused so much trouble."

It was during their hearty meal that Arthur learned that a dispute between two tenants over a cow was the cause of Jonathan's return to Westfield. Apparently, one tenant claimed another tenant stole his cow. The alleged thief said he found the cow six months ago. He said the cow bared no markings and that upon making inquiries within the community, he learned that no one had claimed to lose a cow. The tenant took possession of the cow and cared for it, receiving the fruits of his labor in the milk and the goods it produced. He argued that a real owner would not wait six months to search for a missing cow. He accused the alleged owner of lying, that he only claimed himself the owner when he overheard the alleged thief discuss his good fortune at finding the cow.

Jonathan explained, "My mother tried to settle the dispute by compensating the alleged owner, but he insists that the cow has not been missing for six months and that it is worth more to him than money. The alleged thief is not interested in parting with the cow and neither of them is interested in owning another cow. Apparently, their honors are at stake, each calling the other a liar. They requested a hearing by the local magistrate, who in essence is me, so that is the folly that brought me home."

"Well," said Arthur. "That is some brouhaha. I am all anticipation. Tell me how you ruled."

Jonathan started laughing, explaining, "It turns out the alleged owner insisted that the alleged thief have the cow present at the hearing, so that when a ruling was made, the rightful owner could take possession of the cow. As I waited to hold court, the alleged thief entered the hall wrenching his hat in his hand. It appears the cow was in route to the hearing when it was barreled over by a traveling carriage to the fright of its passengers. Thank goodness no one was hurt, that is, aside from the cow. The alleged thief had the good sense to haul the carcass to the butcher, so I ruled that its bounty be divided equally to the satisfaction of everyone." Jonathan continued,

"Once the tenants learned I was holding court, I have been overwhelmed with tenant issues that kept me from returning to Elinor. I shall, I believe, conclude my business in less than a sev'night. If you wish to stay to visit, I will be glad of your company when I make my way back to Town.

Arthur replied, "I would enjoy the respite. Yes, I will stay and travel with you to London when you are ready.

Less than a fortnight passed before Jonathan and Arthur finally made their way to London. Upon arriving at his town home, Jonathan wasted little time in removing his traveling clothes, bathing and donning himself in his newest coat and breeches. He was excited to see Rebecca. Even though he wanted to make a fine impression, he annoyed his valet by leaving before the man could give a final brushing to his coat. Stuart took his duties seriously and it frustrated him to see his master leave before he finished his administrations. He imagined someone noting a slight crease or a piece of lint on his master's clothes and then being abused for his ill performed services. He promised himself that in the future, he would not allow his master to rush him. His reputation was at stake. If need be, he would lock the door to keep his master prisoner, until he determined the earl was ready to be seen by Society. Anything less, he argued, would be a disservice to the earl.

With more energy than necessary, Jonathan dropped the doorknocker on the Ingall town home. He entered when Palmer admitted him and gleefully asked for Lady Elinor. The butler's stoic face revealed nothing, aside to indicate that the lady in question was not at home. Jonathan announced, "I will wait," and he began to hand the Ingall butler his hat and gloves.

Palmer replied, "Very good, my lord, but I fear it will be quite late. Lady Elinor is attending the Prince Regent's fete."

Jonathan asked, "Who makes up her party?"

Palmer replied, "The Earl and Countess of Ingall, and the Duke of Hartford."

A disgruntled Jonathan left his card, remarking he would call on Lady Elinor tomorrow.

Jonathan headed to his club. He took a seat in a corner and looked around. He was surprised that White's was so thin in company, but then he realized that everyone was probably at Carlton House attending Prinny's gala. He wondered if he had received an invitation and whether he should go. *"It would be great to see Rebecca,"* he thought, though the crush of one of Prinny's parties made him balk at attending.

He was arguing with himself on what to do when Lord Riverdale approached. He brought over a bottle with him and two glasses. He sat down across the table from Jonathan, and said, "Saw you when I came in. I thought you could use the company. Sorry, about Lady Elinor. Thought you two made a fine couple."

It took a couple of minutes for Jonathan to discern Riverdale's comments, before he asked, "What the devil are you talking about?"

Riverdale exclaimed, "Sorry, Westfield! I thought you knew. They closed the books this morning and declared Brentwood the winner amongst Prinny's list. The Prince Regent has granted Brentwood a title, an honorary one I am told until his uncle passes away, but Lord Felton he is. Prinny presents him into Society tonight at Carlton House. The Duke of Hartford and the Ingalls attend him."

Before Riverdale could finish, Jonathan was out of his seat and out the door. "Impossible!" he shouted. "There is some mistake!" Jonathan's countenance changed from fear, to rage, to acceptance by the time he was admitted into Carlton House. He had decided that if he truly loved Rebecca, then her happiness is what mattered. He would not want her, he surmised, if her heart was attached to someone else, to Brentwood to be specific. *"I would not,"* he kept telling himself. Yet, his mind could not accept the idea. He could not grasp the reality of a world where Rebecca was not his wife. He asked himself, *"How could she give her heart away when it belonged me?"*

Jonathan entered Carlton House and walked directly to the ballroom not waiting to be announced. His eyes scanned the entire room until he found for whom he was looking. The newly titled Lord Felton stood at the end of a receiving line. The *bon ton* were offering their congratulations to him, the same fickle aristocrats that had kept him at the fringes of Society because of his association with trade. He thought, *"Now that he is titled, they will acknowledge his lineage and accept him as one of their own, the prodigal son returning home."*

Jonathan saw Rebecca standing next to Lord Felton with her back turned to him. She was engaged in conversation with her parents and her grandfather. Jonathan inhaled to replace the air that was sucked out of him when he saw Rebecca and his rival together. He fortified himself. Then with his most haughty and regal posture, he made his way over to congratulate the new Lord Felton on his good fortune. He strode across the ballroom, keeping his shoulders back and his posture straight. He cut to the front of the line, not caring of the affronted looks at his rudeness. He looked directly into Brentwood's eyes and extended his hand in greeting.

Before he could offer his felicitations, Rebecca turned and exclaimed, "Oh! Finally, my lord, you have returned."

Jonathan was perplexed at Rebecca's exuberance in seeing him and then he was jolted from his astonishment. Edward was shaking his hand with gusto. He said, "Thank you for coming, Westfield. I do appreciate your support. I received the title, but to my misfortune I could not claim Lady Elinor. She informed me that her heart was engaged long before I knew her, but has been kind to offer her friendship, I stand corrected, 'her truest friendship,' yours too, as a matter of fact. I could settle for nothing less. You must call on me tomorrow to learn all that has transpired since I last saw you. For now, I must leave you both, to attend to Prinny who is summoning me."

Confused, happy, curious, and overwhelmed, Jonathan's emotions exhausted him. He looked at Rebecca and noticed she wore the brooch he gave her for her *come-out*. The golden heart shaped pin with a ruby nested in the center was a token of his heart given to her.

Rebecca saw his weariness. Before she could speak, he asked, "I see my heart is exposed, is it safe?"

Rebecca answered with sincerity, "Always." She then asked him, "And how do you keep my heart?"

"Treasured," he responded.

Lord Ingall interrupted them to say, "Westfield, I will expect to see you tomorrow afternoon in my study at two o'clock."

Jonathan was too confused to reply anything except, "As you wish." It was not until Rebecca started laughing that he realized he was finally going to receive permission to pay his addresses to her. He began to laugh heartily as well, but then he stopped abruptly.

Surprised, Rebecca queried, "What is it?"

He asked softly, "You will say, yes?"

Rebecca's eyes beamed with joy. Smiling, she looked deep into his eyes, and replied, "Always."

Acknowledgements

Always Rebecca is my first Regency romance novel and is the inspiration from which my other manuscripts were born. The story precedes my debut novel, "A Love Match, Indeed!" and is Rebecca's and Jonathan's romantic tale.

I must thank my son, Jonathan, who first encouraged me to put pen to paper. Out of recognition, I named my first protagonist after him. I named a character in *A Love Match, Indeed!* after my eldest son Lawrence. No doubt, you will see the names of my other children in future novels. (It's a mom thing.)

I want to thank my amazing editor, Alicia Floyd, for her astute corrections and insightful advice. I appreciate every happy face, correction, and criticism she makes.

Thank you Christina Brusaca for photographing the cover, Debby Ring for answering all my equine queries, and my readers for your most appreciated opinions.

I have amazing friends and family and I want to thank them all for their support and encouragement, especially my husband Larry, my children, and my parents.

About the Author

Teresa Sweeney is a wife and mother of four adult children. She loves to read, write, and a myriad of other pursuits where she can use her creativity and imagination. She takes great pleasure penning historical romance novels that focus on the charm, wit, and banter of courtship. Visit her website www.teresa-sweeney.com for the latest information on her novels.

www.ingramcontent.com/pod-product-compliance
Lightning Source LLC
Chambersburg PA
CBHW030525310726
48979CB00010B/1809/J

9781940319018